DO EVERYTHING IN THE DARK

ALSO BY GARY INDIANA

DO **EVERYTHING**
IN THE **DARK**

GARY INDIANA

ST. MARTIN'S PRESS ≋
NEW YORK

www.stmartins.com

Design by Jonathan Bennett

Library of Congress Cataloging-in-Publication Data

Indiana, Gary.
    Do everything in the dark / Gary Indiana.—1st ed.
        p. cm.
    ISBN 0-312-31205-9
    I. Title.

  PS3559.N335D6 2003
  813'.54—dc21

                                                              2003041382

First Edition: June 2003

10   9   8   7   6   5   4   3   2   1

For Rudolph Wurlitzer

Do all in the dark (as clean glasses, etc.) to save your master's candles.
—Jonathan Swift, *Directions to Servants*

PART
ONE

THE DEBRIS FIELD

1

So people do, as the poet remarked, come here in order to live. Our necropolis with anvils of memory chained to every street and building, every tourist postcard view. All its sunsets and bridges and mutilated dawns. Haunted house of mortal dreams, ectoplasms flickering in obsidian windows. People come here to live, after all. You'd think they were here to die. Well, aren't we all. *I will achieve grandeur,* proclaimed another poet, *but not in this apartment.*

2

Last year I lived in Paris. Now I live here, more or less. People tell me things. I listen. I watch and wait. I have discovered the junction of lapidary beauty and sublime ugliness known as *the spirit of the age.* Like stout Cortez or fat Balboa, whose vicious eyes popped wide in wild surmise, however that dumb poem goes.

Zeitgeist is a historian's favorite hallucination: a confidence trick, quanta leaping over the specific. "These people lived and died clutching statistically measured expectations to their breasts, delusions wired into their brains by lulls in the convulsions of time." We missed the big picture because our eyes locked on some whirling dervish in the lower left corner. All of us, except a few far-thinking individuals, avatars who shift history with their bare hands, starvation protests, atom bombs, religious manias, or the raw will to power.

The rest of us were *caught by surprise* when we woke up buried to our necks in shit.

Let's assume, at least, that the big picture isn't a rectangle, a film of watered silk in a frame, or a mastermind's jump cut, but something more like an urn on a mantelpiece.

Not everyone gets buried. Some burn.

Last spring, an eternity ago, as I passed in front of the Brasserie Lipp, a boy hawking *Le Monde Economique* hollered, "*Bush assassiné! Bush assassiné!,*" hoping to whip up trade. People going in and out of Lipp applauded him. . . .

3

"Alone in the yellow room at last my ankles behind your neck. My ears are between my knees planted in the rug." *I am the deity of this particular universe.* Well, no. I didn't build this horny contortionist out of mud and blow in the breath of life. I'm only a witness, and as witnesses go, maybe not the most credible sort.

A few months ago, a person I hesitate to call close, Jesse W., stayed with me for several weeks, recovering from an ugly incident he doesn't remember. He was beaten senseless, by whom and with what, nobody knows.

Jesse's apartment is two blocks from here. Much bigger and more expensive than mine. It's the kind of building that makes you wish you'd moved to New York years before you did. Or that you'd never come here in the first place. Jesse insisted on yanking piles of notebooks and photographs from shelves and drawers and showing me pictures of people we know. Or knew. Then he dragged them all over here, in boxes. He could've left them there. He wasn't moving, after all. Of course I read his diaries whenever he left the house.

I can't show you all my cards at once, but Jesse's one. Maybe several. A joker and a wild card and sometimes dull as a two of clubs. Like any game using multiple decks there are too many cards to fan out on a cramped surface all at once, and, as somebody once told me, I'm a lousy poker player: my face betrays me every time. I think this is a game of triple solitaire. I'll show you the cards you need to see faceup.

This torn-out journal page seems as typical a place as any to start with Jesse:

"The carpeting in this hotel was last shampooed when Janis Joplin OD'd across the street. The scattered magnolia scent

5

around the balcony. This morning someone asked me what I still loved in this life, what did I have left that I loved. I said: Leroy Brathwaite's penis and Franklin Avenue in springtime. Maybe I always lie when someone asks me what I love."

Undated, like most of Jesse's stuff. Timeless, you tell me.

4

Miles is bitter. Tender sentiments, smooches on his glabrous forehead, Italian vacations, fan letters, good reviews yellowing in a drawer, psychoanalysis, or the diffident kindness of strangers can't bleed out his bitterness. That's finished. The days of masking bitterness are gone. They were gone before I was.

Of all the people he had ever known, Miles announced when he was drunk, Tova Finkelstein was the least aware of what she herself was really like. And then he would tell you what she was really like.

Pathologically cheap, Tova thought of herself as Lady Bountiful.

Callous, rude, unkind to friends and strangers alike, Tova imagined herself generous, warm, friendly, and helpful.

Inflexibly petty in her private dealings, Tova insisted on being viewed in the public eye as nobly concerned with the fate of the world, with other people's sufferings, with every conceivable worthy cause. And somehow, out of brainy imperiousness and a magic trunk of flimsy disguises, Tova got herself written about as her mirror described her, in fawning magazine articles, even when the journalists knew perfectly well what a self-obsessed monster she was. Tova knew how to work the press better than Benjamin Franklin.

I listened to this endlessly. Tova. Her monstrosity. The noble poses she struck, the low impulses she dissembled. There were other monsters lurking in Miles's brain, ghosts flickering on midnight stairwells like the Evil Pretender in a Gothic romance, the gloaming chorus of what I called Miles's two-penny opera. You are too relentless for me, I would tell him. Your desires are too immense. Your frustration exhausts me and your anger swallows up everything.

I can't be with you, I said. I will go mad, I said. And then he howled, or sobbed, pleaded, flung a glass against the wall. You wait, he hissed on our last night together. Wait until the world does you in and then you tell me how relentless *I* am. All right, I said, I'll wait, I'll see. But I won't wait here in hell with you.

5

I used to visit a man who lived in lunar shadow, a man who died in cringing terror.

Jorgen Delmos had written four novels in the distant past, "unjustly obscure" in the estimate of many chronic rediscoverers of the precious. Jorgen loved hiring black hustlers and imagined that writing ornate novels about this enthusiasm was the same thing as striking a blow against racism. A bevy of high-altitude critics who patronized Jorgen without ever earning him a nickel interpreted his work in the same progressive light.

"I am grooming this dummy to take over my responsibilities," he told me whenever I came, dragging it out by a serrated trench in its plaster shoulder that shed white pebbled trails on the cracked floor. Jorgen named his dummy Cuenca, after a city he noticed on a map of Spain. "Cuenca will talk for me and write my books and eat and fuck and shit and piss and sleep for me while I slather makeup on my face and scream."

I used to bring him chicken soup when he was dying, a useless gesture, and furthermore unnoticed. Trying to be vir-tuous and worthy when your impulses run the other way re-quires a patience I've always lacked. Jorgen had arcane nutritional theories he adhered to with an alchemist's fixity. The soup went cold.

Jorgen's purported genius dragged people into his craziness. He spoke so slowly, in such a lugubrious faraway voice, that you hung on every word he managed to ooze out, each one followed by an epic pause, even as you squirmed and hated yourself for your inability to leave his shithole apartment.

He'd stolen the dummy thirty years earlier from Macy's, when he worked on the cleaning crew. Cuenca had everything but a head. A screw of some kind extruded from the center of its neck. It had breasts without nipples. She, if I can call her that, had been used for modeling bras and bustiers, and I remembered that one of Jorgen's wishes had been to write like Virginia Woolf. Had he ever been going to write another novel, I thought, that dummy would have been just the beginning. Thank God, I thought, that thing has no vagina.

6

Dinner in Santa Fe. Denise and Caroline fled New York in the fourth year of their ménage, in search of an ideal desert anachronism where the utopian eccentricities of earlier times didn't scrape against the metal teeth of electronic living. Santa Fe seemed to fit the bill, for the first week or two.

Keeping in touch was never Denise's strong suit. Before their departure, she phoned up after a nine-month silence and said:

"Caroline and I are moving to New Mexico for a while."

"A while? Couple months?"

"Possibly longer," she reluctantly allowed.

"How much longer? Six months?"

"Well, no, actually, maybe kind of permanently," said Denise, who had made withholding a kind of art form. "Depending how it works out."

I didn't hear another word until it was over.

Dinner on the moon. Wasabi-coated dried peas and other dry, unpleasantly crackly snacks as a prelude to something like jerk chicken in grapefruit sauce. Raspberry-scented candles and soft voices and the wistful ruminative memories of middle-aged people who will probably have a similar dinner, similar crunchy dried peas, and the same languid conversations in six months or a year, or three years, or ten years, when one or two of them has died. Mel, the real estate artist (as they often called him), wasted from hepatitis, his skin like waxed fruit, speaks of people who return in dreams from the dark regions where they've drifted, altered in a few particulars.

He enumerates: the people we used to know; the people who died; the people we grew tired of; the people who were waiting for a different life to come along when we knew them; the people none of us really knew; the people who showed up and left again so quickly that they only left an image dissolving in a doorway; the people who hung around for years familiar as an old shoe and one day transformed themselves, changed everything from the ground up, flew off like butterflies or crashed to earth from a preposterous height; the people who withdrew, monastically, into a harsh discipline of silence; people who cleaned up their acts and went nowhere with them; people we envied for their great looks, their money, their mastery of situations, who crumbled physically and mentally collapsed after decades of furtive dissipation; the people we still know but never see; the people we disliked for years, but came to appreciate; the people we liked at first and grew to despise after long periods of almost unconscious study; people we wanted to sleep with but didn't; people we slept with impulsively, more or less by accident; people we yearned for and made fools of ourselves over, who rejected us then, and years later, when everything that inflamed us about them had long sputtered out, attached themselves to us with fierce unwanted desire; the famous who dropped into obscurity, befriended us in those luckless times, and dropped us when fortune smiled again; the people who lived in a different world, and mistook us for other kinds of people than we were; the people we could never quite look in the eye.

Mel roamed the U.S. and Canada six months of the year, buying old houses, gutting them with his boyfriend Sam, revising them the way nouveau i-biz rich people wanted their places, i.e., like antique showrooms scattered with soft pastels, handwoven fabrics, geometric wedges of natural light. A Ross Bleckner over the ten-thousand-dollar sofa, an apple-green AGA stove warming the kitchen all year round. And, in every bathroom, a bidet. As the millennium neared, hip-hop millionaires had discovered the bidet on their first trips to Europe, and now anyone who knew his shit demanded a bidet next to every toilet.

7

According to Miles, Tova Finkelstein, his nemesis, engineered "an impossibly awkward situation" that affected and in fact entirely changed his relations with Paul, his former squeeze, a beloved New York actor dying of AIDS. When Paul became seropositive, he called on Miles, after a silence of several years, to write a one-person play for him, a *summa sexualis* that would serve as Paul's final, deeply personal artistic statement: a thing that would belong, not to the avant-garde ensemble Paul had spent his career working with, but uniquely to Paul, to a lesser extent to Miles, and also to Nigel, the man Paul now lived with, who would direct.

Ours is still the age of irony, whatever you may have read. The piece was entitled *An Evening with Jorgen Delmos*.

Miles and Nigel understood each other straightaway and liked each other, too: no proprietary frictions slipped into the mix. The three men found they could work together all day and still enjoy each other at cocktail time.

They developed the play for a year, forcing a fatalistic patience on themselves. Paul could very well expire in his sleep and that would have been the end of that, but they bore on with an obdurate baseless faith that he'd survive for as long as it took.

"I still remember the lunch in Soho when he asked me," was one of Miles's standard, sentimental rest stops mid-indictment. He reminded me of an old whore in a flowered sundress fanning herself with a theater program while wheezing rhapsodically of a girlhood flirtation. "Oysters and champagne, beluga. Funny what sticks in your mind. All the insane things we'd done years before came back. That year was like a fever dream."

Between the first and second seasons the play ran, Paul's HIV segued into full-blown AIDS. AZT was the sole, piss-poor medication available at the time. Paul was frequently sick, sometimes locked in the toilet vomiting minutes before curtain, but somehow never missed a performance. The show ran on. Crowds lined up for blocks from opening night till closing. The play's success worked better than AZT. Paul often drifted to the edge of death during the days when the theater was dark, but every weekend (*Jorgen Delmos* ran Thursday through Sunday) sprang back impossibly robust and inexhaustible. Paul and Miles won awards, Nigel won awards, it was agreed that they would run the play as long as bookings were offered; these poured in from Amsterdam, Madrid, Paris, Berlin, London, and a dozen American cities.

A few months into the second New York season, Tova began attending the occasional performance. Soon it was every performance, current girlfriend in tow. They frequently joined Paul and Nigel for late dinners and drinks.

"Tova always speaks so highly of you," Paul told Miles. Miles kept his mouth shut. Of course Tova spoke highly of him, she wasn't a fool, Miles knew she had something up her sleeve that not speaking highly of him might very well compromise.

After many such evenings, the sleeve was reached into and out came her trump card. Tova proposed that she and Paul, and Nigel in some capacity, and the young dramaturg, all work up a show together: Paul, alone onstage, in an evening of Beckett monologues. Tova directing. Tova's illustrious name mesmerized Paul, who was, after all, dying, and wanted to go out in the biggest blaze of glory possible. The major triumph of his play with Miles and Nigel began to look an almost puny end, compared to a classy Beckett thing directed by world-renowned Tova. Tova's many theatrical ventures had not been uniformly distinguished, but the name, the proper name—that was sheer ormolu. Paul's physical decay thrown into the mix was kismet wrapped in a maharajah's turban. Paul pictured himself like Antonin Artaud in the throes of apocalyptic insanity, literally rattling apart, dissolving into brilliant morbid particles before a capacity crowd, preferably at Lincoln Center.

8

Late in the summer before the dark, Jesse finds a bale of forgotten photographs, densely bundled as tobacco leaves in a cigar factory. We smoke a joint. He spreads them on his floor with blunt-fingered dispatch, his face scrunched with concentration, keeping up a shaky, self-correcting patter as he stumbles down memory lane.

"These underpass streets choked with ozone," he says, in the spooked whisper of an actor simulating a voodoo trance. "Out along Queens Boulevard, where I used to go cruising with Leon. That's when you know you're old, you even cruise with a sense of irony."

Leon Ivray is a friend we have in common. Still, I wouldn't have guessed he and Jesse were ever close enough to go cruising together. Leon makes movies when he isn't teaching. Years ago he documented theater pieces on video. Jesse acts, or used to act. Maybe then. These pictures must be old.

"I don't know when I took these," Jesse says, catching my thought. "They should have date stamps somewhere. Maybe on the negatives, if I could find them. Dominican joints, Haitian discos, male go-go bars where nothing ever happened."

And he describes the black shadows under the El, the homicidal current in those streets after dark. *Pollo frito* in stainless-steel warming bins, oily under yellow bulbs. Metal accordion bellows padlocked on storefronts. The rusted pylons and rivets of the El slopped with blue paint smeary with dust-furred grease. Events poke out like sharp rocks in the stream. A boy's eyes strafing the sidewalk for an angry blowjob and wishing you dead as his look hits your face. Limpid water races over magnified pebbles in the riverbed, hides itself in the daylight of habit.

Habit conquers everything. Habit "passes the time." It puts you under with a smoky kiss, when you wake the world is older.

This trove of photos spilled off a closet shelf. Others materialized under clothes piled in corners, in boxes long thought to contain old tax receipts and newspaper clippings.

Jesse says he's trying to clear away twenty years of being here, so he can go on living. Memory suffocates him. Look here, he says: People frozen, staring into tomorrow's question mark, with yesterday's answers for a frame. Hopeful faces. Self-assured. These faces that are killing him. The camera snatched them at parties where they were busy sniffing, getting drunk, smoking cigarettes. Planning big things that didn't always work out. "I have it all under control," some faces say, faces owned by the dead. But for a moment—this moment when he had his camera—glamour sparkled all over them like an immortal dancing flame.

Time is a raging river, a torrent of time. In a photo invisible like gelatin. Sometimes clogged and unreadable because of the memories it stirs up. The space between objects: empty. The flicker of a smile: fading. Gestures: what do these fluttering hands say, exactly.

You have your face written all over your face.

Skies smeary with orange clouds. Drive over any of those bridges on a summer night, you arrive at Queens Boulevard. We went out one winter, in Leon's car, and again in summertime, for the strangeness. Between great stretches of darkness the stingy blue neon of a sex bar. Dancers with gleaming pricks kicked over drinks along the sloppy wooden counter.

When you cross those steep bridges into the weird swarming life outside the center of things, and see the template of this city from its approaches, you confront the monumentality of ancient Rome, you become tiny and incidental in the realm of

17

geological time. It takes thousands of faceless beings to build those massive walls and string girders miles above the earth. Thousands of faceless faces, eons of forgotten time, a dark river pulling everything under. Every man for himself and God against all, *toujours c'est vrai, c'est tout.*

9

"This would make the independent little art movie from hell." Miles said this, warming up, or something like this, invariably, leering furiously. "You could get that fat fuck, what's her name, Indie the Pig, to produce it, and call it *A Dyke's Revenge*." Miles pulled the Epic of Tova from his repertoire for strangers, deliberately, in situations where I had to listen, determined to force a cackle from me, despite my disapproval. I thought it disgraced him to give Tova such obvious mental prominence, as if her so-called revenge had occurred the week before instead of ten years earlier.

He sounded like one of the Beat era's antique raconteurs, frozen in the dead past, who greeted every new person he met with the same stale bouquet of self-glorifying memories. Not every writer leaves the best parts of himself on the page, but I'd had the deflating experience of meeting Paul Bowles, whose books I loved, on two separate occasions, a few months apart; I'd been dragged to his Tangiers apartment by two different, zealous groupies. Bowles didn't remember me the second time— I doubt if he remembered anyone who passed through his apartment, unless it was a bona fide celebrity. On both visits he recited the same mantralike tales about Arthur Chester coming to Tangiers with Susan Sontag, Arthur Chester filling his apartment with a truckful of oranges that rotted, Arthur Chester inundating the roof of his building with water that seeped through the masonry, collapsing all the ceilings. I swear Bowles repeated every word without moving a comma. I had no idea who Arthur Chester was, and made no effort to find out. I was depressed to seem so insignificant to Bowles. On the other hand, I disliked him rather much. He played the same broken record for every visitor. Contrived a mystique to draw people in, then claimed to resent their intrusions. One of many strategies for turning an essentially passive life into boilerplate mythology. Bowles was talking to himself, of course, and these were the stories he liked to hear.

"It was an elaborately constructed, very intricate and evil sort of dish eaten cold," Miles would croon in a devilish way, warming to a long-winded effort of character assassination. He didn't sound weary enough to pass for a Living Legend. I should have urged him to visit Tangiers while Bowles was still around, for pointers. "Tova's poison macaroni salad, but it had a fatal flaw built into it—*she just assumed I could never run as cold as she did.*"

10

I am writing these notes in the depths of the fait accompli, in no special order. I hardly need to tell you that the worst has already happened, is happening now, will happen tomorrow, and next month, and a year from Sunday. Like Jesse with his scrambled snapshots, I offer whichever pieces flash in front of me and hope you can baste a quilt if somebody hands you the squares.

People tell me things. I have no idea why. Anna M., for example, a woman I met eight or nine years ago. I never see her. She moves in shadows. No matter where I am on earth she finds me, confides her darkest secrets into the telephone. "You have to know this," she tells me. "You have to know this in case something happens."

What could happen, I wonder. Yet clearly Anna M. has a sense of fatality about *the spirit of the age,* or about herself, about her coding in the matrix. I'm not sure she's wrong, either.

Strange to say, the man she's living with calls me too: I have a long, twined, entirely separate and secret connection with Malcolm, one that began years ago during a weekend I spent in Baltimore, and continued after Malcolm moved here. He hustled then. Perhaps because I wasn't a customer, Malcolm chose me as a confidant. No one has written the script for this sort of thing. Malcolm calls me as if I were a trusted uncle who will listen to his problems and reassure him that his dreams will come true, and while I'm not sure of this at all, I listen, I say what he needs to hear.

11

A letter to Jesse from Arthur, on his summer island:

This morning debris from the crashed Airbus
washed up on Playa Hernando de Soto: some
rubber snorkeling flippers, evidently, a charred
suitcase, a jumbo package of disposable diapers
called Huggies. Therese, the Italian girl who
works mornings in the More Hot above the port,
stumbled across these things while jogging along
the wet sand at five A.M., and turned them in to the
investigators from Madrid who've been swarming all
over these islands since the crash five days ago.

12

Anna M. wakes, shaken by silent-film dreams that have stalked her for a week or more. Images washing through her unconscious like coils of matted seaweed are residue from a silent-era retrospective she recently saw too much of, to please Malcolm. The dreams feature herself and her psychoanalyst, Laurence Seagrave, their dependencies reversed: she's pushing Seagrave in a French invalid chair along the cobbled paths of an English garden. Before long they're screaming at each other. She pushes the chair with such violence that it tips over and dumps Seagrave into an ornamental rock pond.

As she scrambles out of sleep, she feels Malcolm's cock inside her, a hefty bone of heroic proportions and obduracy, riveting into her up to the hilt, his fingers kneading her breasts from behind, his mouth open sucking her shoulder. *He fucks me in my sleep* is another thing she's been meaning to tell Seagrave, though she knows Malcolm prods her vagina wide open to let her know that he loves her.

13

From a fat manila envelope bursting at the seams, Jesse fishes snapshots of Millie Ferguson. He remembers her green eye shadow, glassy Mylar dresses, high wiry whore-blond hair, the array of indelible expressions that wacky woman wore instead of jewelry. Millie exuded an air of hoarding astounding secrets and spiriting special people into dark corners to examine her pussy (which Jesse'd always imagined the lair of rare African snakes or fantastic Amazonian orchids), or to snuffle up an Everest of cocaine. The dope addict rictus, the born sneak's irresistible smirk, the stolid Teutonic jawline that slackened like rubber after two A.M. Millie Ferguson got ambushed by mirrors, stuck to them like a pinned butterfly, and who wouldn't if they looked like her? People wanted either to be Millie or fuck her, or both. Through indefatigable outrageousness and a sense of fun that recognized no moral boundaries, Millie escaped a destiny in lower case her working-class background had laid out for her. She had all that wicked cleverness going on, only closest friends saw her touching insecurity, the naive longing to do something important, to make a big statement, to be something more lasting than the world's greatest party girl.

"I want to forget all this," Jesse says, "but what if one day I want to remember?" Frivolous options.

14

Caroline slips into neocortical badlands like a night-thriving flower choking on sunlight. Santa Fe's harsh sky oppresses her; the desert activates her fear of open space. In the cool of the rented house, the bosky rooms numb her fraying nerves, like a damp cloth laid across a forehead pulsing with migraine. Denise finds the house too gloomy, writes on the back patio. Caroline can no longer place one word next to another. She has nothing further to say using any alphabet she's familiar with. She is waiting. Waiting for a bird, a package wrapped in Christmas paper, lost objects to return by magic, an answer to no question.

15

I should insert here, as it may tell us something, a montage of Anna's typical movements in this city of glass and steel. She frequently takes cabs, and though her destinations are specific— office buildings, restaurants, retail stores—she always tells the driver to take her "anywhere near Thirty-third and Seventh," "somewhere around City Hall Plaza," "Eighty-seventh and Madison or around there," as if prolonging the option of changing her mind, avoiding the person she's meeting, walking off in the opposite direction from the place she's expected. And in truth this happens often lately. The contrary impulse to deflect an encounter, avoid the noise of a particular voice, the banality of a familiar face, has made her absurdly late for a lunch or a business appointment or caused her to blow it off altogether.

Sometimes she circles the block where a date waits for her. She becomes transfixed by ugly, unaccountably horrifying objects in store windows. These merchandise items seize her attention and compel her to stand motionless staring at them, with an incomprehension that fills her with nausea. It's as if, piece by piece, the constituent elements of the universe are forming a picture too alien and unbelievable to contemplate.

Anna M. hasn't yet reached the point where she believes all the pieces lock together. But they are starting to connect. The grotesque handbag in Bergdorf's display case, the movie ad on a passing city bus, stray objects abandoned on sidewalks, the overflow of garbage cans, smartly dressed people stuffing their faces behind restaurant plate glass.

Anna frequently hears voices when she sits in a restaurant or walks in the street, voices she believes address her, cryptic phrases, outright insults, but we shouldn't jump to the conclusion that Anna's delusional, having auditory hallucinations, paranoid. For she has always, for reasons she cannot account for, attracted the attention, the keen and specific personal attention, of insane persons, and others who are, in one way or another, slipping out of control.

Anna also has an uncanny ability to find money in the street. Not just the occasional dime or quarter, but bills, sometimes in high denominations. Only a week ago, stepping out of a cab, she discovered a hundred-dollar note clinging to her shoe. Wiping off it what appeared to be large drops of fresh blood, she treated herself to a pair of Mephistos at Shoe Mania on Fourteenth Street.

16

"An air disaster has no personality," Arthur writes Jesse.

Sad. Even the wreckage is generic. Airliners
don't get named, the way ships do. They're
identified by numbers after they crash. Even
the ways they go down lack that epic dimension. It's either a bomb or a malfunction,
some process that starts before the plane
leaves the runway. The disaster's over in seconds. In cases like this, those "emergencies
over water" for which the passengers are duly
instructed in the placement of evacuation
chutes and inflatable flotation vests, nobody
ever survives.

There isn't any fascinating lore about these
doomed flying vessels. You never hear accounts
of earlier, successful voyages. The successful
flight is precisely one nobody remembers, and
nobody hears about. It isn't even a "voyage,"
but a disagreeable necessity, like having an
MRI or a cardiogram after you faint on a golf
course. The plane is a tin can that one day
flies apart instead of sailing from airport to
airport like a Frisbee. Nobody broke a bottle
over its nose, and no one remembers waltzing
in its grand ballroom.

So far, the most evocative thing to pop to the
surface—besides severed limbs and other body
parts—has been a waterlogged teddy bear from a
hotel gift shop in Tenerife, which the three- and

four-day-old papers that have reached the island
featured on their front pages, to dramatize the
"extra sadness" thought to obtain when small children are among the dead.

17

Tova knew all about Miles's and Paul's love affair from Miles telling her about it. Tova's brainstorm—stitching various Beckett monologues together for Paul to deliver onstage—was, in Miles's view, the mechanism for wreaking a meticulously plotted revenge on himself.

"Don't get me wrong," Miles would qualify, "I'm sure she thought Paul was a great actor. But Tova knows a lot of great actors. Paul just happened to be the only one I had an emotional bond with, and I was one of the few people who ever dumped Tova before she could dump them."

Paul's oncoming death, Paul's artistic legacy—these were the critical things at stake in this endeavor as far as Paul was concerned, and, as Miles put it, Paul had always been wrapped up in Paul like a self-addressed envelope, despite his charm, his joie de vivre, his willingness to get trashed and let the good times roll, even as he fell apart.

When you cut out the sentimental horseshit, Miles sniffed, what you were left with was this: Tova, whose opportunism was the stuff of legend, figured she could get this actor to actually *die onstage* in a production she directed, a publicity windfall of incalculable proportions, and Paul figured it would add sauce, temporally speaking, to his posthumous reputation if he *dropped dead* under Tova Finkelstein's direction.

"An ingenious revenge," Miles declared with rapt disgust, "*hypothetically*. Much as I may have loved Paul, though, and really cherished the emotional intensity of that project, that atmosphere of lethal obstacles overcome, my interest soured right after the play opened. Especially after it went on tour. Imagine, I arrive for the Los Angeles opening and there on my bed is the *LA Weekly,* containing a full-page ad for the thing *without my name on it*."

The dramaturg, a turkey-plump, transparently conniving creature from the black lagoon of Paul's cultlike acting ensemble, as Miles put it, had contrived at every opportunity to subtract Miles's writing credits from the play's ads. Paul, self-involved as always, had only moved to correct this sabotage when Miles threatened legal action.

"Which brought it all back," Miles droned on. "Those years at his beck and call, everything centered on Paul's needs, Paul's demands, Paul's libido, Paul's schedule. Poison had seeped into the thing even before Tova showed up. Which proves," he added, abruptly aiming his monologue at me, "the inadequacy of sentimental narratives we weave around people we fuck on more than one or two occasions."

So, to finish with this particular obsession, Tova's intervention in what had been shaping itself into a soap opera remake of a messily petered-out affair, a "made for TV" kind of dying-homo "closure" ending, relieved Miles of the tiresome duty to trail in Paul's orbit until the medically unpleasant end, spared him from being used all the way to the morgue for the greater glory of Paul. Tova had unintentionally freed Miles to take a distanced view of what had transpired over the previous year between himself and Paul.

"You always disappeared when people were dying anyway," I shot back during one of these recitatives. "You crapped out on Millie Ferguson and a whole bunch of other people."

"Millie couldn't *talk* anymore," Miles screeched defensively. "Our whole *relationship* was based on talking. I said my good-byes," he insisted.

No, I thought, you didn't. Millie had been his muse, his star actress, also one of his best friends. She had lost the power of speech, yes, but had scrawled his name on an envelope when Edith Eddy asked who she wanted to see.

18

Caroline's memory is loaded with toxins, as a gun is loaded with bullets. Ten years ago she expelled her politician father's midnight visits to her bedroom in their Fairfield brick Colonial, regurgitated nine later years of heroin addiction, crystallized her secret inferno into a highly lauded first novel. She had gone into the Program three years earlier. When she sold the book, she'd drunk nothing stronger than ice water since then, and looked askance at any pill stronger than Tylenol.

A few months after she met Denise, she felt "strong enough" to sample a vodka and orange juice. She was, for a while, strong enough. Dis-enabling people was not one of Denise's talents. Some people can look out for other people. Some can't. Denise had her own problems, which happened to require a flair for self-medication. Years older than Caroline and far less reckless by nature, Denise had found her strength, not in overcoming things, but in succumbing to them, riding the waves they rolled through her metabolism, learning her body's reactions to pharmaceuticals.

Caroline believes she's been taking care of herself. She adds an inch of water to her drinks and only on Saturdays allows herself to go as far as groggy incoherence. She lies in her room, fully dressed but limp as a floor mop, opening and closing a notebook of blank pages. She doesn't experience her unwillingness to move from the bed as depression. If you are merely *on* the bed, she tells herself, that's a nap.

19

I'm forgetting the salmon mayonnaise, and a number of other possibly important items: for instance, these lines from Rimbaud that Anna read before going to sleep, before dreaming of Seagrave, before Malcolm's busy prick woke her up: *The day before the Great Day, she fell ill. / Like whispering in the church, dark and high, / She felt a shivering she could not still, / An endless shivering: "I am going to die."* And not only these words, but images from *Les Vampires*: Feuillade's serial was one of the few things Anna appreciated at the silent-film retrospective Malcolm dragged her to; its narrative weirdness, its insistent and continual reversals of fortune for both the police and the villain Vampire Gang, felt like the psychic storms that slammed her every time she left the apartment.

Malcolm, who dreams of directing movies, walks and talks movies almost obsessively, references movies as shorthand for events happening in real life, had insisted that if she really wanted to know how his mind worked, she had to view at least forty hours of silent movies, specific ones he'd circled weeks in advance on the program calendar.

Anna has to admit that a few quirks of Malcolm's personality have unexpectedly fallen into place since she sat through that avalanche of waking dreams, though not the ones she's wondered about since she met him.

20

In the depths of the fait accompli.

"Two hundred and sixty-one dead," Arthur writes.

Mainly burnt, blown, filleted, merged into
chunks and shards of metal and plastic that
forensics experts are reassembling in an abandoned soap factory near Barcelona. (Remind me
to tell you, when I get back, a funny story
about *savon de Marseilles* and the cable in-
staller, if you think of it.) None of us has
television here (though satellite dishes
sprout from the roofs of all the local people's houses, and at night, now, unlike other
summers, the card tables and horseshoe pits
that used to liven the evening alleys and cobbled lanes have more or less disappeared; a
blue glow emits from the white stucco window
frames, whole families blockily outlined
against the cathode fizz), but the progress of
this massive jigsaw puzzle has been the lead
item of radio news every day since the crash.
Three more bodies have been identified, is today's word. I don't know if that means teeth
or it means whole bodies, I couldn't follow
the rest of it in that rapid radio Spanish.

"Look at this one," Jesse insists. "It's Richard Guinness. You wouldn't know about this, but he lived in the Bronx. He had this awful apartment, I mean a nice apartment for middle-class people. I felt so sorry for him, to be so far away from everything."

Jesse says he hated to think of young, eager, ambitious Richard, who had nibbled the fringe of the downtown scene since practically childhood, working the door of various nightclubs, hanging around Burroughs and Ginsberg and all the Bohemian aristocracy, knocking off at five from the publishing job he ended up with to board some airless screeching subway and vanish into Bronx obscurity.

Richard lived alone then, Jesse explains. His plangent distance from things must have bothered him, since as soon as he acquired a best-seller for his company he leased a duplex in Soho, which was still the fulcrum of the art world then, instead of its boutique-encrusted, abandoned shell. Once Richard had a place in town, he also had a boyfriend, a circle of intimates, frequent parties and wacky home decorations, pepper lights and a kidney-shaped coffee table, and a degree of power within the kookier fringes of publishing.

"These pictures fell out of the box," Jesse said, "and landed in your cat litter. Taken, I think, at the only party Richard ever threw, up in the Bronx. The only one he invited me to, anyway. See? You can see Millie Ferguson wasn't sick yet, Edith Eddy's over here in the background, what year would that be? Edith and Eddy."

Edith and Eddy, last of the underground superstars. Lovers of convenience, but their friendship was fiercer, more emotionally volatile than the sexual liaison. A few years after the picture was taken, Millie married a Spanish junkie. Edith spun away on her mysterious gypsy travels, disappearing for as long as six months at a time. When Millie and her husband both got AIDS, though, Edith came back, nursing them with an air of high purpose in Millie's apartment on Bleecker Street. Sometimes Millie and her spouse were hospitalized at the same time, in the same room, a set of bellows pumping glop from the husband's lungs. Edie, for all her self-absorption, could always take better care of other people than herself.

Lyle Lindsay, a spectral fleck of lint from that era, hadn't snagged his first job in fashion yet, because you can see in one of the pictures he's working Richard's party as the bartender. Lyle, beefy in this incarnation, had retreated to the Bronx after his first turn at downtown notoriety or visibility or whatever. People go back where they came from when they don't know what else to do. The moment of the early eighties in this picture was that kind of time for a lot of people. Clean-up time for many of the city's kamikaze harlequins, buy-that-Hamptons-basilica time for others who had cleaned up in the other sense.

Jesse has some other snaps of Lyle, from a bunch that slid behind a dresser fifteen years ago, that the new, fanatical Brazilian lady who cleans his apartment found, pix from the earliest Lyle of Bohemia. Cute-as-a-lemur-Lyle, the first Lyle anybody knew. Cascading black curls, long lashes, lips full enough to qualify as sex organs, "pooky big" brown eyes. No muscles on his wan, skinny body, but in those days, 1978, '79, muscles were hardly de rigueur. Few had them. People who did were considered freaks. One could also have chest hair (soon to become verboten even on straight men), which Lyle, profusely, did.

People fell blindly in love with faces instead of bodies. Faces, at least, gave a closer map of a person's soul than rippled abs.

Though maybe not vastly closer, as time often demonstrated. Lyle fooling with Millie's hair, Lyle dolling his own mug with lip gloss and eye shadow, Lyle spinning on the dance floor at Studio 54.

Lyle later gained so much weight his beauty melted out into something cruder, blunt and thuggish, that conjured a radically different set of expectations when you looked at him. He fattened up on purpose, being sick of people hitting on him. At the same time, an assertive chunkiness refuted any whisper of AIDS.

Lyle arrived on the scene at sixteen, a Puerto Rican fuck bunny, towed by the witty, fantastically cruel, grossly effeminate barge of a poet who wanted to be esteemed as Baudelaire Junior, feared for his evil nature and worshipped for his ready tongue. You wouldn't have inferred that this steamy love machine named Lyle (we learned his family name when the poet let go of him, after months of messy public scenes involving thrown food and jewelry ripped from clothing and body parts) was a bossy bottom by predilection, who only topped as an onerous chore when a date got his signals crossed.

The poet had often screeched across packed restaurant dining rooms that he, the poet, never once took it up the ass except from his father, that he played "the man" every fuck every time. Few credited this entirely accurate boast, but I never doubted it. The top has all the opportunities to inflict physical pain, and Baudelaire Junior was—excuse me, is—a pathological sadist. He spoke, speaks, fluent French, and could, can, mimic Renata Tebaldi's most demanding arias note perfectly. For these and similarly trivial reasons people imagined him anal-receptive, and somehow brushed away the recurring suspicion that he really was as Evil as any Burroughsian centipede or serial killer, even though he told them so himself.

Whatever happened to Baudelaire *fils?* is a seasonally popped query here and there, in the exotic zones of Fairyland where persons over thirty can order a drink without squirming. Nearly always, underscored by an undisguised wish to hear of his unobited demise. I used to wonder how many column inches, if any, the paper of record would award him as its parting humiliation, so often contrived for "people like us" in lieu of physically defecating on our graves, but I'm now convinced that this particular *fleur du mal,* with its Tiffany-blue petals, will outlive even *The New York Times.*

Baudelaire Junior has vast recuperative powers, like all who have sealed a pact with darkness. He's still around, thriving on an ingenious if not entirely original form of extortion, a volunteer minion of Satan who's still hilarious when he cares to be, still ponderously inhuman, the musical-comedy version of Pol Pot or Mussolini: his audiences shift on the tides of his fortunes—but the poet will, I believe, live forever, in more or less the same indestructible form, able to chill a room of any size simply by entering, thoroughly terrorizing any nonmineral organism contained therein. His face has caved in, in the Gallic manner, but what's losing a face when you've always had two?

The idea that there was a center and a periphery to our specific urban geography held powerful sway over everyone in Jesse's old photographs at the time they were taken. An idea for the very young, for sleek and casually coupling mammals swimming in a crowded pool. The people in Jesse's box are all in their twenties and thirties, and even the ugliest among them has a real face, an iconic face. You can read in their eyes the glowing belief that on a given night there is only one, at most two or three, acceptably cool places to be, that "life" is occurring only in Restaurant X, Bar Y, Nightclub Z, and that anyplace else is a kind of unworthy human mulch, a sublife substitute for the authentic *vie de bohème*. Even if you stayed home reading a book in those palpitant nights and starry mornings, you missed "life," absented yourself from the surging rivers of possibility.

Millie Ferguson enslaved herself to this compulsion worse than any pedigreed insider. (Or better than anybody, if you like it that way.) Unless people looked at her, Millie didn't exist. She had to go out every night of her life, had to spend hours preparing for multiple entrances about town, had to believe that wherever she went was the only possible place to be. This could turn tricky, because her own presence anywhere carried enough cachet to lift a mediocre place, a nowhere place, into a simulacrum of "the right place," and could delude the nothing people in that place that they were in the right place, and, worse, that they were the right people. When I hear Millie's lisping voice in my head, which I still do after all these years, what I hear most often is "Leth get out of here."

22

Quite early last summer, I rent a cottage near the beach in Truro, Cape Cod, and abandon it soon afterward out of a dread presentiment. While I'm there, a few familiars surface in the landscape.

"This island is getting to be just like everyplace else," says Edith Eddy one morning. Her quirky insistence that we are on an island, rather than a peninsula, has something to do with Edith picturing herself the Robinson Crusoe of our day and her milieu. Which she sort of is. "ATMs, Burger King, New Balance sneakers, Starbucks."

She says this while sipping a Venti Mocha Frappuccino from the latter establishment, recently opened near the hydrofoil landing where people embark for a large, actual island thirteen nautical miles away. She's stopped by to see if I need any odd paying jobs performed.

Edith Eddy is one of the seasonal people who drift onto the Cape penniless around the end of May, and spend the summer busing tables or tending bar, painting houses, catering parties. Most of these transient workers are students, or just out of college, but Edith has led this footloose existence for decades. She doesn't always leave when the season's over; if she earns enough to make it through the winter, she rents a shack and hangs on during the cold, when the sluggish local pace resumes.

"There sure are a lot more people here this year than any summer I remember."

I have no jobs for Edith. I give her a ceramic mug for her frappuccino. If you ask Edie how she is, you don't have to say another word for at least an hour. This still charismatic woman of fifty-seven, who attempted an acting career many years ago, is so mired in intricate difficulties and convoluted plans for getting out of them that most conversations with her really consist of witnessing a self-flagellating monologue that would make a good audition piece for tryouts of something by Clifford Odets or Eugene O'Neill. She isn't acting. This is how Edith Eddy breathes.

It's pointless to offer advice. The moment her situation becomes anything resembling stable, Edith throws everything away on a caprice, takes sudden flight to New Orleans, or adopts several handicapped animals, as if it were urgent to always start life over from zero, or from a new web of impossible entanglements. On the positive side, Edie isn't self-pitying in any usual way. She doesn't whine. She seldom asks for help, and when she does, the request is heartbreakingly modest. She just torments herself as a sort of performance art.

She hasn't found work in any of the usual bars or restaurants. For the past month, she's helped a contractor gut and rebuild a wing of a house owned by Chrissie Blodgett, the "decadent lifestyle" photographer. Chrissie used to be an old friend of Edith's. Over the past ten years, since becoming a cash cow of the world photography market with glossy pictures of "beautiful and damned" young people in scungy apartments and other settings of decrepitude, Chrissie has turned most of her friends into employees. Some say she always treated them like employees anyway, but now, when she absolutely must, she pays them. They smooth her noisy progress through the realms of strife, so to speak. Bring her magazines and cigarettes, some glassines of smack when she checks into rehab. Mind her bags when she travels. Edith Eddy's bitterness against Chrissie takes the relatively mild form of thin smiles, rolled eyes, "ironic" faces when Chrissie's mentioned. All the same, Chrissie impresses her.

The several permanent members of Chrissie's entourage—Edith's really a temp, and goes her own way, but Chrissie has a core of aging "assistants" Edie will spend the summer around, unless she's lucky—tend to credit every puffy adjective of Chrissie's publicity machine, PMK, as they aren't in the habit of trusting their own perceptions, and confuse their anger at Chrissie's imperious behavior with their own replacement envy. As they all want to become Chrissie or something like her, they need to believe the tripe written about her as the kind of thing that one day will be written about them.

I know Chrissie rather well. We skirl each other warily at public gatherings. She pretends to adore my work and I pretend to adore hers. Chrissie is a genius at bonding with people incapable of emotional detachment from the objects they covet, the people they envy. She has an infallible instinct that tells her when a sycophant is about to flip over into a lifelong enemy, and a thousand proven methods of getting rid of them a week or two before the Awakening.

"Well"—Edith Eddy smirks as she puts her mug aside—"I suppose it's time to go nail Sheetrock for *the Princess*."

23

I am, I think, the grudgingly Too Memorious.

I remember a time when Miles treasured his friendship with Tova, whose mind was a baroque fountain of brilliantly synthesized observations, the kind of gusher you get once a century, as the dying writer with the Macy's dummy, Jorgen Delmos (whom Tova once championed in an essay, and whom Paul incarnated in a play Miles wrote for him), used to say—a Tova with whom he traded books that one or the other had stumbled across in the dozens of used-book stores that used to exist in Manhattan. Arcane, crumbling volumes, decades or centuries out of any literary loop, that lit up vistas of terra incognita to their eager investigation.

A Tova he copped and shared amphetamine with, Obetrol, Eskatrol, Ritalin, and powdered meth, a Tova he gabbed with for hours about Nietzsche, or the *Pillow Book of Sei Shonagon*, or Tommaso Landolfi, chaperoned to midnight kung fu movies in Times Square. Even in that relatively sociable time "in the arts," Miles and Tova did things with a spontaneity and open-headed enthusiasm that was becoming rarer and more circumscribed among Miles's other friends, who were shedding the chaos of their early city days, inking dinners and lunches into Filofaxes, eventually conceiving a real evening out as a little bite of sushi and a nightcap in a nearby tavern. Running wild might include a movie. Moreover, Tova seemed really to love Miles, to place him outside the categories she slotted everybody else into: the walkers, the protégés, the Nobel Prize–winning chums she considered her true peers, and so forth.

Miles's closeness to Tova was something he let people know about, as casually as such a famous connection can be referenced, i.e., not very. He felt special to be special for her, special to receive her almost daily calls and not have to make them himself, special to appear as her "date" at the opera, the theater, the movies.

Tova had tactics for making such dates invisible to exalted figures they bumped into, when it suited her, but she sometimes introduced Miles to important people, when that suited her. She took him places where he'd never be invited on his own, and often praised things he published—at that time, mostly essays and reviews, the occasional poem or short story. Tova didn't like his plays. Once, when he failed to appear at a performance she attended, she dismissed it the following day as "silly," which wounded him to the quick. He quickly rationalized the remark as her pique at his absence.

If my memory is good for anything, that friendship developed when they both felt lonesome and ill-used. Miles scraped writing jobs for pathetic sums of money and mounted many no-budget theater productions and found all his efforts trashed in the press, even when his plays collected huge audiences "downtown." Tova, whose soaring altitude among the international intelligentsia had kept her in radiant public view for decades, had hit a fallow, amphetamine-repetitive impasse in her writing, and at the same time experienced the desertion of her earlier constituency because of a political volte-face she unleashed in a series of essays and speeches. What she actually said and wrote became crudely twisted by journalists who envied her brains.

Their friendship lasted for several years. They met up in Paris, Rome, Berlin. Even when Tova's time ticked at a premium, moments occurred when she listened patiently while Miles recited his latest poems, moments when Tova dropped the demands of her eminence to focus on Miles, suggest directions for his work. Moments, too, when their closeness produced awkward openings for physical intimacy.

Once, flippantly assigned weird boarding arrangements by the Toronto Film Festival, Miles found himself, late one night, in Tova's luxury hotel room, drinking an embarrassed cognac from the minibar (Tova disapproved of alcohol, it rotted the brain), when Tova, stretched out fully dressed on the bed, suggested, as unsuggestively as her gruff masculine side could manage, that Miles "bunk in for the night" with her.

Miles could not picture himself an object of Tova's desire. He was, yes, very handsome. But Tova preferred women, and knew that Miles had only slept with three women in his life, and gotten nothing out of it. There was no misreading what the invitation meant. The phrase "bunk in" repulsed him. Miles improvised what seemed, at the time, a plausibly gnarled excuse to return to the apartment he'd been assigned along with the editor of several films he'd worked on: that this editor would feel slighted, and abandoned to the mercies of the apartment's owner, an earth-mother type who incessantly knitted large, ugly sweaters and offered mugs of herbal tea.

Riding a bus through the black subzero night, Miles realized how easily Tova had seen through his dissembling, straight to his fear of fucking her. It wasn't just fear of fucking her, but fear that fucking her might become a regular event, or a regular expectation, and that this changed dimension of their dealings would pulverize the equilibrium between them.

It might be that Tova could be as casual about a toss as any male trick of his. She had cultivated a mystique of orgies and bisexuality early in her career. As a matter of obdurate and eventually absurd principle, she'd always refused to declare her sexuality in public. Her latter-day attachments to female lovers were obtusely obsessive, abject, manipulative, cruel, and futile

45

in every case Miles had been privy to. She'd even stalked certain women who broke up with her, left ugly organic matter in paper bags on their doorsteps. He'd felt embarrassed for her, as these manias so resembled the ignominious ones he himself developed around unavailable or indifferent men, and he wanted to think Tova more emotionally developed than himself. As he had learned so much from her, he had hoped to glean her supposed sexual sophistication by osmosis. But apparently when a nadir of disappointment had been reached, Tova turned out as clueless as Miles, even stormier and less assuageable.

She didn't metamorphose overnight from friend to enemy, and if Miles had not been hardwired to expect betrayal from people close to him, I think, the sequence of mishaps, many of them accidents, that eventually made it impossible for him to utter a decent word about her might never have had that effect on him. I sometimes wondered if the episode he considered her "ultimate revenge" hadn't been Tova's clumsy attempt to reconcile with him. I'm not a mind reader. As I said before, I'm probably not even a reliable witness.

24

Stuck to the back of one of Jesse's snapshots, a Polaroid of a fist sailing into the camera lens. The deformedly tall, cadaverous photographer who couldn't take his eyes off anything rotten in the corner of a toilet stall, a lump of roadkill on the Interstate, a friend in his funeral casket. His obscure Scandinavian origins, which seemed to include a Dickensian orphanage somewhere, and other soul-crushing varieties of precocious woe, ending in a wall of glass that sliced the space between himself and other people. His professional existence, like that of many photographers, was one of pure predatory aggression, and, as often happens, he had a veritable phobia about being photographed, his hand flying over his face the second he spotted another camera in the room. He was, for someone so fucked up as to seem beyond the pale of anything like normal relations, kind of a nice guy. As long as you didn't try taking his picture.

"I think someone gave me that," Jesse said. "I sure as hell didn't take it."

I don't mind sifting through Jesse's treasures. But I wish he'd throw them out. Whoever said the past is another country didn't know the half of it.

25

Caroline interposed between herself and her father a solid testament she had every right to believe would miniaturize him to a condition of insignificance. Whatever conventional paternal good wishes he held for his daughter's career were handed back in a package that exploded in his face. She had even contrived a life beyond his understanding, one he might very well blame himself for if he disapproved of it, which he probably did, though he was also the sort of man who rented girl-girl porn videos and masturbated to them in his study, as his wife, a Valium zombie, snored obliviously upstairs.

The sales of that first book did not reach the astronomical figure Caroline anticipated. Women with less talent but a firmer grasp of the melodramatic, self-pitying note consumers of the material Caroline was dealing with expected such a book to strike, women who spoke the language of "hurt" and "betrayal" and "the need for closure" had also been raped by their fathers, and wrote books about it that did not engage, as Caroline's did, any irreverent sense of absurdity about the concept of "family" itself, or indicate any extraneous brain activity. Caroline had not adequately depicted herself as a victim hollowed of all substance by violation. She was the least lucrative kind of victim: an intellectual who did not need rescuing by a strong yet gentle man's "healing love," a lesbian who read Kierkegaard, pondered over string theory, and worst of all, did not think forgiveness brought a nice warm feeling in its wake.

The advance had been large and Caroline went through it so pleasantly that two years later she was working at a Kinko's. She outlined another book. She made herself interesting to a powerful agent who engineered another quarter-million deal, despite her disappointing sales history. She invested a substantial part of the new money in what were considered to be conservative stocks.

Denise had inherited money from several maiden aunts she had made it her business to provide with regular company as the aging process inflicted its usual sequential and simultaneous insults. She bought an almost drastically small apartment in a bad neighborhood and felt that at least she owned something. So at first, and for at least three years, the two women lived without egregious external worry, in separate flats. Caroline had episodes of depression and heightened excitement over nothing, clinically known as "bipolar disorder," which she kept in check with psychotropic drugs.

For many years Denise had spent as much time as she could out of the city, in rented houses on Long Island or in upstate New York. Her nerves could only stand the city for limited periods. During a twenty-year relationship with a man she still liked, she'd coped by going away when the chance arose, otherwise by taking drugs. She no longer took drugs, except ones prescribed for her by an admittedly liberal-minded physician. Denise had a pretty clear idea what would happen if she didn't get away and didn't dose herself with calmatives or drink a cocktail when she needed one. The idea of Denise dry held no appeal for her at all. When Caroline entered her life she made it clear that she could not share Caroline's rigid abstemiousness, nor could she act as enforcer, chide, instrument of guilt.

She felt guilty anyway, the first time Caroline ordered a real drink in a bar, she almost said something, but quickly realized that whatever she said she would later have to say a million times, a million ways. Caroline was not provoking her, or angling her into an untenable role. At least, that was how Denise chose to read it. Caroline was simply ordering a drink. As far as Denise was concerned, Caroline ordering a drink was preferable in most respects to Caroline shooting smack. It was legal, easily arranged; up to a point, the effects were no more troublesome.

26

Anna showers. She vigorously swobs her body with a sea sponge drenched in the almond variety of a squeeze-bottle liquid soap whose label enumerates all secrets of the universe. She knows intuitively that we are all one without even reading the label that says so, though of course we aren't, and Anna knows that, too. Heaven and hell are only two ingredients of personal hygiene.

The toothpaste she uses is Rembrandt. She takes a long time on her teeth. It calms her to consider that her teeth won't abandon her, if she doesn't abandon them.

Malcolm has fucked her twice this morning. Once hard and long, the second soft and quick. His balls throb from fucking so much. His prick is numb, a phantom limb. He feels like a manly little girl. Wrapped in a gray cotton robe pinstriped in a subtle orange, he sits on a high stool at the kitchen counter reading volume one of Marx's *Capital* while gulping coffee with half-and-half, no sugar. The gray robe has so much dried come on it that Malcolm has decided never to wash it. He wants to see if it will stand up by itself after a few months.

Anna applies her makeup. She goes for a garish excess of purple eye shadow. Her lipstick is an aggressive rust color. She dabs on a new brand of blush that's transparent in daylight but shades into turquoise speckled with gold flakes in darkish surroundings. As she applies her makeup in the oval bathroom mirror, it's obvious she's painting a mask on a canvas rather than icing the cake of her narcissism. Anna's narcissism never sustains itself over any long haul: it surges up when she's threatened and otherwise hides itself in a mouse hole.

"The value of labor power," Malcolm reads with less than sweeping attention, "can be resolved into the value of a definite quantity of the means of subsistence. It therefore varies with the value of the means of subsistence, i.e., with the quantity of labor-time required to produce them." He scratches his scrotum where various juices have itchily dried, yawns expansively and guesses his breath is foul, forms images of snails and tortoises in his mind.

Anna exits the bathroom and crosses the hall to the bedroom. She has Seagrave in mind as she dresses: a splashy print blouse, a bright green tartan skirt shot through with colored lines, a huge gold safety pin stabbed through the seam. She completes the ensemble with running shoes. It's the ugliest look she can think of quickly. Periodically, when she isn't depressed or freaked out, she works up tricks to throw Seagrave off the scent, trip him up, test his mettle. Clothes are a kind of speech. So is the severe crop she's given her formerly long blond hair.

"Is this me, do you think?" she asks as she enters the main room, executing a slow-mo cancan for Malcolm's appraisal.

Malcolm gazes at her through his sleep-starved glaze. He lays the paperback *Capital* facedown on the countertop with a feeling of relief. He lights a Newport, his third this morning.

"You look impossible," he says approvingly. "Like a legal secretary changing into a whore on her lunch hour. Want some coffee?"

A few details of the apartment. A Manhattan railroad flat with an inner hall that separates a wide loftlike space from a bedroom which can and sometimes is divided by glass-paned doors into two bedrooms, which have a narrower second hall parallel to the main one, terminating at the bathroom. Located on Cedar Street, one of the odd blocks of small residential buildings next to the World Trade Center.

An apartment so clean a piece of lint would look like a theatrical event. Almost phobically clear of clutter. Sparely furnished with fifties "futuristic" chairs, a fat beige leather sofa, mint-green kidney-shaped end tables holding tubby red lamps with pleated white shades. The main open space has wainscoting painted silver, the walls above the chair line canary yellow. A series of Paolozzi prints in red frames hang so close to the ceiling it's a strain to look at them.

Anna pours coffee into a Simpsons mug. She drinks it across the Formica from Malcolm. She slaps at his fingers as if they were little mice. Her brains are scrambled from fucking. She smokes a Newport. She reads the back cover of *Capital* upside down. Malcolm tries gripping a thick rung of the bar stool frame with his toes.

"What I liked," she tells him, picking up a conversation that had never started, "was that scene, I always like scenes like this, where she thinks they recognize her and they don't, and her face goes through this whole morphology—"

At two this morning they put Fassbinder's *The Yearning of Veronika Voss* into the VCR, and watched parts of it while they fucked. Anna supposes she's slept for two hours. Malcolm plans to hit the bed the minute she's out the door.

"Every actor does that scene differently," he says.

"We should make a list," she says. "And rent a whole pile of them and copy them onto the same tape. Just those scenes. I can't think of any offhand."

"I know one. *Nurse Betty.* The waitress brings him the check and he thinks she's asking for his autograph."

"I can't think. I wish we had a little love-me."

"*What Ever Happened to Baby Jane?* Where she thinks Victor Buono knows she's Baby Jane Hudson."

"Yeah." Anna sniffles. "Except she's too nuts to realize he doesn't."

"Stop with the fingers, baby."

"Sorry. I didn't even know I was doing it."

"We can't be too pedantic or it will ruin it. Though I agree ixnay on *Baby Jane.*"

Malcolm scratches his arm. He rubs the sole of his foot against the stool rung. Anna prods the bottom of her nose with the middle joint of her right forefinger. They both have morning-after dope itch.

"What would we call it—the Celebrity Rebuff. The scary thing about *Veronika Voss* was that they usually did know who she was, though."

Malcolm believes he has forty dollars in his wallet. He could call Nahib, go to Neverland.

"I wonder if Larry will guess who I'm impersonating," Anna says. She pours what's left in her mug down the sink.

"Who is it, the former you?"

"Sandy Dennis in *That Cold Day in the Park*. The skirt, not the face. I mean kind of. The blouse isn't anything. If he did guess and got past the makeup, he should get the Lacan Trophy."

"Wow."

"*That Cold Day*—talk about rebuff. Sandy Dennis was like a homicidal boomerang."

"*Cold Day's* not *celebrity* rebuff, though. It's a far cry."

"I only wish my teeth were buck for the occasion."

"Fifty years ago you could get falsies. They made these sugary, chewable wax teeth and lips and mustaches as candy. Like eating some grown-up's face. Kids that loved that stuff probably died of cancer at thirty. Does he see a lot of movies?"

"He pretends to. Alcoholics and shrinks have an aversion to going to movies, I read that once in a dentist's office. He has seen *Suspiria*. I'm not sure why I know that."

"The rebuff moment. I almost wish I was working today."

"Famous rebuff. That's the key, the double double take."

"I could lift all the DVDs that have a famous rebuff scene."

Anna has a passing urge to cancel her shrink appointment.

"Another tape we should make, that thing when actors are so out of character or made up so differently that you don't recognize them. You see their names in the closing credits and think, 'Who the fuck was she?' "

Malcolm's thinking: *No more dope, no more dope, no more dope.*

"Then you have to consider if it's deliberate or they're just not interesting enough for you to notice whether it's them or not."

Anna doesn't want to leave the apartment. A surge of panic seems held back by a thin membrane of reasonableness.

"I wonder," she says, hurrying to the bedroom for her bag before she freaks and cancels, "if they'll make a DVD of *The Forbidden Christ.*"

Malcolm stands up. He finds he has to grab the countertop. He's feeling the vertigo he gets when he's forgotten to eat for several days.

"Probably within our lifetimes," he says loudly. Anna returns with her shoulder bag slung for action. "I mean"—Malcolm drops his voice—"it won't be DVD, will it. DVD will be like eight-track tapes in two or three years. They'll probably have implants. What kills me is how many things were invisible and now they're everywhere. There's a video of *The Brain Eaters* in our three-for-two section."

"That's, oh shit, right, invisible brains suck the brains out of living people."

"It has all this Army stuff in it, too. At the end, I forget how they do it, either they shut off electricity, or turn it way up, and these disembodied brains with spinal columns trailing off behind them fill with ectoplasm so you can see them whizzing around everywhere and smashing into trees and shit."

"Isn't there a farmer, right at the beginning, with like a pitchfork? Really," says Anna, pecking Malcolm's chin and then moving quickly for the door, "you could suck the brains out of half the people in New York and hardly anybody'd notice."

"Word," says Malcolm, giving a sayonara wave from his end of the hallway.

27

When he brought his stuff, the pictures, the notebooks, a suit-case of clothes, after what we eventually referred to as "the incident," lacking a more precise term, when Jesse camped in my alcove for a few weeks (months ago now, in fact, but in the skewed chronology of this story, not quite yet), Jesse told me for the first and last time of the bitter months with "him of the long Polish face and cold narrow eyes," an artist I knew en passant in the middle eighties who died, I think, in 1991, "sus-picious of everything and everybody," Jesse said, "a raving para-noid," though I could not remember Adam Z., the man in question, ever raising his voice, much less raving.

Jesse rummaged through his photographs and found one he'd taken in Paris, in what he called "a winter of freezing shit-tiness." Adam had been, no question about it, weirdly intense. He had a robotic stiffness, an oppressive absence of spontaneity. His thoughts seemed buried deep in his brain, as if he brooded constantly about things too ugly and dark to talk about. I had a few conversations with him, on the street, near the end of his life, but can't recall anything he said. I remember his voice, one of the deepest I've ever heard. He had a cloud over him. You could tell at a glance his life had been shit, shit, and more shit. Even when he smiled he looked as if he expected to be bull-whipped if he smiled too long, or too unguardedly.

Nineteen eighty-three, that autumn, Jesse had drifted close to Adam Z., the attraction based either on mutual admiration or a recognition that they both felt crushed by the same bore-dom. Jesse now denied that he ever "admired" Adam, though I could remember him singing Adam's praises, declaring what a great artist he was. It's odd, but I remembered it in tandem with the memory of going to a Queens cemetery for the burial following my lawyer's funeral. My lawyer had died from an asthma attack, in his sleep.

The cemetery was one of those awful places you can see from the expressway. There was nothing remotely peaceful about this final "resting place." There was, in fact, something grossly abusive to the dead for anyone to be buried there. Except for the headstones, it looked like one of those mass graves we've become so familiar with from newspaper photos. The possibility that I, through some unimaginable circumstance, might be dumped in such a place haunted me for weeks. Little red dots were affixed to some of the stones, like the ones they stick on gallery price lists to indicate that a piece has been sold. I was told they signified "perpetual care." They should call this place the Final Insult, I thought. It was directly under a flight path in and out of La Guardia. It's possible I ran the gamut of the local bars that night and ran into Jesse, exactly when he was falling in love. Or something.

"I got a boner just looking at him," Jesse said. "That lanky frame, and the curvatures of his face, very Middle Europe, and you know he had the biggest cock in the art world. Not that that would bowl anybody over as a recommendation. But he really was huge."

From the outset, Jesse said, Adam set the bar of frustration very low, though perhaps he meant high.

"I had to guess what was going on in there, he never talked. He said things, but he never *talked*. He *inflicted* silence. Sometimes you knew it was a happy silence, but that was rare. I don't mean happy. He never felt happy for a minute. *Contented* silence. Like after he'd eaten something delicious. Sausages, he liked. Anything with greasy meat in it. He wasn't the loner people took him for, you know, he could only be a loner in front of an audience."

He showed up at Jesse's door, when they "became close," whenever the mood took him, and hung around his apartment all day, unless Jesse invented a dentist appointment, or a date with somebody Adam hated. Adam hated many people, Jesse said, if the faces he made when most names came up were any indication.

"I got the feeling I was his only other friend besides Bruce." Bruce was the photographer who lived around the corner, the one who punched people if they took his picture. I knew Bruce, from the neighborhood. He hardly ever spoke a word, unless you mentioned another photographer.

I have always been amazed to hear people work themselves into a frenzy about their ideas being "stolen," as if nothing in their minds could ever occur to anybody else, and Bruce considered himself the victim of idea theft on a gigantic scale. Bruce and Adam used to walk around the neighborhood together, looking like two vampire bats with their wings intertwined. They were equally, unusually, tall and creepy, like the Silent Twins.

Jesse thought Adam desired him. Adam began showing up at Jesse's place every day. Nothing overtly sexual happened, but the unspoken filled so much of the time that Jesse assumed Adam wanted him. Wanted, a funny word. At some juncture Adam began to mention Paris, indicated plans of spending the winter there. Jesse decided, without telling him, that he would winter in Paris as well.

He borrowed an apartment in the Marais from a woman named Donna. Donna had lived in Tribeca in the late seventies. She was one of the strangest people conceivable, a beautiful woman who somehow projected the idea that she thought she smelled bad. I don't know how else to say it. The full range of Donna's pathology would fill a book of its own. One infuriating habit among many: she hounded people to let her do a favor for them, wore them out until they accepted whatever it was she offered simply to make her shut up, and then, if they later declined to do something she asked, ruefully reminded them of what she'd done for them as if they'd squeezed a monumental sacrifice out of her against her better judgment.

She had no female friends. The men she knew all found themselves sexually enmeshed with her in an asphyxiating manner. Surprisingly many people hated her with murderous ferocity, so much so that she was effectively driven out of town. I think I was the only person besides Jesse who perceived anything likable about her, and I can't remember what that was. She was so fucked up that saying hello invited the grip of an octopus. I recall seeing her the week before she fled New York, on Franklin Street near her place in Tribeca; I remember the sky was cold and clear that day; the buildings stuck out in harsh, decrepit relief. The desultory conversation we had no longer comes to mind. Donna hardly seemed "excited," or even especially pleased, to be venturing a new life. Seeing her that day, though, knowing she would quickly disappear, became, unaccountably, one of those ever-recurring memories one thinks of as a "turning point."

Even if Donna was as noxiously insignificant as people thought she was, her imminent absence from the landscape resonated with a vague yearning of my own, I suppose, or a presentiment that the flavor of that time was about to change in ways that her departure, however unimportant, symbolized. Anyway, whenever this memory cropped up later, the whole epoch around it sprang into my head.

I saw Donna frequently in Paris. For two years she lived in the hotel I always stayed in during the early eighties. She fucked the owner to pay the rent. In an effort to ensorcel me into indebtedness, Donna once offered to fuck him more often to pay my rent as well, but I declined. Meanwhile, she set her long-range vision on an uncomely, cripplingly neurotic, pedantic, boring, old, yet queerly likable music critic named Georges, who was fabulously rich, in the secret way certain people with no flair often are. Georges bought her the place in the Marais, a duplex on the Rue Vieille du Temple. Georges lived out in Le Vesinet, a charmless, melancholy suburb I can never picture without a kind of angry sadness.

Donna tormented Georges at every opportunity, needled and sulked and insulted, humiliated him in public, which brought Georges enormous sexual excitement, though I am quite certain he never achieved an erection. He was that type of French masochist. Donna obliged him to buy a veritable palace with twenty-five rooms near Versailles before she condescended to marry him. They kept the Marais apartment as a pied-à-terre, and devoted their no doubt happily tortured pastoral days to the raising of Golden Labradors.

When Jesse arrived in the winter of 1983, the Marais hadn't yet become Homosexualville. It was still a languid district of hushed streets and absurdly narrow sidewalks and precious few agreeable places to eat. He phoned up Adam, who rushed over as if he'd been offered a winning lottery ticket. Jesse threw himself into Adam's arms, imagining they would fuck immediately on Donna's gray wall-to-wall carpet. For months, Jesse had carried a mental image of Adam's penis engulfed by his eager rectum, a film loop cresting in the kind of synchronized orgasm that often spells forever-after romantic bliss for characters in movies.

Adam's body stiffened in resistance. He hugged Jesse in a "friendly" way, one hand rubbing Jesse's back as if stroking a nervous puppy. Adam's patronizing hug simultaneously acknowledged and rejected the carnal intention of Jesse's embrace while affirming an ethereal, superior kind of affection. Jesse realized he had been misreading signals from Adam for a ridiculously long time, and that he still went to the movies much too often.

"That should have been the end." Jesse sighed, a twisted smile creasing his lips. "But it wasn't."

Adam resumed the importunate pattern of the previous fall, while Jesse found himself immobilized by a futile desire. He didn't want to leave Paris, but he did want to leave Adam, let him fade into traffic. If he subtracted the hope of having sex with Adam—a hope that grew increasingly grotesque in Jesse's objective appraisal, at the same time that it flamed into an insistent, impossible wish—Adam was, it turned out, as deeply boring as he was deeply bored. The plenum Jesse imagined behind Adam's habitual silence gradually revealed itself as a vacuum. Adam had, for example, only ever read a particular kind of book, and even though this reading included Genet and Rimbaud and a few other actual writers, it mostly consisted of homoerotic junk and witless pornography. Adam knew nothing about politics, architecture, philosophy, history; it wasn't simply that he hadn't gone to university, Jesse said, Adam genuinely lacked curiosity about anything unrelated to his own career as an artist. He knew a little about painting, but even there his interest extended no earlier than Picasso. He was, in fact, hostile to intellectual effort or inquiry, and thought of himself as a kind of self-sufficient electric generator of "art." Adam believed every possible cliché about the artist as intuitive genius, a being who knew from birth every deep truth of existence, and therefore never needed to learn anything.

I should mention here that Jesse himself often seemed to me a pointless individual, as he'd never really committed himself to a career, or to any serious work. He'd acted in theater and movies, true. Miles had cast him in several plays, and working with Miles had set a "career" into motion, for some reason people sought him for this and that, Jesse fell into acting jobs he did nothing to land. He was the only "actor" I ever knew who didn't have a picture and a résumé to send anywhere. Yet casting types ferreted him out, for movies being shot in Finland or Tahiti or Madagascar. European directors, especially, liked him, for character roles. He'd made scads of money working in Hollywood for five years. Never as a featured player, but he always got speaking parts involving at least four minutes of screen time, sometimes tête-à-tête with the actual star.

Jesse had even lucked into three "supporting" roles that still brought in residual money. Work came to him simply because he knew a lot of people, he looked a certain way that no one else did. The camera liked him. For what Jesse generally had to do, it didn't have to *love* him.

Behind unpredictable spells of being cash poor, though, Jesse owned a quarterly fecundating trust fund and preferred doing nothing. He was a good actor, by the way, but he considered the profession silly. If he worked, it was strictly to meet new people, get laid by beautiful men, hang around.

What Jesse loved, and what often took him out of circulation and away to foreign climes, was investigating odd subjects, for his own enlightenment. He claimed he couldn't write, but that wasn't true. He read constantly, he knew a little about everything and a great deal about subjects like the history of religion, folk art, European literature, nineteenth-century opera, mathematical theory, quantum physics. He knew practical things, too: how houses are built, how to prepare enchiladas from scratch, or beef Wellington, how to repair a broken toilet, wire a ceiling fixture, the kinds of things everybody's father knows how to do. He'd traveled nearly everywhere. I suppose I resented his freedom and his indifference to work, closet puritan that I am.

His sexual life was unlucky or paid for. Like many complicated persons, Jesse wanted what he couldn't have, and seldom wanted what he could. Nebulous gossip had reached me at the time about his winter with Adam, but I'd never heard his side of it. Or Adam's, really. He'd soon learned, he said, that Adam seethed with bitterness about what he perceived as insufficient attention paid to him and his work in the New York art world. Adam saw himself, Jesse said, as the pivotal figure in an "art movement" that had sprung up in storefront galleries in the East Village. For several months, numerous articles had appeared, some in national magazines, supporting this view: I remembered the articles, which often featured large group shots of the "hot young artists" of this burgeoning coven. I recalled thinking that Adam seemed the most prominent because he was taller than anyone else in the photos.

Later, Jesse said, some of these artists started getting written about here and there. Adam thought they were taking up space that was rightfully his. The mere mention of a "competitor" threw Adam into a day-long funk, or an obscene tirade, and yet he was hypnotically driven to learn about the activities of these very people, and dragged Jesse to the Pompidou Center bookstore whenever art magazines from America arrived. There Adam rummaged angrily through all the articles and reviews, bleakly fulminating and turning horror-stricken when a perceived rival got a favorable notice or a reproduction.

"I didn't want to see him. But he phoned every morning and I felt powerless. He always wanted to go to the Flore for breakfast. He'd order a little omelette *mixte*. Strange to say, he always arrived in a good mood. And then he'd say, 'Let's go to Père Lachaise,' or what have you, and we'd figure out the Métro route, and head off, and a little time would pass and he'd clam up. You know how you know when someone's thinking of you as causing them awful discomfort? It just got quieter and quieter, I could feel him getting darker and darker in his mind, this bottomless depression that curdled into total hatred of me. By the middle of the afternoon, I felt like half of a couple that's been up all night fighting, and they can't say another word without killing each other. I never understood why. Except for that first time I never, even once, called him on the telephone. He always called me. Every morning without fail. And he'd stay all day with me, sometimes way into the evening, even though every minute that went by was more miserable than the one before."

"Maybe he needed you and he knew you wanted him and he didn't know how to get what he needed from you without giving you what you needed."

"That's awfully convoluted."

"No, it isn't. It happens all the time."

A month of Adam pushed Jesse over the edge. Jesse hurriedly arranged to attend the Berlin Film Festival as a guest. A film he'd played in was running on the independent program at the Arsenal Kino. Adam, he said, exuded rage and betrayal at the news of his departure. *You're leaving because of me, aren't you?*

"I told him it all came up suddenly and that"—he named an actor well-known in Germany—"needed my emotional support because of legal problems he'd gotten into, the kind that could ruin his career. Well, you know, ——— really did get in trouble over underage boys, it's bad enough he's so fat, but to be a pedophile on top of it, grotesque, and he did practically *beg* me to come to Berlin. He promised to pay my hotel bill, but he never did. Adam didn't believe me but I think he needed to hear a plausible lie, so I told him something true that sounded like a lie he could pretend to believe. I wasn't going to invent a death in the family just to get away from him. As soon as he got back to New York, he wrote this horrible thing about me he published in the *East Village Eye* or one of those underground rags, not printing my name but claiming I was stalking him. Every other word was a lie; of course, some of it was true. I could've sued, I guess. You can see in this picture how attractive he was but how unhappy, too, I know his childhood was a nightmare. He grew up in Midtown. I think his mother was a hooker. Look at all this shit," Jesse said, sifting the hundreds of photos in the box through his hands. "Anyway, it's hardly the best picture of him ever taken. The camera moved. Also I spilled coffee on it."

28

Arthur writes Jesse:

We get on and off those tin cans all the time, it's a matter of sheer luck, though we think it's good odds that we'll make it to our destination. One time in a thousand we just don't, and that's that. You can be on a plane or splashing in your bubble bath, it's the same, you go in a second from being alive to being dead, though today it's expected you'll die in hospital, your vital signs scrawling blips of light and bobbing burps on monitors.

You can't have a death of your own anymore. A death that happens amid death-defying acts, unless you count getting into a car, which is the riskiest thing anybody ever does. Instead we make space around each death. We remove it from life well in advance, we take the guesswork out of death as much as we can. If it's someone else's death we prepare for our loss, withdraw our emotional investment. We kill them while they're still, technically, here. But the death of others crouches inside us, we can't escape. I try to imagine exactly how the passenger, in what this blasted fragment of cramped airline seat used to be, prepared himself for the end, if he had any time to . . .

29

Anna can't be sure if her dreams restage or reconstitute the mental dynamic between herself and Laurence Seagrave at this stage of her therapy. She feels a piddling hostility toward Seagrave at times, but also a dependent affection that is almost love. The love, she thinks, of a dog for the hydrant he pees on every day. Maybe in the dreams, Seagrave is a displacement, a substitute for Malcolm, with whom she's been having inchoate difficulties after a long, happy run of spirited screwing and cohabitation. Or it could be her father: compulsive prankster and raconteur of unnerving abilities, telepathy foremost among them. Larry Seagrave regularly cautions her against reading too much psychiatric literature.

30

"Caroline, Caroline, this can't go on."

Denise hears her own rasping, cracking voice pretending to be less than completely serious and rests her temple against the locked bedroom door of paneled wood. Her will is draining out through the soles of her feet. Her terror of unpleasantness can't sustain her own insistence. She knows that at any moment she'll bolt for the refrigerator downstairs and gobble down a quart of ice cream.

"Omphalos and Thanatos," Caroline yells briskly from inside. Her voice bounces up and down as if she were using a trampoline. "It's *in* there, Denise, it has to be in there, it's hidden in a lake that goes up and down. Omphalos, Thanatos. It's somewhere on the map if I knew where to look."

"Caroline, please."

"I can't let you in here now. There's going to be a manifestation. Think about the others in the ship. They're frightened. They're scared and it's dark. Omphalos, Thanatos. I need absolute, absolute focus until ten o'clock, I am going to complete my search between this minute and then."

"All right," Denise said in a normal, upbeat tone, unable to deal with it any longer. "You complete your search and have your manifestation, I'm going to make an endive salad and boil some tortellinis. I'll leave some for you in the fridge."

31

Arthur's letter to Jesse continues:

From an airplane (not from the unlucky Airbus,
though, which went down in pitch dark), this
island resembles a loosely balled fist, its
middle finger sticking out and pointing at Gibraltar. Did you ever notice? I think we talked
about this one night on the terrace. The
knuckles are a ridge of unimpressive mountains
(the tallest can be scaled in four hours),
with a wide, drought-stricken farming valley
stretched out behind it. Oh, I forgot! You
climbed one of those woodsy micro-peaks on
acid one night, up to the monastery, with Valerie.

Can it be five years ago already? You were
both hoping to end up fucking the Russian Wonder, who panted up there with you. The dawn
broke as you reached the walls of the sacred
order. Giving Dmitri a blowjob while the monks
recited their morning prayers would have been
a lot more tawdry than Aldous Huxley peaking
for the first time in a Rexall's, I think.

You said he sweated all the way up even
though it was chilly and hardly a steep climb.
I could've told you he was junked out far beyond erection territory, but why spoil the
mystery? I knew you would figure it out.

Dmitri has "slept" with everybody on this
island, more or less in shifts, every summer—

still does; his father kicks him out of the
house when supposedly civilized people arrive
for the season. I never heard of anyone getting any action from that evidently large but
limp appendage, though. He did recently piss
on Sylvia White in her bathtub, she begged him
to: he whispered this news in my ear the other
night over mucho mojitos in Saffron Bar, with
hesitant embarrassment and a thicker note of
pride. He told me he'd never pissed on a woman
before, that it disturbed him that he got as
much satisfaction from it as fucking her would
have if he could've gotten it up. Frankly,
that might hold true for anybody who decided
to have sex with Sylvia White. What a pest she
can be. Even so, it's good to have somebody
else from the city around.

Dmitri tells me things he wouldn't tell
other people. I suppose I'm the only person
who ever really listens to what he says. I'm
not claiming this as any sort of virtue, but
as further evidence of how boring everything
is on this island, that deciphering Dmitri's
twaddle becomes a riveting distraction. You do
remember him? The way his voice mumbles and
mutters and trails off, as if he had false
teeth that didn't fit, or was pestered by bees
buzzing around in his skull. It's a strain to
bother making out the words. I need this
strain to keep myself from sliding into a
coma.

He likes telling me about his "sex life,"

because he's gotten it into his fried brain that I "desire" him. He is one of the three or four males on the island who isn't physically grotesque in some way, so a lot of people do desire Dmitri, until they get him, if anybody does. I know you've blown a junkie or two along the trail; if you've blown one you really have blown them all. I'd rather eat ice cream. You can have that engraved on my tombstone, if I happen to go first.

They put Dmitri's twin sister in some spa/nuthouse near Milan. She'd been subsisting entirely on hard-boiled eggs, tins of smoked oysters, and bourbon straight from the bottle for about six months, in some apartment in Lisbon that Boris had forgotten he owned. Go know.

Boris refuses to die. Mental images of Dmitri and the nut job empowered by a vast fortune are probably keeping him alive, to the degree that he still is. He's shrunk about five inches since the last time you were here, he dodders, a crazed mystical gleam crosses his eyes as if he were witnessing the folly of existence diagram itself on the tablecloth. There are millions there. Boris owned three quarters of a Geneva bank at the height of his avarice, then overnight turned spiritual because of some epiphany he changes every time he tells the story, but he kept his assets. That part of the story never changes, and obviously it's true. Boris's Alsatian wife and the mother of his two monsters died in an avalanche, is what Dmitri tells people these days.

Did you know Boris once translated Gogol's *Arabesques* into Spanish? So he ends up with a family and a personality that Gogol would have invented. Is the world small or large? I can never quite decide. Boris can still beat his male nurse at chess, his mind's still nimble, but I don't think he'll be around many more summers. What am I saying. I'm never coming here again.

I wonder what would grow in that desiccated valley, if anything did. Some knobby, pale, uncookable root vegetable, I suppose. Fibrous and tasty as a thyroid tumor. In all the summers we've come here I don't recall ever tasting a fresh vegetable in any restaurant, and here in the shadow of Gibraltar they serve frozen fish shipped in from Japan. Once in a blue moon a stunted local perch or its second cousin netted from a dissolving rowboat turns up on a dinner plate, but the poor thing tastes like the distilled filth of the half-dead sea it's been moping in.

The port, tucked into the corner of that fuck-you finger of mossy laterite, is where the rich live these days, mingling houses with those of the laboring natives, who're never thrilled to see them but simulate an exuberant warmth and festive humanity for the sake of the seasonal cash flow. Stucco boxes, piled on top of each other above the cobbled esplanade, where yachts and sailboats bobble in the filthy harbor, in the wake of giant tour ships that disgorge day trippers from the mainland. Greedy for our local handicrafts. Whichever piles of Singapore-manufactured crap those are. Embroidered portraits of Franco, whatever. I hope you remember all this, or has this sublime shithole fled your memory?

People still talk about you here. Every year they ask when Jesse's coming back. I don't have the energy to tell them never. That could start some depressing riff about the island's less beckoning features, or darken their charming memories of you. You're even quoted, but mainly things you wouldn't remember saying.

That waiter at the Pirate you went nuts over five years ago, Andreas of the pretty mouth and pretty feet, lost his looks in record time. He married a fat German girl with no money, Anita, who used to wash dishes in the More Hot, and now has a pudgy, charmless daughter of three they used to call Sasha and now refer to as Stella. Andreas's feet are still pretty, I suppose, I haven't seen them recently. But everything north of them's a bloated mess.

The lack of soberly available cock is one really rotten feature of this place and it's one thing I can't complain about in mixed company. As you know, all company here is mixed. Mixed and jinxed. Which makes this dutiful annual trip even more a futile exercise in masochism. Of course there are interesting people. Dorothy and her crowd. Dorothy's little spaniel was poisoned by one of her lovely neighbors, that family of apelike fishermen. She's heartbroken. They hated her dog and now she knows they hate her, too. After years of imagining she had a "lovely relationship" with the mustached matriarch of that Neanderthal tribe. Besides the circle of retired British spies and former refugee Jews around Dorothy, all of them in their seventies, nothing runs deep with the seasonal people, after Labor Day it all evaporates like airplane exhaust or a dream you've been trying too long to wake up from.

I miss you. We had some funny times here, those two summers you came, avoiding the Willeys at cocktail hour and sitting on the terrace, watching that slithery orange sun drip and die into the sea and munching carrots with wasabi and throwing martini olive pits in their direction. Even Oliver was fun then. Fun when he was drunk or not. Fuck it.

Now, every year he offers, around the middle of May when the tickets are already paid for, to come by himself. He knows I can't stand this place but that I'll come, if only, stupidly, to save money. Force of habit, inertia, sentimentality, none of the reasons I can come up with are good ones. At first it was to keep Oliver happy, not that my company has made Ol-

iver happy in about seven years. I could pretend it gives him a warm feeling to know I'm
not getting laid for three months, but Oliver
doesn't actually care one way or the other
about that as long as he doesn't have to deal
with it.

He keeps me tired of living a lot of the
time. Stale-feeling, anyway. Trying to have a
conversation that goes anywhere beyond what
I'm cooking for dinner is like licking the
bottom of an ashtray. It gets harder and harder, but I can still for a little while every
day live in the moment of a blank blue sky
and watch the light change on the water down
below.

What does it mean to save yourself.

We hardly talk to each other for days at a
go. I don't know how this happened, it took a
long time, Oliver wasn't always this cold in-
sensitive person and I wasn't always this bag
of resentment. I think Oliver was born to live
in the first chapter of a Zola novel. In the
cozy drabness just before something hideous
happens. And alone, with a chambermaid who
looks in at mealtimes and turns the bed down
when he goes for a walk. He can't boil an egg
by himself, and even though he lives in his
own hermetic world, slopping colors around on
canvases, he's terrified to be alone. The couple thing, being a unit that can leave a party
because of private tensions instead of the essential horror of it all, that's Oliver's thin

defense against being eaten alive by the Willeys—or spit out by them, which is their other favorite party trick, as you well know.

I'm still astounded you could take that trip to Portugal with Valerie and stay on any kind of terms with her for a whole year afterward. Tell me what drug you were on; we should put it in the island's water supply. I know she has charm and intelligence, but they only go so far. After a certain point, the misery seeps out as aggression.

The Willeys just bought another house, on the other side of the port. That makes five they own here. They're also buying the one we're living in from Sandy McKenna, that English woman who used to flash her boobs at the waiters in the More Hot just before closing time. Sandy has cancer, and a lot of money problems. And a twelve-year-old daughter whose dad, you remember, that impossible old drunkard David who thinks he's Noël Coward, is an impossible option after Sandy's gone. How on earth could David take care of anybody? He's a great ruin, but ruins only nurture grown-up melancholics. Sandy and daughter live in Sandy's other house, in the back valley. The Willeys are planning to snap that up, too.

This house mania has made them almost as rich as Henry's paintings have. Since Valerie handles the real estate, I guess that's what you call a working marriage. Still, Valerie hasn't stopped chafing loudly and eternally against the idea of anyone thinking of her as "Mrs. Henry Willey"; she spends at least an afternoon a week in her very own studio, creating imitations of Agnes Martin that will one day reveal her as Henry's equal in the art department. If he croaks, it will probably be rumored that she painted a lot of his things, too, if she thinks she can get that to work.

They use the ranch in New Jersey exclusively for winter holidays. Kwanzaa for the domestic staff, that sort of thing. So far, the twelve-room maisonnette across the harbor is a playhouse for the brats, who're going on ten and twelve, just as scary as when they were smaller. Marie has fleeting moments of resembling a human child, but Antonia is going to wind up a serial killer or a Petra von Kant type of dyke. The rich of Bohemia truly know how to produce spooky kids. Is that deliberate? A Nietzschean sort of hubristic thing? I think the girls both take after the psychotic waitress from Hicksville buried under the seamless parvenu armor-plating that is Valerie Willey, but there's some of Henry's Zen monk/Fu Manchu persona digitized into those DNA codes. That is, if they're actually his. It's a stretch to think Henry ever had sperm that could swim fast enough to penetrate an egg.

I think Oliver figures the first summer he comes here by himself he'll become the annual Designated Victim, and that'll be the end of things with the Willeys. This year the role has fallen to Sylvia, who got roped into renting the place you used to rent from John and Allison Bradley, who got busted last summer for looting a sunken galleon off Sri Lanka. Charged with piracy, pretty classy if you ask me, but a steep felony in places like Sri Lanka. The Bradleys are still fun when they've drunk up all the gin, otherwise a bit stuffily bourgeois, like a lot of criminal enterprise types you run across here. A former Roy Cohn partner they flew in from Honolulu got them out, bribed their way out of the country via "administrative oversight." There's no extradition treaty between Sri Lanka and the continental owner of our little island paradise, as it turns out, and they weren't about to negotiate one over a few hundred-year-old dinner plates and whatever other junk the Bradleys winched out of there. Especially since it was all confiscated and dumped into some basement closet of a Tamil museum. Cost them a pile; now they're crying poverty. Alluding to it, I should say. Valerie, with her usual tact, refers to them as the Pirates whenever they leave the room.

Sylvia, I think, who drinks a little too much to have a glimmer of what she's in for, usually rents one of those Cozy Cabins in East Hampton for July and August, but Henry bought a little drawing from her, and Valerie started taking her to Da Silvano twice a week for lunchtime girl talk; the rest is the usual

pretty history. They haven't got to the part
where they turn on her and make the last two
weeks in August the trigger for ten years of
psychotherapy. To make matters worse, Sylvia
would probably like to be Eve Harrington to
Valerie's Margo Channing, vis-à-vis Henry—
she's in for a lowering surprise, if it gets
as far as the I'll-show-you-mine stage. A
problem person, no question, but it's hard for
me to say anybody deserves what the Willeys
dish out when they're bored with people
they've collected. They convince themselves
the person has failed them in some important
way, taken unfair advantage of them: I sometimes wonder if that could be true. People do
take advantage of Henry, I suppose figuring
he's so rich he doesn't feel things like betrayal, or that Valerie doesn't deserve the
frustration she feels, she can just go shopping to make herself feel better. Her paintings aren't bad at all.

Oliver still thinks he's learning important
things from Henry. Zen purity in contemplation
of the naked canvas, how to make total nothing
look museum-worthy on a wall. I don't see it.
I mean, I see it in Henry's drawings, no one
else makes that kind of line, credit where
it's due. Even though, who cares. But with Oliver I get this sickening sense that his talent is actually moving backward. That he's
been treading water ever since this twisted
mentoring friendship with Henry started. The

only interesting thing out of Oliver all summer wasn't art, but an epic blackout drunk tirade exposing what he really thinks about Henry and Valerie. Not Henry the artist, Henry the passive-aggressive shit, in Oliver's stored-up estimation. And Valerie as whatever it is she is. To be honest, Oliver's never gotten along with women very well, he thinks calling her a cunt is in itself some kind of damning insult.

This letter's a total betrayal of Oliver, obviously, it's just for you to read, I'd appreciate if you'd burn it in the sink when you finish it. If you knew how beyond depression I am, I'd offer that as an excuse.

I would want Oliver's work to be good even if we left each other. And it bums me out to think it just isn't anymore and maybe won't be again. I don't blame Henry's influence. I blame . . . oh, Oliver. Oliver thinking secretly that being Henry's acolyte will somehow replicate the unrepeatable circumstances that made Henry world famous. It would be easier to comprehend and even easier to take if it was just a question of social climbing, schmoozing, winning Henry's endorsement in parts of the art business. It's more twined than that. Henry figured out how to go nowhere special and have it register as a new place every two or three years, he's a brand name, he can do that with a few little tweaks of his formula. You can't say what Henry makes doesn't look like

Art because that's all it looks like. It is
Art. Whereas Oliver's stuff gets prettier and
prettier but it's always the same, the same,
the same, and the size of his brand name might
not get any fatter, maybe it's not fat enough
to get inscribed into history. Oliver could
end up a footnote. He vacillates between terror and placid acceptance of this, but his
preoccupation with it either way has moved him
further and further out of the world of other
people, he's not a social human being anymore,
and when he drinks, he's morose and bitter and
even less present than when he doesn't.

We've rented this broken-down house again,
with two olive trees in a postage-stamp garden, marble terrace facing the sea and the fog-
draped coast of Africa. I dream about Africa.
I was supposed to shoot a documentary in Came-
roon years ago but it fell through. I wish I
could turn black, and go to Africa. I don't
want to go there white. I'd like to live, is
what I'd like to do. Just live, and throw this
life away like a roll of ruined film.

In the garden, everywhere, cicadas raise a
deafening chorus, the creaking of a million
little thoraxes drills into your brain until
you can't hear it. The heat so vile stray dogs
lie panting in any sliver of shade, desperate
for a drop of moisture. Horrible things are
born in this heat. Milky buds of poison plants
burst and spew weightless gossamer seeds into
the fluttering winds.

Nothing new can happen. Ever. Until something does. You never know. Last year a fire jumped the ravine and climbed almost to the monastery. Planes came and scooped water up from the sea and dumped it on the forest. Yes. That happened. You think: I can live another day like this. So you go on living like you'll live forever, and the time goes, and then you're dead.

I can't believe I started this thinking I could entice you into coming over for a week. I miss you, that's all.

32

Anna won't be discussing her secret urge to throw Larry Seagrave from a wheelchair today. Anna always arrives at East
Forty-seventh Street and Third a little ahead of time, long
enough to sit in the coffee shop across the street, eating a Western on white toast that she douses with enough ketchup to raise
the counterman's eyebrows, washing it down with black coffee.

She has, in her tote, objects she finds essential to have on
her person when she leaves the apartment: pens, a small note-
pad, a Canon Elph digital camera, several prescription bottles,
a microcassette recorder, a Palm Pilot with her addresses and
other data, and a global positioning device. This morning, when
she finishes her sandwich, she takes a torn-open Con Edison
envelope from her bag and prints across the back in block letters: I DID NOT KILL ANYBODY LAST SATURDAY.

33

Malcolm sits in Union Square Park, on a bench facing the white tent tops of the farmers' market, braced for another day of floor-walking at the Virgin Megastore. People buying music and video DVDs fall into a trance induced by clustered rows of monitors, clashing streams of music, and a huge Orwellian video grid strategically placed to lure shoppers down to Level One, where three items or two items or four items of the same kind of thing are forever on sale, but never displayed in close enough prox-imity for the sensorily battered to distinguish two for one from three for two or four for three. The calculated illogic of every-thing sends thousands each day into transports of credit card abandon that move a Niagara of cash around the world.

He's recently read a news item about the millions in bootleg CDs that funnel through Ciudad del Este in Paraguay, along with trucks stuffed with counterfeit Marlboros, real marijuana, and heavily disguised convoys of depleted uranium, stolen fuel rods, Kalashnikovs, any species of unthinkable thing desired or sold by shadows traveling under the rose.

At the Megastore, all is legitimate, flawlessly manufactured, factory sealed. Its revenue spills cleanly into the raging river of cash and credit and digital wealth, spinning numbers in and out of corporate bank accounts. Somewhere, no doubt, this river sucks up the tributaries of loot generated by the inau-thentic, the counterfeit, the Jennifer Lopez knockoffs. A spike in the current from the world's numberless laundries sends it all rushing faster to the Falls.

Malcolm doesn't have to persuade people to buy things. They can't help themselves. He merely has to interpret, a few times a day, the sometimes fractured language of the customer's desire, recognize the piece of music or musician whose name they've forgotten or can't quite bring to mind, or figure out from frog-gily hummed signature riffs what album by which performer a song they want appears on. The gross abundance and variety of music and books and movies stimulates an epidemic wish to own a copy of everything. As customers dawdle or race along the wide rows of product bins, their eyes snag on reissued memory tracks, groups they've read about in magazines, music they might not like to hear but which is thought to define the present in an important way. As each moment passes, by the time they get this music home to their audio systems, other, newer music defines the moment they're listening to these ac-quisitions, and still newer music will nail down the moment that replaces that moment. All these moments eventually con-dense into a boxed set as the perfect past, the sound of an era. Memory becomes the sound track of perfection.

Malcolm is most comfortable working on Level One, han-dling DVDs: every week, eons of long-forgotten films fill shelves in reformatted special editions, their sound tracks digitally scrubbed, with clickable sidebar interviews with directors, even the original trailers, optional commentary from stars, material that sparks Malcolm's interest. *Shanghai Express, Eyes Without a Face,* Buñuel, Godard, Fassbinder, *Dracula's Honeymoon, Porky's,* everything from the moronic to the sublime returns from the grave in suavely designed, oblong snap-open cases, even the silents Malcolm cherishes. The only aspect of this eclectic, bo-nanza resurrection of every movie ever made that irritates him is that they're grossly overpriced compared to the vanishing videotape format. However, he gets a substantial store discount. He also steals copiously. Even Anna doesn't know Malcolm hates music. When he moonlights as a DJ, he wears earplugs that virtually deafen him.

34

Something usually happens in the elevator of Seagrave's building, a mid-rise residential structure with a long marble lobby, partly sunken, and a short marble doorman, partly sentient. The people living in this building all appear to have numerous small dogs or wear too much makeup and exude a faintly disreputable quality, as if their money came from looted government treasuries in banana republics or secret arms deals or an extremely elevated level of prostitution. They look normal for the neighborhood, three blocks from the UN.

Today, en route to the twenty-fourth floor, Anna shares the elevator with a couple—no doubt adulterers, given the hour and an air of coy anticipation pooled around them, the man sharply tailored, middle-aged, wearing a sardonic, bored face that might be Panamanian, the woman Spanish, noticeably lifted, draped in an expensive cocktail dress, ornamented with five or perhaps six items of heavy gold jewelry (Anna's count is quick and furtive), hair and makeup expressive of a fierce, contemptuous, frightened defiance of the aging process.

"I forgot the salmon mayonnaise," the woman sighs as the doors shut. Anna wonders if salmon mayonnaise figures in their customary sexual routine.

"It goes like this," says the man. "A homeless guy sees an old friend from college who's doing well passing on the sidewalk and begs him for a few hundred dollars to get back on his feet. The well-off guy gives him the money. A few hours later he walks past a restaurant and sees the homeless guy inside with a plate of salmon mayonnaise in front of him. 'What? I give you money, and then you order salmon mayonnaise?' 'I don't understand you,' says the homeless man. 'If I don't have any money I *can't* eat salmon mayonnaise, and if I have some money

I *mustn't* eat salmon mayonnaise. In that case, when *am* I supposed to eat salmon mayonnaise?' "

It sounds to Anna's ear like a code factored into some scheme to murder the woman's husband, or the man's wife, since neither of them laughs or betrays even slight amusement. They debark on a lower floor than Seagrave's.

This isn't what "happens" to Anna in the elevator, which has a certain physical oddity that always disturbs her, much as the windows she's frequently trapped in front of do: three walls of the elevator above the chair line are not the usual polished metal, but sheets of glass over recessed panels, or dioramas, displaying exceptionally banal examples of folk art: quilts with slightly frayed or torn squares, "naive" paintings, handicrafts of a vaguely Native American aura, antique metal and wooden toys, objects that could be regarded as inoffensively decorative, but strangely troubling presences in the elevator of this emphatically modern building, as there is never a placard or sign identifying them, or, more pertinently, telling why they happen to be there. These displays are changed every few months, for no discernible reason, unless it's because the pleasure or distraction they're assumed to provide the tenants is considered exhausted after some fixed interval. What "happens" in the elevator is that Anna finds a crisp fifty-dollar bill that obviously slipped from the man's pocket when he fished for his apartment keys. Here's half my session, Anna thinks happily.

35

I found Arthur's letters in Jesse's storage boxes. A letter always arrives at its destination. These had passed through Jesse on their way to me, I thought. It's my destiny to collect any evidence that everyone's life hasn't been a hallucination, even if it feels like one.

36

"Sometimes sex is just the memory of sex," Anna tells Seagrave. "It disintegrates. . . . I'll be almost there, and I start floating off. He's screwing me like crazy and I'm thinking, How does a self-cleaning oven actually clean itself? Or I remember what it used to feel like instead of how it feels in the moment. Same cock, same balls, same body, same guy, but all the thoughts of the week come flooding in. It's just enough to turn him into an alien."

"This isn't a relationship you want to let go of," Seagrave muses without making it a question, clasping his fingertips together in a characteristic way.

"I don't know what I want to do," says Anna. "I need to find a job. Not a hacker job either. Or research. I'm afraid of the people who hire me for those things. I think I could get my head blown off."

Anna feels a migraine making tiny threats behind her ear.

"We can get to that, but we were talking about Malcolm."

"It's all tied together."

"No, it isn't," Seagrave says with certainty. "You're bundling."

Seagrave doesn't use jargon, but "bundling" is his own term of art, suggesting the collapse of discrete problems into one large, knotty, insoluble one. He introduced this concept by evoking figures in a Bruegel painting, peasants bent over by firewood bundles carried on their backs. Anna believed at first that Seagrave was saying his patients reminded him of figures out of Bruegel, but she's changed her opinion on this.

"Malcolm's younger than me," she says. "He's a little imma-ture in some ways that don't really bother me. But he's young, he's so sure of himself, but I'm not that sure about him."

"Meaning . . . ?"

"Well, there are things I just can't know about him."

"Can you expand on that a little bit?"

"I can't know what him being this complicated racial mixture is all about when he lives in a white world, more or less. When I got together with him, I never even thought about that."

Seagrave ponders. Or appears to ponder.

"I mean I thought about it but only in terms of how does this person fit into my setting, how does he fit with my life, not how do I fit into his. Staying together or letting it go doesn't seem like the point right now," Anna says. "Even if maybe in some strange way it is."

"What point? How would you define it?"

At times, the air conditioner in Seagrave's office obscures his exasperatingly soft voice.

"Come again?" Anna brays: she's sick of telling him to speak up.

"What do you think is the point right now?"

Anna doesn't bother scraping the underside of her chin with the palm side of her fingers before answering. She sometimes does this to indicate thought when she isn't thinking.

"It's something about being *between*."

"Between?"

"Between enough things that I can't get my bearings. I'm not here, I'm not there. Solid objects have horrible things inside them. I mean, I actually carry this stupid Radio Shack satellite device around with me that tells me where I am on earth. It really only tells where the device is."

The phone rings. Seagrave picks it up. Sometimes he answers calls during session, sometimes lets the machine take them. His voice softens even more. She hears something like "a little after five."

Silence follows the phone call. Anna feels stupid in her ugly clothes. Her inclination to trip Seagrave up now seems childish. She intuits an oncoming insight and feels a kind of mental gasp, afraid it will fade before she brings it into focus.

"What worries you most," Seagrave asks in his "fresh tack" manner, "right now? Today."

"A lot of people would say I have nothing to worry about."

"That's not for a lot of people to decide. What's the situation with your father?"

Anna shrugs. The shrug means, *Maybe it's important, maybe not, you tell me.*

"I guess they plan on keeping him there for a while," she says. "It would be kind of funny, if it was somebody else."

"When and if he gets out of there, does he have anywhere to go?"

Anna has thought about it many times, but never as an imminent problem.

"*If* isn't a question, he comes back from Planet Debby when he's ready to. I don't see him delusional for a whole year." Anna deflects an onslaught of imponderables by running a thumbnail between her front teeth. "I don't see him going back to Quebec or anything drastic," she says carefully. "He put that behind him thirty years ago. In his atlas it's a dead zone."

"What about your brother in Paris?"

"Dad isn't *broke.*" Anna laughs, thinking she's said something in another session to lead Seagrave in this wrong direction. "My brother would take him in, or farm him out to interesting people, but what would be the point? If my father wanted to be in Paris, he could just buy a flat. He can live in the hotel, as far as that goes. He still has controlling shares. They tried to get him declared incompetent at one point, but legally, it turned out, it doesn't matter if he's competent or not."

Seagrave laughs, as Anna expected.

"Would the hotel—I don't mean to laugh—would that be good for him, do you think?"

"The hotel is in *Zug*, Larry," Anna says, feeling like she's inhaled a lot of helium. She wishes she could smoke in the office. "Do I have to say more?"

"I've never been to Zug, but I mean from his point of view. Is the hotel better than his other options?"

Now and then, Seagrave veers absurdly off course for lack of information.

"Larry, from Dad's point of view, he's still *running* the hotel. He thinks that asylum *is* the hotel. The last time we spoke he said, 'We're doing great business! The hotel's full! But just remember, sweetheart, no matter what happens, there's always a room waiting for you here.' You seem to forget, my father is mentally ill."

The session ends in the mutual hilarity that Anna routinely suspects cancels anything accomplished during therapy. It carries her to the elevator and into the street on a cloud of self-control that takes several hours to dissolve into something less wonderful. It's then that she believes that the pattern, the forming figure in the carpet, is big and weird enough to annihilate everything: that it can't be shrunk, Lacanned, domesticated, or stopped.

37

Miles has an idea. Several, in fact. Tall, ascetic, fidgety, charismatic Miles, whose histrionic intensity has convinced many people over many years to take his ideas seriously, to involve themselves in often aborted projects, to lavish their time on plays and movies that Miles sets in motion and abruptly cancels when he thinks they're slipping beyond his control, Miles the aging wunderkind has become circumspect, even fanatically abstemious, about announcing any idea to anyone he might want to involve in that idea: the Boy Who Cried Wolf syndrome has attached itself to Miles's inspirations, a circumstance he's angrily aware of because he knows it's his own fault.

In the recently thickened gloom of his pastoral isolation in Dutchess County, Miles tends to forget that a vast distance separates ideas from expression. He even posts notes on his computer to remind himself that it's better for his reputation to write the script, the play, whatever, instead of talking it up in advance and mobilizing other people's expectations. Not that anybody really counts on Miles to finish anything.

He drives into Manhattan once every week: to see his therapist, dine with friends, collect bills from the plastic bin where the downstairs neighbor puts them. His dismay at Manhattan's overhaul into a playground for the very rich and very young has prolonged an experiment in seclusion that began with a three-month rental and turned into cement when he bought a house, a house he disliked from the moment he moved into it, after an autumn of expensive renovations that were left half-finished by the local contractors.

The desuetude and American-style ugliness of the nearby population centers, the strip malls and chain stores remind him unpleasantly of the grim New England town he grew up in, a place that was farm country in his childhood but rapidly metastasized into a nightmare landscape of commuter housing developments and shopping centers. He now feels, if not completely trapped, gooily wedged between a city he barely recognizes and a country place where he feels surrounded by parasites and werewolves.

Miles's therapist is Laurence Seagrave. Since I'm not only telling this story but figure in it as a character, I think it's probably a good idea to assure the reader that not everybody in this narrative spends time spilling their troubles in Laurence Seagrave's office. It's pure coincidence that Anna M. and Miles see the same shrink.

Miles does confide his ideas to Seagrave, believing this is the opposite of spreading them around, though he's actually rehearsing the way he'll present them to other people later. Idea One, a biopic of German writer and terrorist Ulrike Meinhof. Idea Two, the torrid affair between the Expressionist painter Kokoschka and the much-mated Alma Mahler. Idea Three, a remake of Buñuel's *The Exterminating Angel*. The ideas don't stop at three, but on this occasion, Miles does.

"I met Ulrike Meinhof once," he tells Seagrave. "Under really ordinary circumstances. I was eighteen or nineteen."

"Did you talk to her?"

"I don't remember. Obviously it was before she was a fugitive. I was drunk, wherever it was. Berlin. The Baader-Meinhof people kind of fascinated me. But this idea of someone established as a writer, taking that leap into the void—"

"Well, that's one idea," says Seagrave. "How have you been sleeping?"

Miles shifts uncomfortably in the leather patient's chair.

"Perpetual insomnia," he says. "The weirdest part is that I don't get physically exhausted from it. Before, if I couldn't sleep,

I'd konk out in the middle of the following afternoon. Now I can go twenty-four hours and just do whatever I do."

"I hope you aren't doing it too often," says Seagrave, suspecting that life in the country may be reviving chemical problems from Miles's distant past. Seagrave is allergic to the countryside, the Hamptons, all the places his patients go in summer. When he absolutely has to get away, he hops a flight for Buenos Aires and visits colleagues whose patients have, by and large, more interesting problems than his do.

38

Arthur received a reply to his letter to Jesse, sort of: Jesse mailed his letter to Arthur's loft, where it joined the pile of mail Arthur had to tear through when he returned to New York, quite a bit ahead of schedule. Arthur had spelled out enough desperation that Jesse felt indignant on his behalf. In his vast assortment of pictures, Jesse had numerous shots of Oliver that now seemed to reveal monstrous aspects of that large, formerly amusing man. Jesse saw something intimidating, tyrannical in Oliver's heavy face.

"I'm finished with the Willeys and all that social claustrophobia," Jesse's letter began.

Since they're unavoidable on the island, and it becomes some kind of statement if one sees them or not, I wouldn't care to be on the radar screen of their stupid gossip and backstabbing. Since I barely exist to myself, it's painful to see my own nothingness reflected in the eyes of people I despise. I have never entirely believed that anyone takes note of my presence anywhere. I was the kind of kid other kids didn't like, and if I got invited anywhere, I knew for certain if I arrived a minute late nobody would wait for me. If you've ever wondered why I'm always on time, it goes all the way back to grammar school.

Of course, Arthur, I know this isn't really true in our grown-up lives but we can know things objectively that don't make the smallest difference to the way our emotions run. If

I thought coming there would pull you out of an unbearable reality, I would come, but from your letter I think you're handling things fine and just think of this as your last year there.

Anyway, I'm going to disappear for a while. I am quite sick of myself and need to find something in the world or— I don't know what. But I will think of you.

I know you want to leave Oliver and it terrifies you, the idea of being alone, but we're not going to live forever, and if you don't take a jump, every day that goes by will make it seem harder. Oliver would never stick around if he had to do for you everything you do for him. Think about that for a while. Think about getting really old with somebody you really hate. No one has the right to make you miserable, least of all Oliver, who has no personality left and needs to be pampered like an infant. You have got to make a move.

PART
TWO

MY RECENT DEATH

39

Boredom can be viewed as a kind of fossil fuel, poured into inertia and ignited with fabulous results, but I am skeptical of this view, which reeks of unempirical optimism. We were excited for a while by drugs and sex, sometimes by escape from stultifying provincial childhoods, by ideological manias that were in the wind, by Che Guevara and Mao's *Little Red Book*, by Rolfing massage and Maharishi meditation, by rock and roll, punk rock, hip-hop, marketing brainstorms, junk bonds, liver transplants, by ever-refined electronic gadgets that seemed to afford some control over the gathering chaos. But eventually everything new became a short-lived palliative for the fatal gash of boredom. We began manufacturing problems that sounded deeper, worthier of analysis, than the Oblomov syndrome produced by getting older in an age when everybody had seen too much by the time they were thirty-five.

40

"Are you back from that Dark Place?" Denise asked Caroline hopefully. She could no longer tell, strictly by sight, which side of the moon Caroline was on.

Caroline had pulled on a pair of Levi's and a gray sweatshirt after spending all day and evening in her flannel bathrobe. She'd floated wraithlike down to the kitchen, where Denise was reading Elizabeth Bishop poems. The round oak table where she sat expanded. A leaf for the center rested against a wall in the pantry. But they hadn't had dinner guests in several weeks, for reasons obvious to both of them.

Caroline was tall and skinny, skinnier now than when they'd left New York. Her face had recently developed a strident, fiery hue. It couldn't be sunburn, she took no sun, yet it wasn't the spotty color people get from drinking, either. She set about making tea. She smiled to show Denise that everything was all right. Caroline had a chipped front tooth that made her smile disarming. She was not pretty. Like Denise she had strong, idiosyncratic features, too distinct to be pretty. The misfortune of such faces, sometimes, is that they show every twinge of mood, even when their owners intend to dissemble. Both women wore their hair long to soften this Kabuki effect. Denise's spilled in auburn curls and ringlets around her face. Caroline's fell straight to her shoulders and looked stringy when she drank a lot. Her hair had been chestnut brown. Worry had diluted it profusely with whitish streaks, a few more, it seemed, every week.

"I think," Caroline began to say in a small voice, then cleared her throat and spoke louder, "if I just got some work done. That always *used* to pull me out of these black holes."

Denise lowered her book at an angle, holding it open with her palm against the inner spine.

"It always does wonders for me," she said languidly, "though I can't claim to have written a word since the twelfth of May." She reached for a cigarette pack. She'd taken up smoking again, Gauloises filter tips. The filters seemed wrong, but she couldn't smoke the heavy plain ones anymore. She glanced for matches, but the table held nothing but a black Bakelite ashtray and a salt shaker. She lit up from a burner on the gas range where Caroline was waiting for the kettle to boil. Caroline didn't look at her. Denise was seven inches shorter than Caroline, so avoiding each other's eyes was seldom difficult when they were standing.

"I happen to know that," Denise elaborated, as she padded back to her chair, holding her Gauloise the way Bette Davis handled cigarettes in *Dark Victory*, "because I dated the page."

Caroline carried her tea and deliberated whether to sit at Denise's side, or face her across the table. She opted for the latter. She tried an attentive expression of everyday amity, calm. She joggled the tea bag up and down. Her bony fingers kept busy with themselves: she gripped a finger on one hand with two fingers of the other, then the reverse, twined them nervously in other configurations. Denise puffed her cigarette and glanced at her favorite Elizabeth Bishop poem, the one about Robinson Crusoe.

"It's been so long since I finished something," Caroline sighed. "Or started something, for that matter. And when you go back and look at what you have finished, you can't see how you ever did it."

"Uh-huh," Denise agreed. She made a conscious effort not to finish Caroline's sentences. Denise habitually finished people's sentences, usually guessing correctly which words they would have finished them with, or coming close. But it seemed a bad time to deprive Caroline of any words. "I look at my stuff and

I can never remember how one thing followed another. It's because we revise so much unconsciously in addition to what we're very aware of changing, don't you think? The tracks get covered. I don't suppose it would be of any help to keep a journal, or would it?"

Caroline shook her head emphatically. She pushed errant hair strands behind her ear.

"I've never understood what a journal is supposed to be *for*," said Caroline. "It's either for other people to read, in which case you might as well write a story or a poem, or it's just for yourself, and in that case—"

"Well, some people use a journal to store up material," said Denise. "I jot things down when I can't really write. Not important things," she hastened to qualify, "just maybe what a room looked like, or what color the sky was, if anything like that seems remarkable. It used to be if you were a writer, you just naturally kept a journal. I think that's a thing of the past. I mean there used to be so much information that wasn't recorded anywhere unless you wrote it down yourself. Today you can just go on the Internet and find out if it snowed in Milwaukee that Christmas or any other little piece of data you want to use. I used to try to, you know, write up a whole day, until I realized how totally uneventful my life was. Anyway," she went on, afraid of talking too much, "I think the only thing I ever enjoyed reading in a journal was this line of Kafka, I think— I'm sure it was Kafka, 'Germany declared war on Russia. Went swimming all afternoon.' "

Caroline laughed robotically. Not the upward shift of room tone Denise had hoped for.

"See, I always think if something's worth remembering, it will stay in my head," Caroline said. "Trivial things you forget, little details, I guess . . . one uses a lot of small details in a novel. That is true. You have to really . . . color things up."

"Not if you don't *want* to," Denise said, meaning Caroline didn't need to feel worse if she didn't keep a journal, or write a novel rich in minor details.

Caroline prowled about for a bear-shaped squeeze bottle of honey. She peered into several Navajo-looking cabinets before finding it on the stove where she'd put it down.

"I just don't have any *ideas*," she said. "Not for that book about the court case, anyway. I never even sat in on a trial, which I had planned to. I just sat on my ass for a year expecting some brilliant inspiration to strike."

"I thought the euthanasia book was a very promising idea," Denise said earnestly. "It's such an issue for people with debilitating diseases."

Caroline had written a twenty-page outline, two years earlier, for a novel about a mortally ill tennis champion who seeks out a Jack Kevorkian—like doctor to help him commit suicide. The doctor was charged with murder afterward. Caroline had intended to write it like a P. G. Wodehouse kind of comic novel.

"Maybe right now isn't such a good time to do that one," Denise added after a moment's thought. She couldn't help it, she invariably said what came to mind, whether she meant to or not. She wanted Caroline to see things in perspective, and at least acknowledge her depression as a passing thing. It was probably going overboard to suggest there could be a speck of humor in it.

Stirring a trickle of honey as it drooled lugubriously into her cup, Caroline said:

"I don't know if I'll ever be able to do anything again." Well, Denise thought, so much for a speck of humor. "Let's face it,"

Caroline went on, staring at her tea, unable to shrug off the vibe of a losing battle, "I'm a mess, I should probably be in a hospital. I know I'm slipping over the side. People don't stay this way this long and get better by themselves. You know I try every day to get a grip on this, this spiral of shit, there's moments when I remember crawling out of holes in the past, I almost believe I can crawl out of this one. The thing is, I don't think I can. I mean, I don't claim I can see anything objectively. I can't, that's the trouble. I know it's going to go too far if I just try to weather it out on my own. I hate what it's doing to you. I don't have the right to inflict this on you."

Denise held her breath for a moment. She didn't want it to be true, but it was true, so what should she say?

"Well, let's think about this for a minute," she said. "If you *did* need to spend some time in a hospital, would you want to be in a hospital out here, or go to a place in New York?"

Caroline was, suddenly, weeping. Tears streamed in even lines from her eyes, rolled down her narrow cheeks, dripped off her chin and puddled on the beige linen place mat under her teacup. She cried so freely and frequently now, without sobbing or wailing or any of the sounds that accompany a fulsome cry, that Denise no longer felt it necessary or appropriate to hold or hug her. Caroline's crying apparently didn't signify an upsurge of unhappiness or the need to be comforted. It was, by now, a spasm of nervous release, like a sneeze, that unwelcomely interrupted her in conversation. It stopped abruptly. She swobbed her face with her hands.

"I think New York," she said. She licked honey off her spoon. She closed her eyes and pushed them with her narrow thumbs, opened them, and shook her head, as if annoyed by a tic. Her sudden brightness looked more desperate than tears. "I mean we're not planning to stay here forever, are we?"

As often happened lately, Denise caught herself gaping at Caroline when Caroline looked elsewhere, unable to reconcile the mess she'd become with the stubbornly confident young woman she remembered occupying Caroline's body what seemed like a few months earlier. In reality, Caroline had been sliding downhill for at least two years. Denise probed her mouth's inner surfaces with her tongue, intent on dislodging a sliver of endive trapped between two lower teeth.

They had ruminated on this mental hospital topic before, though more as a remote possibility. It now hit home that hospitalization was nearly as much a problem for Denise as it was for Caroline. They'd lose half the summer rental if it happened immediately, not that that mattered in itself. Denise had quickly grown tired of Santa Fe and the butch-femme lesbian throwbacks abounding among their new acquaintances there, and the twee home-decorating mania that possessed male and female couples alike. Denise had immediately sensed that no one in the area they'd met or would meet had ever read anything more thought-provoking than the latest Anne Rice novel. Those kinds of people were okay for a weekend, if heavy drinking went with it, but anything beyond that was torture. She knew she and Caroline had been objects of incessant gossip since they arrived; the so-called gay community was so insular and deprived of real otherness that all it had was gossip and a collective fixation on Mission furniture. She missed her slum apartment. Selfish though it was, she missed living alone. She had no thought of deserting Caroline, but she desperately needed time away from her, and here she never got any.

"We need to find out," Denise said, "if your insurance covers that kind of hospitalization."

Caroline nodded.

"I'm almost sure it does," she said uncertainly. She sipped

tea. She tossed her shoulders back. She underwent a quick, familiar metamorphosis. Caroline wasn't consistently in an abyss; in a blink, she often came back to herself and remained legibly present and sensible for hours at a time. She certainly doesn't *want* to be crazy, thought Denise. "On the other hand, it's possible it doesn't. Actually, to be honest, I don't think it does cover psychiatric. They'll pay for a chiropractor, but I think it's your own problem if you're going nuts." Caroline shrugged. She walked around the room, rinsed her cup. She looked over her shoulder at Denise.

"I know this sounds awful," she said, "but I'm going to have a gin and tonic."

Denise smiled crookedly.

"I'll have one too," she said, to banish any hint of disapproval. She craved one, anyway. She smoked, rocked her shoulders backward and forward as she habitually did as a friendly, contented type of body movement. She mentally calculated what remained of her assets. Caroline had taken a bath in the stock market and barely had a dime left. No, Denise thought, there's no way I can pay for it. If I even tried to cover *some* of it, I'd lose the apartment and be out on the street.

It came to her, not for the first time, that the only person close enough to Caroline sufficiently rich and obligated to pay for her mental care was also the only person Caroline could never call. Denise felt a headache inching from her nape across her left temple to her forehead, along with the freaky thought that Caroline might not have any choice in the matter.

41

Chorus girl legs and flapping arms sprout from three hamburger buns stuffed with delicious patties and whorls of lettuce and glassy tomato slices. The hamburgers dance and sing an excited song about fresh new toppings.

Jesse can't remember where he is. In the seething night-light of the TV commercial he could be in several places. He has an impression of heavy air, starched sheets rustling pleasantly against his legs, a fuzzy recollection of a narrow room in the Gabrielli. He's woken with the taste of Bellinis souring his mouth. The night clerk shakes him, he thinks, or just stands near the bed calling him out of sleep: the taxi he ordered the night before is waiting.

He sees that he nodded out, sordidly, with his clothes and all the lights on, that he knocked the phone off the hook in his sleep. Magical Venice. The water cab to the airport, across a stinking lagoon in the blear blue hour before dawn, costs him eighty dollars. It's a trip for throwing away money, losing and letting go of things.

There was another time in a different Venice room, one with a similar groggy, underwater incoherence, shutters closed to maximize the feeble air-conditioning. Through chinks in the shutters helixes of gray light threw circling webs against the wall. Stillness and silence make it impossible to guess the time. Distant bells echo on the water, one reverberating sequence following another, marking the day's first devotions. Jesse has never learned the order of these Catholic clangings—vespers, matins, he doesn't know all their names, either. He found them all one time in a poem by Auden, or maybe Yeats, but even though he normally soaks up any fact or peculiarity of any religion, Jesse's never been able to keep the order of the bells straight.

A man he wasn't in love with breathed aggressively against the adjacent pillow. He slapped Jesse's arm when it accidentally brushed his back. Anthony traveled with him to Venice, later to Naples, finally to Rome. They slept together in the Santa Lucia and in the Locarno, and in the bar garden of the Locarno their friendship ended, even though they didn't put that into words. Anthony went upstairs. He packed and left the hotel while Jesse watched the flight of evening swallows.

He orders a light Bacardi and Coke. He feels more relieved than he felt many years earlier in Rome when, after a week of sleeping in parks for the dirty fun of it, he cashed some American Express checks and checked into a five-star hotel. Anthony is a prickly companion, unused to travel. He didn't bring enough money of his own. Jesse has picked up the check at almost every meal. All the same, Anthony keeps a log of every lira he spends. In hotel rooms Jesse wakes to see Anthony, sitting at the escritoire in a jockstrap, fretting over his budget and silently forming the angry thought that his money's evaporating because of Jesse. Jesse's insistence on a good hotel, Jesse's choice of a decent restaurant. Jesse could easily read Anthony's mind.

He'd met Anthony in Barcelona, another American. He never cared to travel with Americans, but Anthony's helplessness abroad, his guileless sexy smile, his extreme perversities in bed won Jesse over. Coming from Spain, Anthony slipped into some kind of travel panic less than an hour after the plane dropped them in Milan. Jesse might've thought it was Stendhal syndrome, but Anthony's disorientation seemed uglier than that. A sullen pig of a taxi driver who drove them to the train station took Anthony for something like fifty dollars.

"Are you crazy? You never should've given him that much money."

Things had moved too quickly for Anthony ever since. He began hating Jesse and fucking him meanly, with more violence than Jesse could handle. By the time they reached Rome, Jesse knew the next step would be real violence: Anthony was the type who either imploded or knocked the shit out of you. Since the Locarno was one of Jesse's many second homes, he felt calm enough there to suggest inexpensive ways for Anthony to go back to New York. They parted civilly, brutally tamping down the affection they felt for each other. Jesse knew he would despise this three-week lover for a long time, miss him while despising him. He wished his own nasty mouth had some kind of breatholator attached that wouldn't let him talk after too many cocktails.

He now has the garden to himself. He watches the barman's white shirt move through mottled reflections in the windows of the inside bar and wonders why almost any bartender or waiter in a clean white shirt makes him think about fucking. He ventures to say, in a whisper: "I am really so alone." He remembers sitting at the same wrought-iron table five years ago. The words fade in the damp air. The swallows change into bats. The soft falling twilight feels hollow and the wet air has a miasmic deadness, something like the sweat that pours out of people coming down from LSD. Jesse recalls that Rome was built on a vast swamp. He studies the narrow street through the padlocked garden gate, wishing someone he knew would turn up at the hotel. Few cars pass. Even fewer people. The Locarno period is long finished for anyone Jesse knows, if indeed he still knows them. In his mind, Rome will forever be a late-seventies city. All the aristocrat junkies died long ago; the artists have moved away. He considers booking a night train for Paris.

He stares at a leonine gargoyle spitting cool clear water into a marble scallop. His eye follows a pointy ribbon of jade ivy up the garden wall. Solitude makes him shy, hesitant to move. He speaks enough Italian to pass for an imbecile. Alone, he feels others' eyes when he walks around to the Piazza del Popolo. Even familiar places turn foreign when he feels vulnerable to the gaze of strangers. An annoying surge of gratitude washes over him when the Rosati maître d' greets him with recognition.

He takes a corner table. He remembers festive meals at Rosati with parties of fifteen and twenty friends. He remembers being much younger, excited by the world he traveled in. The familiarity of everything hasn't ripened into a feeling of being at home in the world, however. It weights him with the knowledge that he could go anywhere and never be surprised again by anything.

The world has become too twined, too insalubrious with suffering, to float through it, as if one had the right to be anywhere.

Jesse eats a heavy meal, avoiding wine to keep the edge from creeping near. He's prey to histrionic inner turmoil after several drinks. He gets excited, aggrieved, sad, stupid. Jesse needs clarity. He hasn't thought about where he'll go after Rome. If he drinks beyond a fixed threshold, in the wrong place, he knows he'll start to perceive himself as an interesting person, and want to involve a stranger in his subjectivity. This would not be dangerous in Rome, as it might be in South America, but it would be obnoxious. Jesse has become economical about giving himself ugly memories.

He considers that in the years he's been coming to Rome, he has always handled his own luggage. He has never ordered room service at the Locarno. He travels like a self-effacing mouse, he thinks, or just a cheap one.

42

Decades after the German terrorist debacle, Miles found it scandalous that the reams of committed journalism written by Ulrike Meinhof before her clumsy conversion to "direct action" had been totally eclipsed, on the Internet, by references to the Baader-Meinhof Gang. I confess that his fascination with Ulrike Meinhof fascinated me. I never knew where Miles's fitful mind would go. When he lived full-time in the country, Miles phoned when getting drunk. I could hear ice trays cracking open, Miles pouring whichever drink he favored at the time.

I recalled my last conversation with him. I heard the ice clinking in the background. He complained bitterly that all his attempts to write a "drama" about Ulrike Meinhof had come to naught.

"I suppose I could go back to my Kokoschka story," he said, when his Meinhof monologue suddenly flagged. Miles had a backup scenario based on an episode in the life of the great, tormented German painter Kokoschka. "You know, he had a replica of Alma Mahler made for him after she left him. There's a whole correspondence between him and the woman who built it for him: how he wanted the vagina shaped just so, the exact armature behind the breasts, every anatomical detail. After months of anticipation, what he got was this sort of hairy dummy, something like a damaged Hans Bellmer sculpture. It didn't look anything like Alma Mahler, but he was too far gone to care. He brought it with him to restaurants, had them set a place for it at the table, dragged it along to art exhibitions. He called it Alma and carried on conversations with it."

"Kind of a leap from Ulrike Meinhof," I said. I'm sure I sounded dismissive and bored. I was.

"What, you think I can only have one idea at a time?" Miles

became expansive, challenging. "I have dozens of good ideas that have had to atrophy and die. If I had a *producer,* if I had people I could *rely* on, if it wouldn't always be people looking at me as the *father figure* who takes care of everybody's emotional problems, scrapes up the cash, grabs the bar bill after every rehearsal, but it's always that way. Actors regress to infancy the minute a director's there to tell them what to do. People become passive-aggressive, and it's the one pathology I can't deal with. The technical people are all right. It doesn't take weeks of existential torment to hang a lighting fixture or nail up a scrim, but—"

"Not that I don't love her dearly," I said, "but you always insisted on working with people like Edith Eddy, so what did you expect?"

"I know, that's my weakness. When I was directing, I could only cast people I could visualize onstage. I could only write if I heard their voices in my head. Millie Ferguson, case in point. She was the most undisciplined, self-indulgent, passive-aggressive, infuriating human being I ever knew, she sabotaged me at every opportunity, that disastrous production of *Salome,* my God, I even tried to strangle her."

He had, too.

"She was even a rotten friend," he went on. "She had no loyalty. She wouldn't pick you out of the gutter if you were lying there in your own puke. I could give you a dozen examples. But when she was onstage, with her wild-ass hair flying and all that Cleopatra maquillage caked on her face, with that fucking *lisp* giving all her lines that tweak of irony. Edith's the same way. Once they're in front of an audience, you couldn't get that effect in a million years with any of these so-called professional actors. The only actor I ever fired was also the only professional actor I ever hired." Miles sighed. "Friend of Millie

Ferguson's, come to think of it. A former child star on Broadway who threw a tantrum whenever he thought his blocking was off."

Miles still had satanic good looks. When people saw him and pointed out how handsome he still was, he simply said he "wasn't taking the Lyle Lindsay way out," though by then Lyle had slimmed down to 130 and regained his mop-haired adorableness. Lyle had climbed the fashion business ladder. He was booking models for, I think, Eileen Ford Agency. People would have hit on him no matter what he looked like. He would never be loved for himself, I suppose he figured, so he might as well look good again.

As life's little ironies go, Miles's appearance at my front door buzzer the afternoon after I arrived home from Truro later seemed part and parcel of Arthur's premature return to the city. I had not expected Miles. The cool weather had shifted that morning into scorching heat.

"You're so thin," I told him as he wheezed through the door after climbing six flights. "Do you ever eat anything?"

"No"—he scowled—"and neither do you. You're thinner than I am. I'll bet that freezer's full of Stouffer's vegetable lasagna."

"Well, you'd bet wrong. That freezer's been iced solid for two years."

"I'm sick of eating," Miles went on without listening, "pissing, shaving, everything else a person has to do every day. I don't even *bathe* in the country, or change clothes. What's the point? I just forget to do it until I really stink."

Miles did not stink, but I could tell it pleased him to think so. His black hair was shorn to caplike stubble. His wide brown eyes looked sunken. He wore a Ramones T-shirt and the olive cargo pants popular that summer, that gathered with pull-strings at the waist and ankles and sported innumerable Velcro pockets. And leather sandals, to show off his long, high-arched, pedicured feet.

I didn't ask to what I owed his visit. As far as Miles was concerned, I owed him everything and anything, and always would.

43

Anna M.'s rich biography includes a sister named Claudia, a sister Anna never knew. Anna was born eighteen years after Claudia. Their parents, Christophe and Miranda M., married young, at university. A second child, David, was born seven years after Claudia. That year, Miranda finished a Ph.D. in anthropology at McGill. Eleven years later, on the cusp of menopause, she risked a final pregnancy, in Switzerland.

The family had originally lived in Montreal. Christophe had ideas about making fortunes from grand hotels. Shortly before Anna's birth, they moved to Switzerland. Anna had no real memory of Claudia. When Anna was three, Claudia drifted off on the peace-and-love trail to enlightenment. First she lived in an Ibiza commune, later in Tuscany with a small-time drug dealer. She summoned money out of air, odd jobs: dressmaker, waitress, masseuse, chef, nanny, drug runner—a typical love child of the counterculture. Her parents didn't disapprove. They were intellectuals. Or rather, Miranda was. Christophe simply hated convention and stupid methods of raising kids. They opposed the Vietnam War. Miranda smoked dope. They didn't mind Claudia rejecting Western values. Western values had caused most of the misery in the world, Miranda often said.

Claudia backpacked overland through Albania and Greece, Israel and Syria, Afghanistan and Kashmir. These were nice places then, except Albania, a Stalinist holdover. And poor deposed King Zog had to drive a taxi in Paris, he'd once taken Miranda from the Rue du Seine to Place de l'Opéra and poured his royal heart out to her. " '*Pour moi*,' " the typical Albanian peasant had formerly asserted with pride, King Zog averred, " 'le roi est Dieu.' Et maintenant?" Zog lamented as his cab meter ticked. "Regardez-moi. Méchant, c'est tout."

The Afghans of Claudia's sparse letters were welcoming tribes of ancient habits, who decorated their flesh with henna, smoked the strongest hashish in the world, and fucked like inexhaustible gods of libido any white thing that wandered through. Srinagar, in Kashmir, featured a tomb reputed to house Jesus' remains, the Savior having drifted east after his staged death and resurrection, becoming a fervent Buddhist. You could rent a houseboat on Lake Dal, complete with maid service and cook, for practically nothing. Claudia survived four months in a Poona ashram on lentils and the occasional onion. She crossed and recrossed India by rail, bus, and on foot, suffered epics of the runs. She made the obligatory trip to Kathmandu, which had thicker smog than Los Angeles, she wrote, crawled with addicts and brainless American hippies. At some point, she went down to Chiang Mai by taxi, copping super dope in the Golden Triangle. Claudia finally, fatally, ended up in Bangkok.

Where she met her death, her senseless awful death. Her throat slashed with a razor, her body dumped in the shallows off Pattaya Beach. For months it lay unidentified in the Bangkok morgue, until an enterprising Dutch diplomat, interested in a spate of tourist murders, determined her nationality from items of clothing, had dental impressions made and sent all over Europe.

Claudia had met up with a bad monkey. Two bad monkeys: a dashing con man who passed for French but was really Indian-Vietnamese, and an Indian youth with no criminal past who became a symbiotic henchman. Amphetamines figured in the murder frenzy they played out over five months; so did a twistedly channeled, closeted-homo folie à deux. Their exploits crippled Thailand's tourist industry for a year.

These bad monkeys were named Charles and Ajay. Charles was later imprisoned in India for twenty years on a variety of

118

nonlethal local charges. Quite incredibly, by outwaiting a non-renewable extradition order in Delhi's Tihar Prison, Charles walked out free after serving his time. He flew to Paris the day after his release. Ajay had vanished when he and Charles and Charles's mistress fled to Malaysia, then to India after the murders. It was claimed by the mistress—a pathetic Canadian nurse who denied any knowledge of her boyfriend's homicides, painting herself as a duped slave of love, even winning support from Indira Gandhi, as well as a large contingent of Quebec separatists—that Charles had killed Ajay in Malaysia, burying him in a swamp. It was believed by others that Ajay currently managed a Honda dealership in Georgetown, Virginia. Anna meant to look into all this, someday.

Claudia's death crippled Miranda's spirits for several years. It splintered Christophe's mind, one part of which went on working like a flawless piece of business machinery while the other was steeped in dissociative melancholia, occasionally tripping into schizophrenia. The business end of Christophe formed lucrative partnerships to restore and operate grand, decrepit luxury hotels. The dissociative side of him exuded too much pain and strangeness for Miranda to absorb. When he slipped into fugues, or had to check into a clinic for a month or two, Miranda left Zurich and disappeared for the duration, leaving Anna and David in the care of various nannies.

One afternoon, as Christophe strolled out of the Gare du Nord into a raging downpour, a bolt of lightning zapped through him. He survived with perfunctory physical damage, a pinkish fissure on his chest that had a paler double on his shoulder blade, a few weeks of therapy, tests, a mild passing aphasia and difficulty passing water. A welcome miracle, but also unsettlingly improbable, a suggestion of invisible powers at work which neither Miranda nor Christophe believed in.

Six months later, when the miracle had shrunk to the size of a dinner anecdote, Christophe, walking beside the river in Zurich, was hit by lightning again. Against incalculable odds, and, weirder still, he again survived, though this time some of his innards were scorched, his organ systems scrambled and temporarily failed, there was talk of dialysis and brain damage, hearing loss, possible vision impairment, some bad moments in the emergency room and exploratory surgery occurred, yet after some weeks of intensive care his physical envelope defiantly rallied and healed. "Twice is really too much," Anna heard Miranda muttering on one occasion. Miranda found herself thinking of Christophe as a reanimated dead person.

After the second lightning strike, Christophe's normal melancholia was replaced by unnatural ebullience. For several weeks, though, he stumbled around in an abstracted haze, smiling strangely to himself, running his hands over household objects as if skeptical of their reality. He also heard sounds out of normal auditory range. He developed an extreme sensitivity to weather: wind shirring in trees, the interval between dusk and nightfall. This often manifested itself in song. Christophe uncontrollably burst into song when the weather went a certain way. Five or six songs, always the same ones, all from the 1924 Broadway production of *The Shanghai Gesture* starring Florence Reid.

He appeared without warning in darkened rooms of their vast apartment, in a red silk bathrobe he wore for an entire month.

He soon manifested a disturbing array of new mental skills, aberrant abilities of the type usually faked by magicians. In Christophe's case, these were indisputably authentic. Walking into one of his hotel kitchens, for example, he might declare the exact number of spoons, knives, and forks in the cutlery drawers, how many of each flatware item in which drawer, how many tarnished, how many of a certain style. When the utensils were counted they tallied exactly with Christophe's psychic inventory. If Miranda went shopping with Anna, Christophe might name, upon their return, the streets they'd walked on, in what sequence. He described objects they'd seen in shop windows, the boxed items they'd purchased. The novelty of these powers quickly ceased to amaze the family, their friends, and employees. They began to stir everybody's deepest apprehensions.

When family members traveled without him, if Christophe phoned he could describe in lavish detail any objects in their hotel rooms, hotels he'd never seen, colors and patterns of drapes and bedcovers, even the water pressure in the bathroom.

Growing up, Anna believed her father omniscient, omnipresent, and more or less omnipotent, like God. As no one in the M. family had any religious superstitions, Christophe's expanded mind undermined their faith in the rational values of the Enlightenment and plagued them with haunting evidence, which it possibly was, of an invisible world, a parallel universe that Christophe's brain, or part of it, occupied while his body inhabited physical reality. Sometimes Miranda speculated that Christophe had been zapped into alignment with unknown chemical reactions in nearby organisms, or undiscovered quiddities of physics that might, if adequately investigated, reveal entirely new, possibly horrible properties of time and space.

Anna's father's most alarming faculty was his evolving acuity as a telepath. He really did know what people privately thought, and would tell them. It unnerved them. These extra senses convinced Miranda, Anna, and David that they were fatally cursed, that some type of god existed after all and hated their particular guts with a diabolical loathing only a Supreme Being could possibly manifest in this unique fashion. For a telepath, Christophe remained surprisingly oblivious to his family's growing wish that a third bolt from the blue would fully remove him from the realm of the living.

David fled Zurich and entered a university in western France. He believed that the variegated geography between there and Zurich, and the density of electrical interference (he speculated that the two lightning bolts had connected his father's synapses to generated AC current), would shield him from egregious surveillance.

Miranda found daily life with him insupportably invasive, even though he gradually learned, at least now and then, to keep his revelations to himself. Their divorce was not exactly amicable but not exactly hostile, either. It was a divorce of confusion that seemed to involve large metaphysical questions rather than the usual issues of incompatibility. She moved to the United States with Anna, first to Providence, Rhode Island, where she'd been offered a job in the Brown anthropology department. She then sought out and landed a tenure-track position at UCLA.

44

Malcolm squandered a lot of dream capital that summer filming a movie in his head. Anna had given him a digital camcorder for his twenty-sixth birthday. He taped things, all manner of things, trying to make the camera follow the vagaries of his perception. It was quite tricky to make a motion camera produce something worth looking at. (Still photography, he believed, could be done as artfully as Irving Penn or Richard Avedon by any of the higher primates, with a little basic training.) Malcolm loved silent movies. He also loved postsilent directors like William Wyler, who told stories purely through pictures, even when a lot of dialogue went with them.

Malcolm considered silence the most wonderful thing in the world. New York was twenty-four-hour noise that shot through your bloodstream like crystal meth. It reduced your thoughts to flying fragments. Even the World Trade Center, looming in their bedroom windows, squalled noises all night, hydraulic squeaks and high-pitched creaking like metal scraping metal, in bed they also heard massive volumes of some liquid whooshing and gurgling, which he thought must be the air-conditioning system or some related internal process. Buildings that massive are like sleepless living organisms, stuffed with hidden switches and circuits and signals that snap and flash continually through thousands of miles of pipes and wires. Their neighborhood was one of the city's most desolate places after dark, and it made an infernal racket all the same. The soaring buildings created a wind tunnel in the surrounding streets, and every piece of hanging signage in the area, every traffic light and stop sign bent and creaked mightily when you walked home at night. This tsunami of noise crashed over you ceaselessly and you gradually heard it subliminally instead of as a conscious irritation. It shot through you like gamma rays. It throbbed in your blood and got you used to being rattled and distracted all the time, without even feeling how stressed out you were.

Malcolm suspected that he hated New York City and one day would leave and never look back. Odds were good that he would be here for several years, however, so he didn't frame the suspicion as a certain fact. People came here and made their mark, and then they could leave for years without anyone suspecting they were gone. You only had to read articles about famous musicians and artists and writers to discover that most names you thought synonymous with "New York City" belonged to people who lived in villages two or three hours out of town, or in other states, other countries altogether. Malcolm didn't think he could live in a village or some country town. His idea was somewhere like Madrid or Paris, even Mexico City, some foreign metropolis where he didn't feel directly affected by what went on around.

He had, for now, his irregular job at the Virgin Megastore. He did many other things to stay solvent. He worked the door of a Loisaida nightclub three or four nights a month, maybe twice a month DJ'd inside the same club. He made headbands and metal jewelry that he sold on the street, or put on consignment at one or two little shops. When money got uncomfortably tight he danced at the Adonis.

In Baltimore, Malcolm had danced at the Atlantis, where the dancers performed right on the bar, naked except for white socks the customers stuffed with tips. Here you had to keep your package covered. Malcolm did the odd date with a customer, top only, no condom, no fuck; he'd paid for a year at NYU Film Studies that way. Now he was taking a year off. He didn't have hang-ups about whoring around, but he lacked the kind of energy it needed, somehow. For a while he ran deliveries for Nahib, but that scared him: if you were black they locked you up for a long time even if you only had a "personal use" quantity on you when they busted you.

Malcolm's father, Ginger, a local blues singer, had done time in the Baltimore lockup, the one right beside the freeway, assault and battery on a cop. As he had no priors, Ginger wasn't in long, but it left scars; Malcolm didn't want scars.

When they let Ginger out, Malcolm's mother split. Left him, left Ginger, left the country. She was half-Swedish, half-Japanese. Malcolm barely remembered her. Ginger was half-Nigerian, half-Indonesian. That was the short version. His parents' parents had been mongrels too: the Japanese part was mixed with Peruvian, the Swedish with Spanish; his Nigerian grandfather had been half-English, the Indonesian grandmother half-French. Some people have nothing to give their kids besides exotic names—Maximilian, Swaneesha, names to confound booking clerks in police stations. Malcolm's parents gave him a little more. He looked like something all those strange names should hang on.

People spun around to stare at Malcolm in the street, not simply because he was beautiful, but because he seemed to belong to a new human species. A narrow skull, puffy Negroid lips in the middle of a sharply tapered Japanese-shaped mouth. Oval eyes a fraction wider than Japanese but radically slanted at the edges. Ingrid Bergman's nose, an explosion of red and gold-brown dreadlocks. Up close, people sneaked glances at him and hoped he didn't notice, as if he were a movie star.

Unique Malcolm. Unique as he was, he understood early that Baltimore would kill him if he stayed there, Funkytown full of guns and knives and every type of lethal possibility. One dumb word in a bar, the wrong eyeball action on the street, took less than a second to jack into homicide.

He lived with Ginger until he finished high school. Ginger drank all day and sang all night; the dull business of raising Malcolm was left to a succession of Ginger's girlfriends who taught him everything a boy needed to know. More, really, but it was all good. At least he got through high school. Before he was old enough to buy liquor, he moved into a girlfriend's basement dump on South Dallas Street. Malcolm clerked for a while in a used-record store in Fells Point; he tried blending with the gentrifying sandbars in the deep blue sea of race trouble. But at night, Malcolm knew, every nigger is a nigger to a nigger. The Atlantis Club and the jail where his father did time are separated by a long potholed parking lot in a scary-empty pocket of town. For Malcolm, the parking lot would never be long enough.

He sent Ginger a snapshot of him and Anna on the Coney Island boardwalk. "Pretty girl," Ginger said on the phone. "Good family, I bet, too. You stick with that. Stay off all them ho's only after your money." What money? Malcolm wanted to say, but skipped it. He knew "good family" translated into "white"; he left it at that.

45

As Jesse's Venice reverie dissolves into consciousness he recognizes the darkness around him as belonging to a suite at the Gramercy Park Hotel: if he switches the light on, he'll find his wallet and keys and a Perrier gone flat on the night stand, and a copy of Genet's *Journal du voleur*. His slacks, underpants, and a print shirt are heaped over his shoes on the carpet. The dancing hamburgers and car ads have segued into Marlene Dietrich and Orson Welles on the television.

"You look like you've been eating too many candy bars," Dietrich is telling Welles.

"I'd rather be getting fat on your chili," Welles says. Jesse has never understood how Welles got Charlton Heston to play a Mexican in this film, but there it is.

Un soir il dut se battre. He thinks about dead people in the dark: Millie Ferguson, Bruce the photographer, Adam Z. Millie was cremated, Bruce interred somewhere in Wisconsin. Adam, he thought, probably had set aside some cash for a party, and had margarita glasses rimmed in his ashes. Some people are a flicker of lightning. Some have faded to a single facial expression, a faint breath, a photograph, a quick tug of the heart. He will go to the airport tomorrow and buy a ticket for the first place he thinks of: but he's startled to realize he hasn't embarked already, but simply managed to leave his apartment with a suitcase. He watches soundless Janet Leigh terrorized by hophead Mexicans in her motel room. On the bedspread near his arm, a current issue of *Next* lies folded open to the escort and masseur ads. Jesse's circled some in pencil. He gropes for the light and settles the magazine on his chest. The Mexicans approach Janet Leigh with a giant syringe. The escort ads seem slim pickings. Only Hung Like a Horse, who gives his name as Ivan, and

Ten Hard Inches, known as Angelo, have tackled the composition of their ads with a feeling of brevity and directness. He isn't calling either of them, even so.

sometimes you're mistaken about things & it makes you crazy you wake up & hear yourself thinking the same thing over and over & it's terrible being alone & how old you've become my pretty pretty

If anyone asked why he was in this hotel, he would tell them it was for the view. At night, out the window, he sees the canopy of leaves over the small private park, the street where taxis pull up to the hotel. The view is so minimal he can lose the sense of where he is, sometimes forget who he is.

i've failed to piece together something. i terrorize myself with fantasies of doom. i've become strange to my own strangeness

The park below represents a flawless state of order. Only property owners around the park have keys. Jesse remembers being in the park once, four years ago, on a Sunday: some structural work was under way, so the park had been opened to the public for one afternoon. There were prams and pink balloons and a little orchestra. Jesse is glad they aren't there anymore.

A California blond with perfect pale lips drives through a storm to his girlfriend's house. Every time he sees the commercial Jesse imagines pressing his cock into the actor's mouth. He thinks the car being advertised is a piece of shit, it said so in *Consumer Reports*. Maybe the actor is a piece of shit, too. But he still buys the fantasy they're selling along with the car.

He remembers things he forgot to buy. He wanted candles. He's never burned candles in a hotel room, except Third World places during blackouts, and in the Athens Grand Bretagne, where they stock candles in the bathrooms. He remembers that the doorman at the Grand Bretagne is Cat Stevens's brother. He remembers power failures in Bogotá and Quito and La Paz. He wishes New York had frequent blackouts. Jesse recalls epic electrical storms in Cartagena, in Cuenca, in Saigon. He avoids thinking about why he happened to be in some of those places, but he likes remembering the places. And if he burned candles in the Gramercy, he could imagine being nowhere at all.

voices the same as other voices. you're on a bus for instance or in a crowd somebody from your childhood adolescence who knows when, you turn and expect a familiar face aged with the years along with yours & it's the face of a total stranger

46

In Los Angeles, when Anna was fifteen, Miranda married a physicist ten years her junior, Wallace W., whom she met in the course of a fender bender on Melrose near Cahuenga. Wallace's unassuming, easygoing personality, his solid position at a private research firm, his sanguine blandness, gave no indication of his festering obsession with a species of nudibranch, a shell-less marine snail that fed on jellyfish. The nudibranch digested the jellyfish's stinger cells in such a way that they formed part of the nudibranch's outer surface, hence forming a third sea creature: not a parasite, but an instant hybrid.

Wallace had the kind of synergistic, some would say paranoid, mental structure that projects obscure, unaccountable facts into cognates of more important things, and eventually expands them into universal principles. He theorized that mutations akin to the nudibranch's partial assimilation of the jellyfish occurred in unknowable variants among aquatic and terrestrial life forms yet to be discovered—but, most subtly and frequently, he announced one day, when the inductive leap became irresistible, in human beings, through psychic contact. In Wallace's ever-enlarging view, human mammals mutated on a continuous and invisible basis: any individual's contact with any other deposited significant psychic residue in each from the other. Therefore, he said, there could be no such thing as an integrated human personality, only an amorphously congealed human species, randomly broken up into perpetually hybridizing monads—all pieces of a vast, multitasking, single consciousness, akin to that of fire ants or honey bees. "Therefore," Wallace concluded, "we could say that it is really not at all random but an intrinsic structure of human nature." Wallace called the composite nature of personality "the Interhuman."

Once Wallace had fully articulated his theory, Miranda realized that her bad luck must have been the yang to the yin of Christophe's surviving two separate lightning bolts.

Wallace's other obsession was betting on wrong horses at Santa Anita racetrack—over time, a less theoretical, deleterious source of family tension. Anna didn't mind Wallace. She'd noticed that people did seem to melt into each other until they were all the same. She didn't mind California. Anna tried to be *sportif* about things she had no control over. Still, she knew she could easily resent her entire life if she played it out in Westwood past the age of eighteen.

Miranda was a decent but unengaged mother, too distant and involved with her husbands and her studies, with her hobby—a translation of Levi-Strauss's *La pensée sauvage* into Italian—and with a Martha Stewart–like perfectionism in trivial matters like the proper shape and depth of a fish poacher, when to plant tulip bulbs in Southern California. Too distant to appear keen on Anna's happiness. She was, Anna thought, unaware that anyone *could* be unhappy who hadn't already been married to a mind reader, and then married to a man who found the meaning of life in snails without shells.

Anna sometimes thought Miranda had loved Claudia so fiercely that she'd hoped a second female child would turn out a close approximation of Claudia. Anna imagined she'd been found wanting in whatever had made Claudia special. This hurt. A bit. But Anna sensibly told herself that wanting to please Miranda was not one of her life's goals.

After high school, Anna went to Yale. This put several thousand miles between herself and either parent. She wanted to study law, not to become a lawyer, but so she'd know what lawyers knew. She became a computer hacker because she dated hackers at school, hackers who weren't geeks but in fact had a piratically sexy aura. She wanted to know what other people besides lawyers knew, people who ran corporations and banks and used back channels of intelligence to secretly rule the world. It had been her observation that most people had no idea what sort of world they were living in, or that it was ruled by any particular group of people. Anna wanted a precise grasp of how reality was shaped and manipulated. She couldn't just tap into other people's brain waves like her father, but still, she wanted to know.

Anna was confident that she'd distinguish herself somewhere along the road in some more or less conventional manner, in the arts, maybe, or as an actress, or something cultural, but saw her immediate destiny in those murky technological regions where information travels from place to place with the thinnest veneer of legality.

47

The hotel in Istanbul used to be a palatial rest stop on the Grand Tour. Marble everything, scaled for Byzantine autocrats and British royalty. In the majestic lobby, yellowed newspaper clippings about Agatha Christie, who wrote some books there, occupy a glass vitrine. The staff moves at an unhurried pace that never varies. Chairs, lamps, paintings, chandeliers, all spaced at soporifically long distances. The shabby grandeur of the hotel and its pretentious history hang in the air like soot, absorbing and shrinking every modern thing. It turns the American Express forms and Madonna songs playing in the bar into piquant debris from a world destroyed centuries past. Paper currency crumbles between his fingers. Jesse thinks Turkish coins are pressed from recycled soda cans.

The hotel is wildly expensive. It does not feel like a haven of safety and graciousness. The concierge is rude. The staff at the main desk ignore him when he asks for a cab or directions. His room overlooks the dining room terrace and, beyond that, a wide, double-tiered cement park where hotel guests sometimes drink tea. The park fills with local teenagers and old people at night, who stay until two or three in the morning. At five, when starry darkness covers the immense valley to the left of the park, prayers are yodeled by faraway imams, through crackling loudspeakers. The town appears coated in fine dust. The streets light up in sunset hues and carry odors of burning rubber and rotting meat.

The room contains two single beds with rock-hard mattresses and cheap linen sheets, a giant oak armoire, a uselessly tiny writing table. The bathroom has glistening, chipped white tile. Green oxidation smears around the bidet and bathtub drains disturb him. He thinks the city's putrid matter could seethe up through the plumbing. The room's vaulted ceiling and excessive empty space heighten the impression of frugality. Surfaces look crisp yet faded, like museum pieces under glass. He imagined Istanbul differently. He had been told a certain erotic easiness prevailed there, but he imagined that differently, too.

Every man he passes in the street gives him a look of flagrant sexual appraisal, men of seventeen, men of eighty. At first this quickens his interest. But the general condition of the city precludes going just anywhere with strangers. He doubts that just anybody can enter the hotel. The city resembles an immense hive that's been compressed in a vise. He knows he can't acquire the radar to move around in it freely, so he sticks to large, wide, well-lighted streets. At night, even these streets dip without warning into valleys of blackness.

The Third World is intrinsically hateful. It is hateful to be rich among so many poor, hateful to desire men who will sell him their bodies for the price of a pack of cigarettes. It is hateful to be hated by these people and hateful to pretend to love them, as Jesse often does, hoping to be loved back for a few hours or days, knowing he'll forget any promise that he makes as soon as his plane takes off. There was a time when Jesse believed what Third World people always told him, that he "wasn't like an American," meaning that he wasn't arrogant, that he showed his emotions, that he didn't treat the local people like scum. But I am, he thinks, exactly an American, taking what I want from the country and paying for it with chump change, faking sincerity and niceness so these simple people will think I'm put together the way they are. I'm just an American with better manners.

48

"When I first moved upstate," Miles ruminated that afternoon, when he showed up without warning, sipping from a can of Coke he'd brought with him, "I got into all that city exile shit. Planted a spice garden, whipped up complicated meals, I used to drive to Massachusetts for groceries and have the neighbors in for dinner. I did the food thing, the garden thing, the interior decorating thing, I've done all the things you can do."

Yes. I remembered entire months when Miles spoke of nothing but food on the telephone, rattling obsessively about pressing his own gravlax or working a new twist in an osso buco recipe. He spent a fortune on specialty cookware, Crock-Pots and sauté pans. He was too aware of himself not to bend this into a joke, but he did it, all the same. After a while the air drained out of that balloon, and he spoke in withering terms about the countrified rage for haute cuisine running rampant in Dutchess County, the related fetish for antiques, the blather expended on decorating rooms.

As a person who had trafficked for years with set designers, Miles was not indifferent to a room's look, but enough, as he increasingly griped, was enough. "It's all any of these people talk about up here," he would growl, banishing all thought of interior design with an audible splash of vodka, an emphatic rattle of ice. "They yammer on about where they got a footstool, or a hand-painted chest of drawers, or a cedar cabinet, how lucky they were to find this auction over in Catskill, how these peach curtains go just perfect with these impossibly shaped windows, it's all straight people who sound like fags," Miles said, "and fags who sound like the Stepford Wives."

Well, he'd reached the end, evidently.

"I'm in therapy with Seagrave again," he told me, meaningfully. "I've been having these dreams."

He checked my dubious expression, stretched his long legs out in the one chair I didn't use at my desk, a director's chair with black leather seat and backrest. He stared at his sandaled toes as he flexed them agitatedly. I looked at Miles awkwardly from my desk swivel chair, thinking this configuration too formal and cramped and itself almost psychiatric, as if we had a fixed amount of time to sit there. I can't claim that my apartment has a very welcoming arrangement of furniture.

In this matter of dreams, I suppose it is necessary to reveal that I'd given up my summer rental in Truro, in large part, because I found myself waking up from terrible dreams about death, the same dreams over and over, and the sadness of these dreams suggested, for reasons I still can't articulate in a coherent way, that I had traveled too much and stayed away from "my life," whatever that really was, way too long—and when Miles alluded to his dreams, I had the disturbing feeling that I knew what he was going to say.

My air conditioner had perished the previous summer. Our clothes spotted with sweat. I would have asked Miles into the bedroom where a Vornado fan, at least, swirled the damp air around, but there was nowhere to sit except the bed. I have never trusted myself on a bed with Miles.

"Except they're not really dreams, but this . . . mental thing that happens as I wake up," he said, and the words could have come from my mouth. "You know that moment when you know you aren't dreaming, you're in reality, you're conscious, but you haven't pushed yourself forward yet, you're still lying there, it's almost a meditative state. At first it happened when I woke up from a night's sleep, but now even if I take a nap— it's not overpowering, that's too dramatic, it's more this neutral, resigned, melancholic . . . apprehension of mortality. A suffocating sensation of being dead already. And with it a bewilderment about death, like, how is it possible, one day I won't be here?"

I already knew that *something was taking its course,* though I did not want to know about it.

"I had the feeling these dreams were telling me to leave the country house," Miles said.

I considered showing him the letter I'd received from Arthur. He had described an eerily similar disturbance in virtually the same words: "A resigned acceptance of my own death," he'd written, "and at the same time this confusion about how it's possible to die, to not be here anymore."

I opened my mouth to mention it. I couldn't.

"Anyway." Miles sighed. "Nothing springs to mind about Ulrike Meinhof down here, either."

He looked at the Coke can in his fingers as if he'd never seen it before, and set it on the floor. Just then, from the courtyard of the music school down the block, came a startling clamor of instruments. Some student orchestra was playing a jazzy version of "Amazing Grace."

"Marx was right about one thing," Miles said.

"What was that?" I was startled that Miles, of all people, had reduced what Marx had been right about to one thing.

"Religion *is* the opium of the people."

"Too true," I said. "And then there's Opium, from Yves Saint Laurent. Oh, I have to show you something." I climbed over his legs. "Just wait, I ran across this the other day."

Deliberately excavating anything from the sediment of my apartment, anything of more than two or three months' vintage, on a brutally hot day, could usually reduce me to a muttering blob of regret for every decision I'd made in my life, or not made, since everything in the apartment pointed to a systemic disorder, an inability to discard what I no longer needed, some perverse tendency to cling to messy clumps of never-to-be-revisited past. I had uncovered a relic the night before by accident, in a shoe box. I brought it out to show him: a puppet.

A puppet. It had the face of a shriveled human fetus, or somebody very old whose face has wrinkled its way back to babyhood, with a rude brain holding it in place, made from wire mesh and clock innards. Lidless blue doll's eyes you could move around with a wire soldered to a tiny gear, a jaw that opened and closed using another wire. Its body was a stuffing of metal coils, wax-molded steel wool, shards of wood painted blue. You could work it using ordinary string-and-wood attachments, make it walk, bend, move its arms—protractors, screwed to odd lengths of hinged copper; if you fiddled with it properly, it danced.

I swung the puppet in front of Miles's face and dropped it in his lap. I had bought it twenty years earlier, at a fund-raiser for Miles's theater company. He'd made it himself, for a little puppet show he'd used to illustrate a reading of Kleist's *Essay on the Puppet Theater.*

Miles held it up for inspection, then tentatively manipulated the strings and wires, making the puppet amble along his thighs, spread out its arms, rub its hands together. As he played with it his face tightened, unpleasantly determined. The more he fooled with it the more supple and expressive the puppet's movements became. And then, as if snapping free of a trance, Miles shoved it back into the shoe box, shut the lid, and slid it under his chair. He smiled at me somehow pityingly.

"I don't want to remember all that," he said matter-of-factly. He picked up his Coke can, gently crushed it, waggled it back and forth. "Here's today's little dummy. I'm amazed you held on to that all this time. It's probably worth less now than you paid

138

for it." Miles looked at his Swatch watch as a matter of form. "I have to meet somebody on the West Side."

He organized his long, loping body into motion, his expression, as far as I could read it, a twinge of annoyance playing across his face.

"I'll call you," he said as he left.

49

Denise squeezed her eyes shut. When she closed them no light penetrated her lids, no phosphenes radiated in her inner sight. An ink-solid blackness draped her visual field. Mentally she pictured her city apartment windows. They stared out on an expanse of waste space separating five tenement buildings, an unintended courtyard full of unplanned vegetation. It enclosed four sickly elms, a rampant growth of crape myrtle, and one white birch, its striated bark peeling off in black and white strips. She could see the windows of her neighbors and restage their habitual oddities, gleaned from years of idle spying. If she looked up she saw a ragged wedge of sky.

It wasn't much; sometimes it was everything. A rubble-strewn dustiness and a stagnant odor hung in the street outside, which was gentrifying at a snail's pace compared with the blocks west, north, and south. Recalcitrant minority people with rent-stabilized places had made the block their final barricade in fending off expulsion by the better-off. For many of them the landlords' offered buyouts would climb to some irresistible figure. Denise would miss her loser neighbors. She liked sitting on her stoop gabbing with eighteen-year-old Puerto Rican girls who already had two babies. She liked the desuetude and the company; she hated being old among such young people.

She juxtaposed daily life in that space (comforting as any well-worn rut, dulling as novocaine in its unvarying Denise-ness; the apartment, however clean and spartan-empty she kept it, defeated bright schemes of self-improvement and energized productivity she conjured when she was away from it, exactly as though it were stuffed with all the detritus she'd ditched at the end of her twenty-year common-law marriage; Denise's calculations never glossed over the torpor that place tossed over wishes and ambitions like a thick, fuzzy blanket) with the wide, cool, dusky rooms of the chocolate-shingled, California-craftsman-style jewel box—a rare example in the Southwest—on the outskirts of Santa Fe.

Here she could wander for miles into the desert pondering a single undistracted thought like an expertly balanced tray of champagne glasses, loosely packed sand crunching underfoot, mesquite and lizards and mineral-indifferent cacti the only decor, an occasional rattler slithering away at her steps' vibrations, under a limitless sky, a blue color that stung the eyes like pure white during the day, retracting after dark to reveal an awesome planetarium. Denise had never seen so many stars and satellites and cosmic spirals, planets and constellations the locals pointed out in a proprietary way, and the fact that everything out there was as dead as the chunks of quartz the local New Age emporium sold as "healing crystals" made her living existence feel like an unrepeatable miracle.

The flat, uninflected desert spread out in every direction. The dry heat, the weightlessness of empty space, relieved time of any meaning. Denise's history, any history, never impinged or accumulated. But she would never be here without Caroline, she reflected, could never adapt or take pleasure in this exceptional solitude as she could back home. Without Caroline's difficulties and their shared aversions, Denise would swiftly have been absorbed in a "scene," one of the networks of coastal exiles who imagined this flat world to be frothing with "cultural ferment."

The New Yorkers and Angelenos who'd fled here had burned out on city life, and embraced the usual aporias to soften the harsh fact of their defeat: they immersed themselves in local Indian lore, dabbled in wicca covens, treated their ailments with herbal poultices and homeopathic drops, scouring nearby towns and adjacent states for furniture, pottery, turquoise jewelry and handicrafts, or like Mel and Sam vanished for weeks or months to other incipiently trendy backwaters of the country, to snap up real estate bargains, revamp buildings bought for a song, resell them at giant profits. This particular form of entrepreneurship exerted a strong allure as an alternative endeavor for Denise, who was not handy at gutting houses or reassembling them, but thought she could prove a quick study. Denise used the vulnerable-girl thing for convenience, it invited protection by men, usually protection from other men, but she figured anything two alcoholic fags could pull off wouldn't be beyond her reach. Plumbing fascinated her, for instance. Denise had all her life been spellbound by the intricate varieties of waste disposal. Wiring, tearing out walls, the wielding of dangerous tools were mysterious activities she hoped to master before she became a doddering wraith in some nursing home. Her books earned nothing, and her various inheritances wouldn't keep her much longer.

She would have to teach writing in various ill-paid positions in and around New York, as she'd done for years before taking this indefinite leave. Caroline taught writing in even less lucrative venues around Manhattan. Her students were fiercely loyal, for Caroline had a gift for tact, and measured praise, and gentle criticism. Denise took a rather more ruthless approach to the brats she dealt with at the New School, half of them debutantes killing time, the other half good-looking Jewish princes from Connecticut, arrogant with mingy testosterone and delusions of genius.

Invariably, the oddball shunned by the more fiercely assertive would-be literati proved the only student worth cultivating, but he or she quite often slid into alienation, followed by druggy indifference and other strategies of insulation.

Caroline's classes attracted the insecure, unbeautiful, shyly affectionate types who responded gratefully to nurturing and sometimes even learned to write interesting things. Denise's drew impossible kamikazes destined to drop out after first year, returning in irregular semesters from near-death adventures to chalk up a few more grade points. But those audacious fetuses, as Denise called them, were the very ones who risked disaster and came back with something real to write about. Denise hated teaching. Her deranged students were its sole reward, and hardly worth it in the end, she thought.

50

I have, I see, stranded Arthur on the Isle of the Dead. As he wrote Jesse, nothing at all ever did or could happen there, until something did: those islands are all the same. People drink too much and idle away their time. They throw pointless dinners to alleviate the sunny boredom. Reconstructing things from his overlong missives to Jesse, I find that the diurnal routines, the charter boat picnics, the habitual, queasy attempts at "fun" ran their stultifying course for a few weeks. Then, to Arthur's amazement, something did, indeed, happen. But that wasn't written up in a letter. I heard it from Arthur's mouth, a bit later on. I'll get to it, but the time is not yet.

51

Existence in Santa Fe was a slaw of non sequiturs. Flash points spaced between eons of static. This noiseless stasis, Denise thought, had triggered the premonitions, or whatever they were, the morning signals that she'd left her real life and might never find it again. Caroline's erratic spells of calm and her firestorms of madness were almost equally nerve-racking motes in a time-less eddy of dust: unconnected, meaningless, so lacking in any-thing Denise recognized as narrative coherence that she couldn't recall, with recountable certainty, the sequence in which any-thing happened.

The meals she cooked for herself, for Caroline when Caroline ate (almost never), formerly a day's endeavor, became rapidly eaten, quick, simple vegetarian fare, these days more often than not frozen and microwaved, the vegetable emphasis a silly pre-tense of "staying healthy," like the occasional yoga class or acu-puncture treatment with which they punctuated the tedium. On what passed as a good night, they played Laura Nyro and Nina Simone CDs and sang along with the most freighted songs when they drank together. Denise picked up and put aside the books she ordered on Amazon.com after ten or twenty pages. The worlds they painted seemed impossibly distant and unreachable from where they found themselves.

The relief from the city's war of nerves the two women had hungered for, the implied option of staying on in New Mexico indefinitely, even permanently, had collapsed like slow-leaking birthday balloons. Any prolonged future had crept away from the house, the desert, the stasis. Impatience now haunted the place; irritating questions hung from the light fixtures. When she woke from a full night's sleep, or even a short nap, Denise heard the same dire, unbearable thoughts enunciate themselves as if she were speaking aloud. I will be dead someday. Maybe not so long from now. This "me" won't exist anymore. The world will exist, if it does exist, but I will know nothing about it.

One morning late in June, Denise lay on a plastic chaise behind the house looking at the paintings in Mary Woronov's *Wake for the Angels,* paintings that caught with synecdochic flair a flesh-ravaged world of drug vampires, sex madness, anomie, and estrangement that Denise recognized from her former residence in Los Angeles, a city with which she maintained an ambivalent romance. Woronov conjured the three A.M. madness and daybreak pathos of the downfall precincts of Los Angeles. Which still existed, Denise felt certain, though she hadn't dipped into that world for a long time. Denise's eyes roved over desolate bodies in dope pads and heartbreak hotel rooms as if peering into her own bathroom mirror at the Los Altos in 1978, or the Asbury in 1982.

It was the only book Denise had opened all summer without wanting to toss it in the Frank Lloyd Wright–inspired, copper-hooded fireplace. The short stories Woronov had written to illustrate the paintings reminded Denise of a time when her life had actually been fun. A reckless fun one inevitably stopped having, but Denise recalled it without a heavy heart. Although it was ten A.M., Denise sipped a gin and tonic without guilt. She shrieked loudly at Woronov's story of coke-crazy women shaving their heads in a dump on Western Avenue.

Drawn to the flagstone patio from her barricaded room as if by occult force, Caroline pressed her face against the door screen. She asked almost rudely what Denise found so funny.

"I was laughing at something I read," Denise found it necessary to explain. "It wasn't a private sort of laugh."

"I just found it strange, laughing to yourself."

"Want me to read you some of this? I'm sure it would make you laugh, too."

"Not right now," said Caroline. "In fact, I think we should be careful about what we say to each other. I think today we should maybe only hum and point and gesture."

Denise twisted her short neck around to see if she could guess from her look what Caroline could possibly mean. Caroline's recent utterances had assumed the opacity of arbitrary noise.

Caroline stepped around the chaise and crouched near Denise's right ear. In a rapid, urgent whisper, she informed Denise that the KGB was monitoring their brain activities with implanted sensors. They should make every effort to empty their minds of all but the most ordinary thoughts.

Agents tailed her when she drove into town, where operatives disguised as obese housewives pushed supermarket carts, as elderly men wearing hearing aids at Rexall's pharmacy counter, as cashiers in Starbucks. They talked inside her, almost like celestial presences, instructing her which stores to avoid, what streets to navigate through Santa Fe. Certain drivers, pedestrians, persons crossing her visual path were identified as enemies tracking her moves, though some, they said, were "on our side," "one of us"; if these partisans happened to make a gesture of some kind, it meant she should roll down her window, or light a cigarette, or pee in her jeans. Which she had the day before, arriving home splotched with a sharp-smelling stain spreading from her crotch to her knees.

In ensuing days, surveillance intensified. Caroline fled upstairs at the sound of the mail delivery, scrambled down to the cellar at the hissing of the automatic lawn sprinklers. When cars passed she ducked under windows, or dropped to the floor, or crouched in the hall closet where the landlord had, imprudently, Denise reflected, left his double-barreled shotgun resting against shelves of pickled cactus and quince jellies.

Denise noted this escalating paranoia without clearly focusing on it as the four-alarm blaze an outsider might have recognized. The monologues that ran at the tail end of dream time suffused her waking hours. They were telling her something important, like Caroline's voices, but the voice of Denise's half-dreams was her own. Some corner had been turned, some lethal line crossed. *Got nothing for you, I had nothing before*—the Dylan song was the faint nasal background of I'm-going-to-die ruminations—*Don't even have anything for myself anymore.*

52

Anna can never adequately picture for Seagrave the atmosphere she and Malcolm slip into at night. A magic stasis, unpredictably jarred into disarray when the phone rings, when friends say they're coming over (this might or might not happen), the hours open to any vibration. They live more in the random moment than Anna feels comfortable about, it isn't just being young and full of restless energy but arch ambivalence about everything as well.

Her sense of personal coherence is so fragile that weeks pass when she only leaves the apartment for cigarettes and groceries, unplugs the phone, lets all arrangements with other people run askew, at times Malcolm is her only line to the world outside. Sometimes, when he isn't working, he joins her in radio silence.

During such hermetic missing days what passes between them varies like weather. They never blame each other for "messing up," but the drug thing, the speedball thing, Nahib's little waxed paper folders of H and tiny blue plastic bags of C— at first these were novelty items, weekend party favors, now there's one or the other and most of the time both on the premises all the time.

They retreat from their own uneasiness about it. Neither wants to seem to reproach the other when they both know they've fallen down a hole. So far, it's a shallow hole that can feel comforting. Strong lights in the room can be quelled to a mellow Victorian dimness. Tangled blankets, accordioned flannel sheets, cozily lumpy pillows, TV/VCR tinting the bed with the glow of a dubbed Italian horror film. A quart bottle of Fruitopia, cigarettes, and, sometimes, miraculously, a working lighter: this is all they need, more than they need, to feel "happiness." They sleep with their bodies curled together like cats in a basket.

The stillness. The indifference to clock time. Lately, instances of sudden chill. Silences of uncustomary awkwardness.

"Something bad is going to happen," Anna tells Seagrave unequivocally.

"Why do you say that, Anna?" Seagrave wears his owl look, his fingers clasped in a clumsy fashion, a look that makes him particularly loveable.

"I can feel it," she says. "In the street. I see the way everything is kind of, kind of—"

"Yes?"

"Spread out around me and lying in wait."

"Back up, what do you mean by everything?"

"Things. Objects. Cars. Lights. See, I can't articulate it. Something is taking its course. Something's completing itself."

Seagrave presses his left-hand index finger against his lips. He should be able to sort this out, he thinks, but he has absolutely no idea what Anna's talking about.

53

One night in the dining room, a waiter lays a heavy palm on Jesse's shoulder and asks him, almost inaudibly, if he'd like to go to a disco later. The waiter has achingly beautiful brown skin, dusty like skin someone's blowing smoke on. Quick eyes. Sinuous smile. In New York, this man would be considered extraordinarily beautiful. In Istanbul, he doesn't even know he's pretty. Jesse imagines the waiter mounting him with acrobatic skill. He doesn't want to go to a disco but says yes. He goes to his room and falls asleep.

Hours later the phone wakes him. He hears the waiter's voice.

"No, I . . . I'm too tired."

"Don't want disco?"

"No."

"May I come to the room?"

"All right."

Seconds later the waiter taps on the door. When Jesse opens it the man slips inside and rushes to the alcove off the bathroom.

"I like you," he declares, unfastening a purple sash around his pants waist.

"I like you too," Jesse assures him, bewildered by the speed at which things are moving.

"In here," the waiter whispers urgently, motioning him into the bathroom.

In the bathroom the waiter lowers his pants, liberating a thick, stubby, hard prong that sticks straight out, and fat, tight balls.

"Please do not kiss me," he says, locking eyes with Jesse. Jesse can't tell if it's a command or an entreaty. He compliantly perches on the toilet rim and licks the penis and balls. He notices that the pubic hairs are clipped into a tidy triangle, about a quarter-inch in length. He wonders if this is an Islamic custom, or just a weird personal habit.

"Kiss," the guy instructs, drawing a line with his thumbnail across his lower abdomen.

Jesse dutifully kisses the salt-tasting stomach below the navel. The frantic quality of the moment disturbs him. A chasm opens between idea and action. The waiter draws away, beckons him to the tub. He gestures for Jesse to lower his own pants and bend over the tub rim. Then he searches for Jesse's hole with his cock, without using his hands, as if it'll naturally sink in upon contact, unlubricated. After a few abrasive pokes he gives up and settles himself on the toilet seat with his legs open.

Jesse steps between the waiter's legs and turns around facing a mirror over the sink. He lowers himself. The waiter pulls him closer, steering Jesse's ass toward his penis. This position is useless. The waiter stands, pushes Jesse to his knees, sticks his cock into Jesse's mouth. Jesse gags, expelling the penis.

"Look," he says, fed up, "there are two beds in the other room. We don't need to do this in here."

"People see," says the waiter. "Close the windows."

Jesse walks out and draws the heavy drapes at the sides of the huge windows. He hasn't noticed the drapes until now, only the sheer white curtains that don't retract. He now realizes the room is wholly visible from the park. From the alcove the waiter says, "Lock the door."

"It's locked," Jesse tells him.

"No, lock it."

"It's locked, I tell you."

The waiter opens the door. He gives the outer hall a nervous once-over and shuts the door. He's pulled up his pants. Now he removes them completely, unbuttons the lower buttons of his shirt, pulls the shirt up around his nipples. He flounces on the bed farther from the windows, knees raised, legs spread. Jesse takes off his clothes. He kneels between the waiter's legs. He sucks the now half-hard penis with grim concentration. Seconds pass. The waiter springs to his feet, pulls Jesse into dog position at the mattress edge, stands behind him, spits on his fingers, greases his cock, and accurately rams it in. He fucks Jesse's ass for about thirty seconds. Jesse tightens himself around the pounding, slippery meat. He feels pleasure, even ecstasy, for the half-minute or so that it lasts, he craves an abundance of this stranger's need filling his willingly surrendered flesh, for the man to take him with some insistent demand for love. The waiter pulls free. Slips into his pants and shoes with absurd haste.

"Can you give me some money?" he whispers.

"No."

"Cigarettes?"

Jesse takes two for himself and hands over the pack.

"I'm going to get a drink," says the waiter.

"You're going for a drink."

"I'll come back," the waiter says.

"All right."

"I'll come tomorrow," the waiter promises.

"All right."

"I like you."

"That's nice. I like you."

He wonders what exact element of this farce has given the man so much anxiety. He doesn't think he'll return the following day. He hopes not, anyway. He regrets not offering money. Jesse calculates that the whole encounter has taken about seven minutes. He's curious about the dark roasted-walnut smell of the waiter's balls. He replays the scene many times in his head, touched and disappointed by it. Eventually he jerks off in the bathroom.

54

Malcolm called his movie *Floating Particles*. Over the winter he'd skimmed several books on chaos theory, read debates about the order of the universe, whether it was an expanding pancake or retracting into itself, or twenty-dimensional, or a ganglion of separate space-time continuums. Malcolm wanted to film these ideas using human beings.

He saw himself as Particle A, skirling the edges of a cosmic Tilt-A-Whirl hidden in the clouds of space. When he came across other potential particles, people living radically different kinds of lives, plugged into the system in an unfamiliar way, he debated whether they fit, if links could be drawn, the way stars clustered to resemble mythic forms. He pictured flickering human lights, sunspots, quasars flaring out of certain souls, or brains, forming the spokes of a Ferris wheel.

When he wanted to see objects, bodies, movements in space clearly, Malcolm pretended to be deaf, or visiting a country whose language he didn't know. He pretended language was involuntary noise made by pipes and tubes in people's bodies. Sometimes he assumed the identity of a Tuareg with a primitive grasp of English. In seizures of giddy impudence he walked up to strangers with his camera, and quizzed them about any nonsense that came into his head. Depending on what he was wearing, his physical approach could trigger raw terror or an eager grin. Occasionally the question *What's this chink nigger doing here?* rolled across white people's eyeballs like an LED sign.

55

One afternoon, Caroline strolled out of the house naked and walked a half-mile along the highway shoulder before Denise realized she was gone. Denise momentarily considered an apathetic approach, instead dutifully searched the road from the rented green Toyota. She saw Caroline's loping, skinny, milk-white body, the pale globes of her jiggling buttocks, tramping down the roadbed like something in a bad art movie, pulled over, and coaxed the lover-turned-stranger into the backseat.

As Denise pulled into the driveway, Caroline revealed that Jesus, too, now spoke to her. Jesus had called her out, explained the hidden meaning of her life as she made her way. He showed how events that appeared to mean one thing were signs of quite other things Caroline was too jittery and misdirected to interpret. "When your father came to you," Jesus had told her that afternoon, "it was never your father, but Myself assuming your father's form." Jesus had said to shed all things of this world, including her clothes, and follow him into the light.

The waking dread continued. Denise believed it was urging her away from this wilderness, back to her apartment, the city, its jumbled density, a different disorder she could share with millions of others. *I'm in a mood to crash and burn*: the song line wove through morbid inner verbiage. The father thing had sprung from its box like a grotesque toy after Caroline had practically ripped her guts out squishing it in and slamming the lid. The Second Coming. Now the Republican bastard wore Jesus's flowing amber hair and pansy-ass robe and turned Evian into Muscadet. Denise prodded herself off the couch where she'd drifted off and launched her body into the day's pointless motions.

Caroline, throughout much of this period, had a bewildering

ability to observe her actions from outside, as if some region of her brain were exempt from the defects of chemistry swirling through the rest of it. After swallowing a Klonopin and smoking half a spliff, or sedating herself with a few vodka gimlets, her new drink of choice, she resumed, convincingly, her lucid personality, like a member of the *Star Trek* crew beaming down to terra firma in a blizzard of whizzing molecules. Long pauses interrupted the psychotic flow of Caroline's . . . Caroline's what, Denise couldn't name it, Caroline's . . . *naufrage* was the word that came to mind. When these ruptures occurred, Caroline might stretch facedown on the living room sofa, or pace the kitchen as torrents of bright talk restored the sense that madness aside, Caroline owned a brilliant mind, and in large part existed at a tragically dissociative or, contrariwise, redemptive distance from the rag-doll version of herself currently quaking apart into jigsaw pieces. She could analyze her disintegration and its gnarled mechanisms, offer theories, speculate about fine points of causality, even have the presence of mind to say that she might be completely wrong about all of it: the steps leading to this uncontrollably deviant toboggan ride to hell might be found somewhere entirely else.

Denise found these colloquia relieving for the first few hours, thinking that if Caroline could maintain a foothold in reality long enough to resume some productive activity, she might find the brake pedal on her careening mental vehicle. As evenings progressed, however, Caroline's self-analysis gradually developed an ominous circularity. She insisted that she had, as Denise well knew, "burned a lot of bridges" between herself and certain powerful figures who had been involved in Caroline's promotion as a noteworthy-and-soon-to-be-important literary novelist until Caroline poured kerosene on the pylons and lit a match. This was, Denise conceded, at least temporarily true; on

the other hand, it had all been part and parcel of her break-
down, she'd been certifiably bonkers when she placed a three
A.M. phone call to the agent handling her proposed next book,
accusing him of sabotaging her chances of a National Book Critics Circle award nomination by promoting for said nomination,
instead, in Caroline's words, "a piece of doody festering with
maggots that's only ninety pages long by yet another square-
chinned photogenic WASP cocksucker with no lips from Yale
whose lousy book could've been written by any hack at *The
New Yorker*": this partial steal from William Burroughs regarding
Capote's *In Cold Blood* had, alas, not been Caroline's only surprise Hour of the Wolf phone visit with highly placed contacts
who had lent support to her work in the past; Caroline believed
that "objectively," she'd immolated her future and would soon
be reduced to manual labor ("I'm not Simone Weil," she lamented, "I can't just go work in a Ford factory"; Denise had
started to reply that all the Ford factories were being moved to
Mexico and other centers of global peonage, but skipped it), as
she had no intention of begging for jobs in journalism ("Lord
Maucaulay said he would rather wash his face in a mud puddle
than write journalism," Caroline defiantly pointed out whenever
the suggestion arose), and her teaching gigs paid laughably minuscule salaries.

On this score, Denise really didn't know if Caroline's fears
were realistic. Perhaps she'd said things she hadn't told Denise
about, things people really didn't forgive. If what she reported
saying was what she had said, however, Denise thought a fulsome letter of apology to each of the offended parties, with an
explanation of the condition she'd been in—without striking
the note of self-pity, but honestly stating the facts—might soften
any attitudes that had hardened against her. Perhaps not, but it
was worth a try. Especially since Caroline *was* sorry for spinning

out of control, with them or anybody else. Anyone who'd read Caroline's books realized this woman's life hadn't been any day at the beach; even rather unfeeling individuals understood that an incest child is prone to attacks of depression and more serious mental illness, and runs a much higher than average risk of suicide. The crapulous facts of Caroline's childhood and adolescence were precisely what people knew about her, she'd laid them out in gruesome amplitude in that first novel—and they also knew, they had to know, that in her right mind, Caroline was an extraordinarily kind, considerate person, a person who remembered birthdays, unflaggingly encouraged colleagues, expressed genuine pleasure when someone got a prize, an advance, or the kind of rare, thoughtful review she herself would have liked getting. *That* Caroline felt a duty to lighten other people's disappointments. She was admired for tenacity, fairness, generosity, inflexible honesty, tact, and a rare ability to listen and come through for practically anyone with a helpful word, an affectionate gesture. But she did expect wider fame, bigger sales, a higher status in the literary world than had been dealt her so far, and her fear that her talent would dry up and her work be forgotten had become insidiously coiled with the fear of an eight-year-old hearing her father's heavy steps approaching her bedroom door.

Denise handled her own publishing matters in an understated way, without great expectations, sticking with the small press that had produced her three books to date. Denise was phobic about being pushy. She happened to know several prominent editors at major firms, as friends—Denise came from a wildly eclectic showbiz family that included film directors, pop lyricists, one movie-star cousin, stage producers, and, certainly, a writer or two. She'd known some major players all over the board since shortly after her birth, and had never asked any of them for a career favor—and soliciting opinions about how people they did business with might react to hysterical accusatory phone calls in the middle of the night was something well off her personal reservation. She might ask her own editor, whose socializing within the business was considerably less than frenzied, but he'd be guessing, too. People get over these things, was Denise's sense of it; if everyone was petty enough to carry a grudge beyond twenty-four hours over anything that stupid, nobody could survive New York. In Denise's childhood memories of grown-up parties, people in showbiz screamed accusations at each other all the time. The next time their paths crossed, the antagonists bought each other drinks and behaved as if nothing had ever happened. Denise considered modern publishing to be a sidebar asset of showbiz: unlike Caroline, she wasn't at all mystified, much less indignant, over why a highly photogenic, under-thirty WASP with inch-deep talent became a best-selling author, when his other career option was print modeling rather than Kinko's.

Denise didn't consider this facet of Caroline's distress necessarily insane, because she knew numerous writers who nursed paranoid suspicions they claimed to be verifiable facts—against, for example, weirdly balkanized and haphazardly attentive institutions like the *Sunday Times Book Review*. One writer she knew swore that his name flashed a red, pulsating warning message on any *New York Times* computer it was typed into.

Many writers believed in Machiavellian conspiracies directed against them by critics they'd written nasty letters to, or other exalted folk they'd confronted in public. Denise had never found herself in the inquisitional mind-set these writers stoked every year or two when they brought out a book; she wrote and published books at a lumbering pace, they materialized in bookstores without much fanfare, simply finishing a novel struck her as such an unlikely conclusion to her torturous endeavors that getting it published was nearly the full extent of her ambition.

For Caroline, the publishing world had far more personal urgency, she felt her very life was at stake. Her "enemies" were certain to destroy her, eradicate her, nullify her. Yet she no longer admitted needing help. Everything about her screamed for help, but the "sane" Caroline had fused with her addled double. She could not go into hospital, she explained. Her myriad enemies, the people hunting her, wanted precisely to trap her there, to make her crazier and push her to suicide. Government agents, foreign assassins, her father, the Church of Scientology, Satan: a horde of whisperers steered her this way and that; it took a herculean effort to resist them.

56

In front of the Blue Mosque, a small, ugly man with rotten teeth tries to sell Jesse a carpet. He says his name is Genghis, as in Genghis Khan. He says his brother owns a shop in the basement of the mosque. Jesse tells Genghis that he doesn't need a carpet. His brother also sells silver jewelry. Jesse says he doesn't need any silver jewelry, either. Genghis looks like trouble. Jesse has met a number of Genghises in his travels: not sharks, exactly, but smaller, parasitical pilot fish who mistake themselves for sharks. Jesse knows if he doesn't get rid of this person, he will end up separating Jesse from a lot of money. He will not use violence, but intimidation and guilt.

It has been so many days since Jesse spoke to someone fluent in English that he equivocates at a crucial moment when a little hostility would have sent Genghis on the trail of a different tourist. They go into the mosque together and look at the vast floor of carpets, the columns, the windows. Genghis points out the abundance of blue tiles. Some restoration work is taking place. Many columns are draped with green netting. Genghis explains many details of the mosque that Jesse already knows.

When they're outside retrieving their shoes, Genghis proposes showing Jesse around the area. Jesse again thinks he should ditch the guy. The area is, after all, world-famous, and Jesse knows what all the buildings are. Genghis also strikes him as a bore, a bore with peasant cunning. Jesse calculates the amount of cash he can safely blow on a superfluous guided tour. He feels himself giving in. It's easier than getting away from this creep. He'll have somebody to talk to, even if it's Genghis.

They slog through the Topkapi and the Aya Sofya. The most important jewels of the Topkapi are away on loan, and the Aya

Sofya hums with Japanese tourists. The streets dense with bad air and traffic. Genghis takes Jesse into the cavernous cistern under the basilica. Water trickles, splutters down through the darkness, pooling to a meter's depth beneath the clay walkways, around dozens of arched columns. At the base of two columns deep in the cistern they see chiseled heads of Medusa: one upside down, the other resting on one cheek. As they leave, loudspeakers blare "The Ride of the Valkyries."

Genghis proposes a trip to the Dolmabahce Palace, in the same quarter as Jesse's hotel. Jesse thinks he's seen enough for one day but can't think of anything better to do. At the Dolmabahce Palace, they wait on line for forty minutes for the mandatory guided tour to take them through. The air is cool here, near the water, and Jesse would like to sit under a tree, thinking his own thoughts. Genghis asks if he minds taking the tour in Turkish, instead of waiting an extra twenty minutes for the tour in English. Jesse doesn't care. They herd from room to room with twenty others. Sometimes Genghis translates, says what the rooms are. Then he becomes, if not exactly thoughtful, absorbed in the grandeur of the decor. The sultans did many of their rooms in crystal. Crystal wall panels. Fat crystal bannisters on the staircases.

During the tour Genghis chats with another Turkish boy. The new boy has better teeth and better clothes. He keeps a ring of car keys looped in his fingers and plays with them. Jesse wonders if Genghis is hustling this boy, but the boy seems too smart for that to happen. He's from a better class and obviously regards Genghis as amusing scum. Outside the palace, Jesse asks the new boy if he's hungry. He hopes to shake off Genghis. Genghis translates that the boy has to go home. He lives on the Asian side of the city. Jesse and Genghis go to Jesse's hotel in a cab. Jesse tries paying Genghis for the tour.

"Not now, not here," Genghis says sharply, jabbing a finger at the driver's back. Once they're out, Genghis tells him never to let a cab driver see his money. They walk up the road away from the hotel. They go into the cement park. After some haggling Jesse gives him what he originally asked for. Genghis insists on another sixty thousand lire. He says the tour lasted an extra two hours. Jesse points out that the Dolmabahce Palace was Genghis's idea.

"You could have said no," Genghis replies smoothly. "Besides, we all need money, and you're rich."

Jesse feels too worn from walking and sunlight to argue. He supposes he is rich, by comparison.

"And," Genghis persists after Jesse gives him the sixty thousand lire, "another twenty thousand for the tour tickets."

"Oh please," says Jesse, who paid for the tour tickets. "Go fuck yourself."

"That's nothing to you, twenty thousand!" Genghis replies with an air of indignation Jesse can't help admiring.

"All the same, fuck off."

And what if it were me, Jesse asks a polished mirror he slows down for in the Pera Palas lobby, to see if he still reflects in mirrors. What if twenty thousand lire put a lamb chop on the table. What can possibly be fair or unfair when everybody's prey.

57

A few weeks after her naked quest for Jesus on the Interstate, a sudden hiatus in Caroline's manias presented Denise with a reprieve from melodrama, one she made optimum use of by finishing a chapter of her novel. Caroline's demons had either stopped whispering grotesque suggestions, or Caroline had recognized them as auditory hallucinations and ignored them. She seemed, relatively speaking, stable. Denise even sensed a faintly suspicious serenity. She welcomed the change, of course; she felt her blood pressure drop; the thought even came that the storm had broken for good, though she pushed this idea aside. She tried to resume the thin but somewhat fortifying routines they'd settled into in their first days there, renewed some social contacts, assumed a lightly patterned regularity.

It took more than ten days for Denise to surmise that Caroline had found a reliable heroin dealer in Santa Fe. This was a remarkably long time for Denise to fail to scent drugs: she'd done them all, and normally one look at a person told her exactly what he or she was on, how much of it, how often. Whichever vein Caroline shot in was one Denise hadn't noticed the few times they'd had sex, probably because they usually did it in the dark. What passed for normality was just Caroline being trashed. She'd stayed off it a decade, but being trashed on junk, Denise considered, *was* normality for Caroline, a home she'd fled but never burned down behind her. Denise recalled the first vodka tonic Caroline ordered after years in the program, and wondered about fate, and tried not to let Caroline's suicidal folly colonize every waking thought.

58

Jesse walks beyond the park into a narrow, winding bazaar he explored on his first day in Istanbul. In a lane of vegetable and butcher stalls he finds a vendor selling freshly killed fish and tinned food. He buys a half-pound of Beluga caviar: thirty-five dollars.

At the Pera Palas he walks into the kitchen off the dining room. His presence violates some rigid hotel protocol; immediately, several waiters cluster around him, absurdly solicitous, as if he'd just been run over. Jesse asks the handsomest one to open the caviar and bring it to his room.

In the room, closely observed, the waiter, who introduces himself as Marco, looks beautiful as a movie star. His hair's curly and brown, with red highlights. His face is adorable, more rounded and Western than the sharper profiles around the hotel. He arranges the caviar on a bowl of ice on the table, turns to leave, pauses, asks Jesse a question Jesse doesn't catch, shrugs, moves to the door, turns, Jesse moves close to him and touches Marco's sleeve. Marco indicates that he'd like to smoke a cigarette before going back to the kitchen.

They try to talk. Jesse knows no Turkish words. Marco knows the phrases he needs for his job. Marco sits down at the table. Jesse repositions his chair so the table isn't between them. He glances at the caviar. He thinks it will quickly go bad in the heat. He doesn't know how to make anything happen. He watches Marco smoke. Marco's waiting. Jesse hooks Marco's right ankle with the toe of his sneaker and brings Marco's shoe to the chair cushion between his legs. He unlaces the boy's leather shoe and slides it off his foot. It's a narrow, elegant foot, with long, bony toes. Jesse grips it with both hands, massaging it through the black rayon sock. The sock exudes an expanding smell of mildew and sweat. Marco shuts his eyes ecstatically.

"I come to you tonight," he says.

"Yes."

"I fuck you tonight," Marco elaborates.

"Yes, definitely."

The massaged foot moves back to its shoe. Marco raises his other shoe, pulls it off. He pushes his foot between Jesse's legs. Jesse massages the new foot. Marco presses it into Jesse's crotch, squeezes the hump of Jesse's erection with his toes. Marco lights another cigarette and watches Jesse dreamily through clouds of smoke.

Jesse squeezes his thighs around Marco's foot. Marco rubs it up and down, squeezing the shape of Jesse's penis with his toes. Jesse comes. Marco replaces his shoe and stands up. He points at the caviar.

"Eat," he says.

Jesse kisses Marco on the mouth. Marco's tongue snakes into Jesse's mouth and they stand locked together, Marco guiding Jesse's hand to his cock. Jesse feels the long, thick lump through Marco's pants. He kneels down and kisses it. He runs his hands over Marco's buttocks.

59

"I thought you were in Portugal," Leon said on the phone. After thirty years in New York, he still spoke English with a slight accent, so slight you could no longer tell what language it came from.

In the first several weeks after I left Cape Cod for Manhattan, I kept to my neighborhood more or less, and didn't phone anyone, assuming all my friends were flung across the globe. Anna, who never left the city, as usual knew exactly where I was, and must have mentioned it to Malcolm, so separate calls came from that ménage, usually at unwelcome hours, and from some of their friends I knew less than well. Besides two of my building neighbors, with whom I had an occasional drink or a meal, I saw nobody. I had, of course, had my dour visit from Miles, whose indifference to my travels persuaded him that I was always home. But that had been a lowering exception. Quite suddenly, however, people came crowding in.

"I never said I was going to Portugal," I said. That's it, I thought: nobody really listens to anybody, we never pay attention to each other's plans, and so we eventually feel like balls of matter spinning alone through space, colliding at random intervals. Days become confused with weeks. I can't even tell if something happened a year ago, or ten. "I *was* on the Cape, but I changed my mind about spending the summer."

"Yes," Leon said, in a drifting voice. "The Cape is too full of vacationers," he went on, as if I could have no other reason to leave. "I've never cared about the Cape."

"I thought you might be off somewhere."

"I just came back," Leon said. "I was in Ecuador, Peru, Argentina."

He would ask in a moment if I had seen some obscure movie playing at the Film Forum. I would say no. He would tell me that I "must" see it. I would promise to, never convincingly.

"Are you around?" Another vague question.

"I don't have any plans," I said. It occurred to me that I had fewer plans than I had ever had in my life.

"Let me look in my book," he said. "Oh, yes, I don't know if this interests you, there's an opening tomorrow night of this artist"—he cited a name and nationality I didn't catch—"in Chelsea, would you feel like going?"

"Sure," I said, meaning not really, but I skipped events, movies, openings, every kind of "cultural" or social gathering so routinely that I often felt doing anything at all would be "good for me" in some unspecifiable way.

When I clicked off the phone, it rang again instantly. It's that weird shit, I thought. Phone service in New York had degenerated to Third World chaos and dysfunction, thanks to deregulation, and often my phone rang automatically when I finished a call, though no call was coming in. I answered it anyway.

It was a call, for a change. I heard Arthur's voice, surprised first that he was here, and surprised that he'd called, for he almost never did. Arthur maintained a snail's inaccessibility. I always had to call him and wheedle him out of his shell. Arthur would do anything for me, except keep in touch. Edith Eddy was the same kind of friend. So was Denise. In fact, I seemed to have precious few other kinds of friends. I never knew if they were sparing me the uncontrollable outpourings of clinical depression, or living out a new and unexpected drama so intensely that they only found time for me in its margins. Or, perhaps, simply didn't much like me. Strangely, I had just opened a letter Arthur had sent me from the island.

Arthur's speech tripped over itself in a sour rush to spill recent happenings: the Willeys, Oliver, I couldn't follow it all, Arthur said he'd just got in from JFK in a state of sleepless rage and jet lag.

"Look, couldn't we meet somewhere? I want to hear this but I think you need some sleep before you tell me about it."

"Can you come here?"

"You mean your place?" I dreaded going to their place.

"Oliver won't be around," Arthur quickly said, catching my hesitation. "Like tomorrow night, I'll make some dinner?"

"All right. No. Wait. I just told someone I'd meet him tomorrow. What about Saturday night?"

Yes, he said, fine, and I said instantly, "Just because it's two nights away don't forget about it, I'm coming there at seven whether we talk between now and then or not." Because it really had come to that over the years with Arthur, if you fixed something less than immediate, even two days in the future, the arrangement could easily dissolve, quite aside from his real problems with Oliver. Arthur manufactured crises that wiped his calendar clean.

60

Many small, malignantly cheerful, powerfully smelly boys with shoe-shine kits surround him the minute he sits down in Taksim Square. He shows them he's wearing sneakers, but the kids plant themselves in front of his bench anyway, squatting on their wooden boxes, jabbering the English words they know. The bench faces the sunken heart of the square, an expanse of uninflected poured cement lined with slatted tubs of geraniums. The Turks, Jesse thinks, are overly appreciative of cement and its aesthetic uses.

A boy insists on selling him a glass of tea. He drinks it, noticing the glass has been used many times without being washed.

A tall youth in cheap Western clothes approaches, beaming the broad smile of a born hustler. He sits down near Jesse and claps him on the back. He has pale, thick lips, a fleshy nose, scads of curly auburn hair. Jesse eyes him wearily. The boy has an eerie resemblance to Tony Bravo, a porn star whose career Jesse has followed in various magazines and videos.

"I am Shamir," the boy announces.

"I am Jesse," Jesse mimics, wasting sarcasm. Shamir's smile broadens. His teeth are not as bad as the waiter's from a few nights earlier, but they are not good.

Shamir has arrived with a friend his own age, who hovers interestedly at a discreet remove. People stroll back and forth in the shade of the elms. Shamir shouts something at a group of men who look at them appraisingly as they pass.

"I don't like these people looking at you," Shamir explains. "I don't like them looking when I talk to you."

"Uh-huh."

"All people look at you. Why they look at you?"

"Maybe because I'm a blond," Jesse says.

Shamir emits a snorty laugh.

"I know America," he says. "In America I know San Francisco, Palo Alto. You know Palo Alto?"

"Not really," Jesse says.

"Now work at American Army base. But soon go to Germany. Not from Istanbul. Shamir from Adana. Adana people good people. Not like Istanbul people. Here the people, they lie, they rob. My father worry about Shamir all alone in Istanbul. Thinks, Shamir, maybe he's killed, maybe he's dead."

"Maybe you should give him a call," Jesse suggests, thinking that Shamir is very pretty but also very boring.

"I know, right now, you think: Is Shamir a good man? Is he bad man? You don't know. Same for me. I look at you, think, Are you good, are you bad? If I go with you, do you hurt me? And you too, thinking, if I go with Shamir, maybe he hurts me."

Shamir has brown saucer eyes that don't miss anything. Jesse feels his gaze and grows uncomfortably conscious of his own face arranging itself into various expressions. He wills himself to relax. He doesn't want to go through with anything but he wants Shamir to want him.

"I tell you Shamir is a good man. Like you very much. Maybe like you too much. Where is your hotel?"

Jesse tells him. Shamir's eyes sparkle. Jesse knows the look.

"Maybe," Shamir says, "you take me to Pera Palas."

Jesse looks into space. The numb geometry of the cement.

"But," Shamir adds, "maybe is big problem for me. Because I am Turk. Maybe we go in bar, drink, you go to room. I follow, they see, they come, they say, 'Leave now, you are Turk.' "

"I think they probably would," Jesse says. He considers that one of the virtues of the Pera Palas is that it has its own hustlers in-house.

"Where I stay," Shamir continues, "not so nice hotel. But man at desk from Adana. His house in Adana, close by my house, I know him, you come there, is no problem. Pay for room, maybe you sleep, maybe I come in your room, maybe you come in my room. No problem. I like you, no problem. Drink, no problem. Friend, no problem. Sex, no problem."

Jesse doesn't understand why people all over the world have such a thing about saying "no problem." He does not think there would be no problem with the scenario Shamir is describing.

Shamir waves away his hovering friend. Jesse walks with him along a wide street where the airline offices are. At a café, Shamir drinks a beer and quickly orders another while Jesse sips a glass of mineral water. In the streaked sunlight flowing through the fringe of the Campari parasol, Shamir's beauty seems almost awesome. His gestures have an overdrawn masculine crudeness that goes with his cheap clothes and discolored teeth. This kid will die young, Jesse thinks. He senses that other people in the café have taken note of them. In Istanbul, there could be no reason besides sex or drugs for two such people to be drinking together. Jesse suddenly feels the threat of this in a new way.

He doesn't think Shamir will be violent. But Shamir has already calculated the wad of money in Jesse's wallet, and maybe it will be a point of pride for him to get all of it. Jesse feels no particular pride in the matter, but the imprudence of blowing two hundred dollars on a fuck in Turkey seems like the beginning of some fatal indifference to protocol.

When they resume walking, Jesse decides to ditch the boy

when they get near the Pera Palas. Shamir purposefully turns up a side street. Jesse remains at the corner, waiting for him to disappear. Shamir turns, then comes back for him.

They reach a scungy doorway in a small alley. It's pretty much the way Jesse pictured it. He goes in behind Shamir, wondering if he'll ever come out again.

He sits in a filthy sitting room while Shamir haggles with the desk clerk, a man with livid boils covering his nose. They do not give the impression of being old neighbors from Adana. One wall of the room is papered with a peeling photomural of an autumnal forest in New England. In front of it, an ancient black-and-white television with an elaborately padlocked metal grille clamped over the picture tube stares at nothing. The haggling ceases and Jesse has to give the clerk twenty thousand lire. Shamir follows him up four flights of twisted stairs, across crackling fluorescent halls that smell of urine and stale farts.

The room contains a narrow cot and two sheets and a window that stares into a dark hovel where someone is hanging out laundry. Shamir finds a blanket under the cot and drapes it across the window. He moves to lock the door. Jesse stops him.

"I don't want the door locked."

"No, why, someone can come in."

"Look, I'm going to be nervous if that door is locked."

Shamir gives up on locking the door and unbuttons his shirt. He throws it on the floor, kicks off his shoes, drops his pants. His cock is already stiff. He moves again to the door.

"No, I said."

"Please." Shamir turns the lock.

Now, Jesse thinks. Now out comes the knife.

Shamir keeps his torn athletic socks on. Jesse slips out of his clothes. Shamir's thinner than he imagined. Jesse kisses his balls and licks him up and down, from his asshole to the tip of his penis. Shamir's asshole doesn't smell. After a while Shamir fucks him, with Jesse's legs pressed against his narrow chest. Shamir fucks in long, emphatic strokes. He comes after about five minutes. He kisses Jesse's face and embraces him. They're sweating like pigs. Shamir stands up and snaps his shirt in the air, making a breeze to dry Jesse off.

Jesse pays him eighty thousand lire. Shamir asks for forty thousand more and twenty thousand additional for the desk clerk. Jesse doesn't know what kind of trouble Shamir would think to cause, though he seems pretty benign at the moment. Jesse gives him the money.

In the street Shamir kisses him and tells him to watch out for strangers on his way back to the Pera Palas. He asks him to meet him in Taksim at nine P.M. Jesse says he will. Shamir looks at him skeptically. Jesse asks if they can fuck again at Shamir's hotel. This to postpone the final shakedown. Shamir assures him that this is possible. Jesse promises he'll be in Taksim Square between nine and nine-thirty. They will never see each other again. In a few minutes, probably, Shamir will meet a friend, and together they will plan Jesse's murder. At the hour when he's supposed to be murdered, Jesse will be stroking the balls of the wine steward at the Pera Palas.

61

At dinner at Mel and Sam's, Caroline wandered out of the rustic dining room into the kitchen and slipped out the back door. As she lifted a forkful of chimichanga to her mouth, Denise heard Mel's ignition turn, followed by the unmistakable sound of his Mercedes roaring into the desert.

"Um," Denise told her oblivious hosts, who'd both smoked too much hash and drunk most of a fifth of Remy, "I think I need to tell you what just happened."

The state police contacted Mel, who contacted Denise, two days later. Caroline had driven all the way to Albuquerque. They had found her naked, clinging to a wooden pylon of the Electromagnetic Pulse Test Trestle on Kirtland Air Base. Fortunately for her, they were not testing any electromagnetic pulses that week. She'd been placed in a local hospital for observation.

The hospital kept her for ten days, on Thorazine, which chased off the hallucinations and brought her back down where the iguanas live, a place her feet had barely scraped for three months. Denise took a bus in, paid an exasperated visit to the hospital, and bailed Mel's car out of the police impound. Since Caroline's insurance turned out not to cover this type of hospitalization, Denise forked over the remains of her emergency cash to pay for it. For her own daily maintenance, she had to sell most of her few stock investments at a loss. Caroline was given prescriptions for several antipsychotics and discharged into Denise's care.

"I'm really all right now." As Denise drove them back to Santa Fe, Caroline's slender face wore a rictus of mortification. "I do not have words to tell you how sorry I am I've put you through this."

Denise continued driving, her expression frozen in a bleak

attempt to convey understanding, patience, whatever you were supposed to feel. What she felt was confused and threatened, angry, sad, with love and hatred floating somewhere in the pool like irrelevant fallen leaves.

"Don't apologize," she said. Denise also felt as if she were sliding into shock. Her life had totally unraveled a few times, long ago, when her parents had still been alive and willing to help her through the worst. Having the sensation again, much later in life, was not a welcome thing. "What's done is done. You need to get back into therapy somewhere, and you need to take care of yourself."

A while later she said, "I'll always stick by you. I mean, we can always talk. But I have to go back to New York. I don't know if you want to stay on here, or what you want to do."

Caroline lit a cigarette and puffed it rapidly down.

"Oh, God," she said, "I want nothing more than to get the fuck out of here. This would have been a great thing if we'd just come for a month, that's happened so many times in my life, something that starts out good gets dragged out way too long."

Denise reached for the tactful formulation, but supposed there really was no tactful way to proceed.

"Speaking of that," she said. "I'm sorry to have to say this right now, but you'll have to find your own place."

Caroline hadn't owned her New York apartment, and had given it up instead of subletting. She struggled with her face.

"We can't live together," Denise continued. This had to be said. Denise couldn't soften it. "I'll help with whatever I can help with. But you've got to understand, and I'm not blaming you for anything, I'm kind of . . . kissing the edge myself."

And, she refrained from saying, you have managed to drain my bank account, and if I end up broke, I'll go just as crazy as you have. My God, she then thought, why did I use the word "kissing"?

Caroline nodded, Caroline smiled. She was trying hard to be Caroline again. Good, competent Caroline, unburdensome and self-sufficient Caroline.

"No, Denise, of course, I mean I understood that a while ago, I'm not selfish enough to deliberately subject anybody—I mean, I knew the same time you did, I understood that. I just didn't know *when*."

62

Something was taking its vile course.

I felt it in waves, in my sleep, when I woke.

I replaced the air conditioner. I got a haircut.

What news? I asked my demon. What news? What now?

It rippled the air as I walked down the Bowery to Leon Ivray's loft.

In the waning light, rainbow-skulled couples morphed into Micronesian cannibals. Tin ornaments and tattoos skewed flesh into mosaic dreamscapes. Weirdly angled dormitories, thrown up like mineralized shark fins over the parking lots where Joel Rifkin, mousy thrill killer, used to strangle prostitutes before taking their corpses for joyrides in his panelled truck. The buildings spewed a continuous stream of dewy cutenesses, cell phones sprouting from their ears. These podlike mammals draped themselves in product logos and designer alphabets, like free-ranging billboards. Men wearing sandwich boards used to roam sidewalks as ambulating publicity. Now millions did it for free, like serfs declaring fealty to corporate gods. All right. Something vile *was* taking its course.

Did I really want to scream into those moist rodent faces, *HOW FUCKING SOLD OUT CAN YOU BE? IS IT A COMPETITION?* No. If I opened my mouth to scream, a blast of silence would fill my head and a moray eel I mistook for my tongue would slither out. People were turning into things, had already turned into things. Electric wires and plastic organs grew inside their bodies. If you sliced them open with a scalpel, you'd uncover a factory of blue winking lights and cathode tubes and microchips and fiber optic cables fused with scattered organic matter.

This is how it was, or how I was, that summer: I wanted to

accept the world in its true condition, as it hurtled to its stony end. To meet it on its own filthy terms. Even force some pleasure out of it, though I couldn't. I did not believe that Oxfam, Doctors Without Borders, Greenpeace, or the Nature Conservancy could rescue this lemming species and its cell phones. I wrote checks to these organizations as a futile, half-assed gesture. It was too late, too late, too late.

Office workers moved in ziggurat patterns toward the black cube in Astor Place, sucked into the subway like lint gobbled by a vacuum cleaner. Ruminant tourists dreamed of killing and dismemberment. Sleepwalkers armed with credit cards spilled along the sidewalks, filling outdoor tables of fifth-rate pizzerias and bistros—the East Village's Kmart parody of Montmartre. In the gray innards of a rockabilly joint, its facade open to the street, a band tuned its instruments, squawking feedback into the hum and gurgle of deaf automatons. A crackle of incipient mayhem strafed the area as the summer twilight blackened into night. The Bowery was a treadmill for exhibitionists and the criminally insane.

Sky, clotted clouds. As I reach Leon's corner, the temperature spills down, the clouds rip apart. Rain rakes the sidewalk, just enough to wilt my clothes. Then it falls hard, soaking me as I wait for Leon's sluggish new elevator to reach the lobby. Through the wire mesh in the street door windows, I watch the elevator numbers light and fade, stalling at each digit long enough for thirty people to load the elevator with furniture.

If I have only mentioned Leon Ivray in passing until now, it's probably because, among the people most in evidence, in one sense or another, that summer, Leon, uniquely, did not drag an unending drama around with him.

Here is Leon: gentle, erudite, shrewd. Occasionally befuddled. Prone to lose his place in conversations. He has the normal share of turmoil, sadness, frustration. He doesn't insist on his difficulties. A stable life. Realistic ambitions. A displaced Argentinian, Leon has a European worldliness. (Argentina is, as far as I'm concerned, a European country, and one of the better ones, when it isn't plunged into horror.)

"What will you have? A scotch?"

The elevator opens into an alcove containing a picnic table covered in papers, bills, bowls of fruit, peonies in Mexican vases. Glass bookcases, a coat rack, a ten-speed bicycle. The vast square footage right and left of this alcove neat as a pin, tasteful in a minimalist way. Leon raises Brazilian orchids behind clear Mylar sheets. The pinkish grow-lights emit a festive threat of vegetation reclaiming the building.

"A brandy," I say.

"What do you mean when you say 'brandy'?" he asks, as if he's never heard of it, or anything resembling it. Leon has an aphasic tendency. "Something like Metaxa?"

"No, like Rémy Martin. Hennessy. It's brown."

"Metaxa is brown," he argues.

"I suppose it's brandy, too, but I can't stand it."

He sticks his head into the lower compartment of an armoire. Bottles clank. In Levi's, Leon's ass looks firmer than mine. It's not fair, I think. He's older than me. My ass has a crease in the left buttock. Or even some kind of cellulite.

"I can made Midori sours," he cries out.

"We're not in *India*, haven't you got something that doesn't taste like watermelon?"

Leon's ass backs away from the cabinet. He rises majestically, gripping a bottle of Bacardi like a bishop's miter.

"We can make mojitos," he says. "I have mint from the farmers' market."

"Oh. Oh. Mojitos."

We sigh in unison. A duet of comic longing. We both love Havana, the way you love sex you want every night but can only have in a hotel room, on the sly, once or twice a year.

Tossing cubes in a blender, Leon briefly moans about money trouble as the ice smashes around.

"Credit cards," he says. "The triumph of Satan."

"Every time I leave the house," I say. "One hundred, two hundred dollars. On *nothing*."

"Life is impossible. And in Buenos Aires now, shit on top of shit. You need to go and look at the Chris Marker, this documentary at Film Forum—it's called, the smile, I forget—"

"I know I should. I hate going to movies anymore."

"But you *have* to see this. Oh, you must. You must. It tears your heart from your chest."

"It's *four hours long*," I protest, with calculated philistinism. "I don't want my heart torn out from my chest."

"Well, neither do I. I want a nice little sexy Puerto Rican boy with an ass smooth like a baby's, but the Marker film, he shows the whole history of the Left, it's devastating."

The terms *Left* and *Right* have lost any meaning for me.

"I'm already devastated," I say. "Aren't you?" A recurring subject. "We have no dreams left. Nobody cares about equality, or any utopian anything. We're all just *fucked*. The guys who own the world won't let anything happen anymore."

I release this tirade in the way one breathes in and out. We've breathed in and out through the same history, and seen our wishes trampled to death. Including any wishes we ever entertained about Cuba.

"We should go," Leon says. "Otherwise we will sit here getting drunk and think of all the starving peasants and begin to hate ourselves."

Yes, I think, time to go. You have to flee the ghosts of old disappointments, before they make you sad.

63

For a summer show, the gallery draws a crush. A familiar throng. Here and there, an unfamiliar Spaniard in the works. It is a small world, the art world. Small-minded. Smarmy. Fake. Backbiting, corrupt, meretricious, shallow, howlingly pretentious, infantile, devoted to a worship of wealth and celebrity that reduces everyone in it to the mentality of a concierge or a subway pickpocket. The few authentically educated, earnest people in the art world wake up contemplating suicide five mornings every week.

All the same, it has its reverse, perverse side. A smudge of quixotic idealism. A hangnail of parody in relation to the economic system. Worthless objects become conduits for millions of dollars. The superrich are conned by their own ignorance into shitty, tossed-off junk that hangs all over their posh houses, which resemble mausoleums, and pay through the nose for it. The artists hold out the better pieces, for museums. Once in a while, something important is exhibited and celebrated. Important to what, you tell me.

I notice the show's title stenciled on the foyer: *Napalm und Pudding*. This defrosts a frozen memory cell. Of course. It's the title of an Ulrike Meinhof article about someone's attempt to smash a bowl of pudding in the German chancellor's face. Or perhaps the target was Franz-Josef Strauss, the Kleine Hitler of Lower Bavaria.

An assortment of evenly spaced light boxes runs in a straight line across three of the gallery's four walls. Clear plastic color images clamped to the glowing boxes like X rays. Computer-manipulated press photographs of Ulrike Meinhof, Gudrun Ennslin, Andreas Baader, Holger Meins, and other members of the Red Army Faction.

"Classic," I tell Leon. "Miles gets an idea, broods about it for ten years, eventually somebody else does something with the same idea."

"Who is Miles?" Leon's eyes scour the room for boys.

"You know Miles."

"Remind me," says Leon, but his attention wanders to a tall Jamaican guy in John Lennon glasses he recognizes at the drinks table. "I take a glass of wine," he says, moving off as a fortiesh art critic cuts through blue-rinse collectors to say hello. The critic is a mole, pale, slouchy, like most critics out in public pretending he's guarding a nuclear secret. He wears a stricken expression, as if openings were funerals.

"These are okay." He approvingly nods. Shrugs, smiles like a Komodo dragon. "Not bad."

"I wish I could see them better."

On the critic's advice I zigzag to the wall for a better look. This is logistically difficult. Not because there are *that* many people around, but at any New York opening the problem is figuring out how to cross the room while avoiding certain individuals without being obvious about it: not one of my better-developed skills. On closer view, texts in Helvetica type overlie the transparent images in English, French, and German. CAPITALISM PROVIDES US WITH THE TOOLS WE NEED TO DESTROY OURSELVES.

I saw the famous Gerhard Richter paintings in Paris, in 1993. These boxes are the only recent works about Baader-Meinhof, I'm pretty sure. If the show gets a lot of attention, it's sure to sully Miles's nebulous project; he has to be counting on the "transgressive" surprise of the subject. Miles once worked up a head of steam, though nothing less vaporous, about a *Titanic* opera, years before the Broadway musical scooped him, a musical quickly eclipsed by the blockbuster movie.

Anna M. materializes.

"Hey," she says, punching my arm.

"Hey," I reply, gripping her bony frame. She feels like ribs will shatter if I hug too hard. I haven't seen the face attached to the telephone voice for half a year. It looks chemically enhanced. "How are you?"

"Okay. Fucked up. You know. How's shit in Indianaville?"

"I wish I knew. Everything feels a little off. I'm surviving. Do you know this artist?"

"Yeah, we met him, like, last year. He's close to that guy who lives in Barcelona? Marc? You met him at our place."

"Marc—"

"Super cute guy, he's got warrants out on him, domestic abuse of his dickhead boyfriend? Felony assault?"

I remember Marc. A smoothie, as they used to say. One of those guys so blessed with looks that he confuses them with brains. He projected a Genet-like criminal sophistication. I assumed he was a spoiled turd from Connecticut.

"This guy Ernesto, you'll meet him—Marc's living in Spain until the statute of limitations runs out or the boyfriend drops the assault charges. He slips into New York, you know, travels in black, like that night you met him. Pretty rad shit, huh?" She means the light boxes.

I see Malcolm hovering near Gracie Mansion, the art dealer, moving his video camera back and forth. He called me a couple nights earlier to tell me that Anna's previous boyfriend had joined them in a three-way.

"I fucked her ex in the ass," he said with a giggle, knowing it would irk me. We have nothing to do with each other that way, but I dislike hearing about his conquests: it makes me feel ancient. "So I guess I'm the man, right?" He'd sounded rabid for approval. "I'm the man."

"You're the man, Malcolm, but you're also *such* a little girl," I told him.

"So? I can be both, can't I?"

Keith Sonnier, one of my favorite artists, rolls his eyes for my benefit at the opposite end of the gallery. Hovering beside him, talking a blue streak, is a world-class bore Keith and I have shared a little joke about for twenty years. The bore has to stand on tiptoe to reach Keith's ear. Keith seems to be the tallest person in the room. He endures his ennui with inflexible Southern politeness.

"You should see us," Anna's saying.

"You should answer your phone once in a while."

"We've had trouble with that phone," Anna says.

"So has everyone who tries to reach you, I'm sure," I say.

"Listen," she says, moving her face close. "I need a favor."

"Anything," I say. Except, I think, B&E on some corporate headquarters.

"My dad's coming over to visit," she says. "They're letting him out of the, uh, *spa*. Like, soon. Maybe a couple weeks. I was hoping the three of us could have dinner. I mean four, if Malcolm comes."

I shrugged. "Sure," I say. "But why me in particular? Why not a bunch of people, have a little party?"

"He'll like you. He won't like our other friends. You're kind of an established person, you've written books. That will impress him. That I have friends at your level."

"I doubt if my level would impress your father," I say.

"No, no," she protests. "You're like, a celebrity."

This is getting awkward.

"Maybe to you, but in the larger picture, I'm absolutely nothing."

"That's just not true." Malcolm's voice sends shivers down my back. His camera lens fixes on me like a Glock automatic.

"You're like, really admired," Malcolm says.

"Super admired," Anna amplifies.

"Why don't you just admit, you want me to meet him because I'm the only friend you have who's close to his age?"

"Well," says Anna, "there's that, too."

"Okay, fine," I say. "I mean I'd like to meet him. As long as he doesn't tell me when I'm going to die."

Anna laughs.

"Dad keeps that kind of information to himself," she says. "Come see us. If my dad comes soon, I'll call you, and set something up."

Leon is making himself interesting to a pencil-thin youth with ash-blond ringlets, and a face out of Zurbarán: Ernesto, the artist. Smiling, wide-eyed, feigning excessive modesty, dazed by the turnout. Femme, I decide. Leon's type.

"This is a very . . . ballsy show," I tell him.

"You think the show is balls?" he asks. He makes a hurt face.

"No, no," Leon explains. "In America, this means bold, brave."

"It made for me a lot of trouble in Europe," Ernesto says. A touch of smug there.

"If you're lucky," I say, "it will make a lot of trouble for you here as well."

In my journalist days, I would have rung up a right-wing reptile at the *Post*, or some turd at *The New Criterion*, and lit a fire of indignation under his or her ass, to bring Ernesto a little profitable scandal. I used to do that sort of thing all the time, assuming the identity of a basket case I knew in a VA hospital on Long Island. Hydrocephalic members of the press always fell for it.

"I served this great country in Vietnam," I'd rasp manfully into the phone between tubercular coughs, "and lost both legs, I've got shrapnel in my ass and lost half a lung and it wasn't to defend this kind of outrage. This anti-American Marxist-atheist crapola. Freedom of speech isn't the same thing as a license to defecate all over our flag or our country. What is this telling our young people, what message does this give people, is what I'd like to know."

On two occasions, I was able to mobilize actual picket demonstrations against various cultural artifacts that would otherwise have come and gone unnoticed. My indignant-veteran impersonation launched numerous scathing, brainless tabloid editorials, and reviews in a range of publications of such foaming viciousness that crowds rushed to the scene of the crime— among them, usually, two or three collectors with deep pockets. It was my idea of fun.

Scanning the gallery, I count nine people I never want to see again in my life. The gigantic white space generates a familiar pinball-machine confusion.

"Many people have forgotten Ulrike Meinhof," Ernesto laments, more to Leon than me.

"People forget everything," Leon answers brightly, "except their childhood wishes and dreams."

This is probably intelligent. In fact, I think Leon stole the line from me. But I want to gag, to run out of there. I've noticed a particularly slimy writer lurking in a corner, picking his moment to pounce on me. He often does, locking me in a stranglehold of boredom without surcease. A half hour is the absolute maximum I can stand any opening. Nothing resembling normal social interaction happens at these things. Everyone pirouettes on display for everybody else, asserting that they still exist, whether other people like it or not.

"I'm going," I tell Leon.

"Oh, but you must come to the dinner," says Ernesto. It occurs to me that, apart from Leon, I am probably the only person in the gallery who has the slightest idea what the Baader-Meinhof Gang was. The crowd, I think, has turned out because the gallery has cutting-edge cachet, and powerful air-conditioning.

"Forgive me," I sigh. "I'm very tired. If you're in New York for a while, get my number from Leon, we could meet for a coffee. I just can't do anything tonight. Congratulations, it's a beautiful show."

I think Leon stands a fair chance of nailing him, since they both speak Spanish as their first language, and Ernesto might as well have BOTTOM printed across his green silk shirt.

On the sidewalk I run smack into Miles. He has already looked at the show, he says, went for a beer, and is going back in. I don't know how to interpret his contented look. I guess he feels relieved that someone has usurped his current mania.

"This guy's really talented," Miles says. "He's also saved me a lot of work. You know, Squat Theater did a piece about Ulrike Meinhof back in the late seventies, I'd forgotten all about it until the other day, she had a rubber penis glued to her forehead and shot a guy dressed as Andy Warhol. Maybe that's where they got the I Shot Andy Warhol idea from. One thing I don't want to be is redundant."

"I think they got the idea from the fact that someone did shoot Andy Warhol," I say, but Miles ignores it.

The frazzled smile, the shrugging acceptance of another project aborted, isn't unprecedented. Still, something's changed about Miles, some major shift in his gear works. I glimpsed it the day he dropped over. Now I recognize what it is.

"You don't think there's room for a play after this," I say.

"I can't write that play," Miles confesses, shaking his head, still smiling, as if it's always been obvious to everyone but him.

I have seen this change in others. A subtle inner movement from stubborn ambition marred by ambivalence, to the dark acceptance of utter, hopeless, permanent defeat. It comes with the ruined cheer of someone who doesn't mind letting go, as if he's swallowed futility as the last bitter pill. I have seen it in people who killed themselves: the film producer Dieter Schidor, quite a few others.

After our affair, or whatever it was, my certainty of being ill-used had inspired a wish that Miles would look in the mirror and see a burnout instead of a genius. I never considered how I'd feel if it actually happened: not wonderful, it turns out. What I loved, what once made me light-headed with something—forget happiness, but some sort of warming complicity, mutuality, I don't know what to call it—was Miles's obstinate refusal of reality. Not denial. Refusal. Even his refusal of the reality of failure, its weight and implications, was reason enough to love him. Miles saw that in a place where all the peaks were third-rate successes, failure could be a kind of beatitude. I saw it because he'd shown it to me.

"There's always Kokoschka," I laugh.

Miles laughs too, but he's laughing at me as well as the whole situation. His laughter is a Snidely Whiplash sort of villainous croaking noise. He wraps an arm around my waist. With force. He pulls me into the gallery's recessed delivery doorway.

"You know what happened to that dummy?" he breathes in my ear. I laugh, to neutralize an unexpected sexual heat that glues our bodies together.

"Kokoschka," Miles says, growling seduction, pushing so I

feel the erection in his pants, "finally got fed up with his Alma Mahler dummy, this baboonlike mockery of the cunt who brought him so much anguish. Some baroness or count, or the Duke of Saxony or some such high, mighty arsehole threw a weekend gala in the artist's honor. They set vast tables in the French garden of this nobleman's palace. Kokoschka brought along the dummy, of course—by this time his obsession was a national joke, and a tragedy, too. But he hadn't taken Alma out to the garden for dinner; everyone found that odd.

"Then, somewhere during that gilded garden party, in fourteen courses, sorbets studded with emeralds as party favors, the artist bolted from his chair and sprinted across the fabled garden, sprinted from the great columned stairs to the palace, down the Carrara marble floor to the Carrara marble staircase, knocking servants and sconces and scattering candelabras, reeling as if seized by St. Vitus' dance, back and forth along the second-floor hall, crashing into the immutable wall, staggering to crash against sconces and tapestries like a thing possessed until he reached his suite of rooms. The guests on the lawn, dripping with jewels and stuffing their mouths with pheasant and caviar and wild boar, froze for a moment, dumb, as the artist whirled from them, quickly resuming their endless meal, their rattled blather, swallowing whole magnums of champagne; in a matter of seconds they forgot all about him. He's mad, they all said, Oskar is stark raving mad, you have only to look at the storms and the tortured figures, the wild strokes of hepatic colors in his paintings to see that he's mad, all artists are mad as March hares, but Oskar is crazier than ten artists rolled into one.

"A half hour passed. Suddenly, Kokoschka flailed and screamed down the palace steps and stormed across the garden, clutching the Alma dummy with his fingers buried in her furry vagina, screaming, 'We've got to burn her! We've got to destroy this filth, this parasite!' And the thirty or forty guests instantly caught the spirit of the mad artist and his rage; they all raised their voices in a chant, across the entire countryside you could hear a mob shouting 'Burn the bitch, burn the bitch!' It became a kind of fever dream, Kokoschka thrashing about and finally climbing on the table with his fist buried in this rubber twat attached to a hairy life-size doll, screaming that she had to burn, this demonic virago, this female Lucifer had to be sent back to hell.

"The servants scrambled to a woodpile, and right there at the end of the garden built an immense bonfire. The guests threw chairs, tablecloths, anything flammable they could grab, flung it all onto the fire; all the while servants popped open champagne bottles, others carried old furniture from a barn, crates, a stack of hay, everything thrown on the fire, and all these aristocrats danced around the crackling flames, thousands of splinters sputtered high above the trees and pinwheeled about the garden. The chant built with violence, 'Burn the bitch, burn the bitch!'

"And once the flames were roaring in blue and orange arabesques high into the starry sky, great thick tongues of fire reaching up like devil's fingers, throwing heat in all directions and lighting the branches and hedges like a searchlight, licking the mirror of a vast reflecting pool, Kokoschka tore off the dummy's arms, then its legs, and with superhuman strength tore her head off and tossed these pieces of Alma to the conflagration, and then, with his fist embedded in her cunt, he swung the torso around and around above his head, making it spin on its own sex, at last letting go at such a pitch that her cunt and the rest of her flew off his hand and shot through the air, dropping into the infernal center of the conflagration. Everyone joined hands, circling the fire in a mesmerized dance, chanting the doom of Alma's dummy until the holled-out, once-beloved thing was reduced to a carcass of popping cinders.

"He regained his sanity after that."

Miles pulls me close. He rams his tongue into my mouth. We French each other like animals ripping their prey apart. I lick his face all over, inside his nose, his ears. He spits on my eyelids and then licks the spit off. We attack each other so hungrily I don't care if he fucks me in the doorway, or on the sidewalk, I don't care if everybody watches, and for a moment or so I want people to see all the things I will let this man do to me and what I do to him. But we're locked into this thing, this feral possession of each other, with our clothes on, and keep doing it, it is so intense that even ripping our clothes off would break the feeling. Miles lowers me to the ground under him, smashing the lump in his pants against my groin. He dry-humps me for a long time. When he stops, and gasps, I know that he's come in his pants. I hear passing steps, a car, the soughing of traffic up the street on Tenth Avenue.

"It's a beautiful story," I lie as he rolls off me and staggers to his feet. I stand up and try to smack dirt off the seat of my pants. It would take nothing for me to burst into tears. *He's going to throw himself away,* I realize.

"Maybe someday I'll tell you another one," Miles says.

A kind of miasma floats around me.

"Did we just have sex?" I ask. I feel like I've been grazed by a fast-moving car.

"I'm pretty sure *I* did," says Miles. "Whether you did or not, that's your call. I mean"—he laughs—"every person has to answer that question for himself."

We both laugh, a little hysterically. It's such a strange, stupid moment. I say I have to go. I back away from him a few paces to show I have to go.

"We should all burn our dummies when they don't support our delusions anymore."

Miles bites his lip. He looks himself over to see if he has dirt patches. He looks away from me and nods.

"I second that emotion," he says, in a dry voice, as if nothing at all just happened. He gives my arm a squeeze as he walks past me, and then walks into the gallery.

64

Glazed the next morning, I wanted to hold Arthur to our ren-
dezvous. He could easily drop out of contact. I liked to spare
myself the drop of resentment that sat on my stomach when
he did.

Oliver and Arthur had migrated from a largish basement flat
in the West Village to a large skylit loft in the offal stench of
the meat market, just before the slaughterhouse district
sprouted art galleries and pseudo-European restaurants. They
paid usurious rent. There was a bad story behind that, involving
Oliver's refusal to rent a more modest apartment and maintain
a separate studio, but I'll leave it aside.

They took the place in raw condition. The architectural renovations mirrored their relationship in every detail. Arthur's office filled a narrow sliver on the street end of their ground-floor
Shangri-la, just off the bedroom. They had installed, at breath-
taking expense—Arthur's—a high-tech gallery kitchen. A Hy-
drostone counter opened on the dining area. The dining area
had no discernible separation from the remaining two-thirds of
the loft, used entirely as Oliver's studio. It always had at least
ten canvases in progress on the walls, and a dozen more stacked
under them. Directly under a skylight, Oliver's trolley-wheeled
worktable, covered in painting supplies, charcoals, pastel sticks,
brushes poking from coffee cans, squatted like some boil-
skinned bullfrog.

Arthur's space: cramped, narrow, segregated from everything
else, at one end. Oliver's space: massive, unlimitedly merging
into where he ate the meals Arthur cooked three times a day,
in a kitchen open to Oliver's continual surveillance.

I had visited this address enough to notice that objects were
out of place. The dining table was boxed in by Arthur's stacked

editing decks and a bank of monitors, the table strewn with folded brochures for X-Stream Video's latest offerings, mailing stickers, envelopes.

The young Arthur had been a sleek, dangerous-looking man, with the violent good looks of a Mafia scion. Which is what he would've been if he hadn't turned out queer. Arthur had recently coupled up with Oliver when I met him. For several years I didn't know that Arthur operated a gay porno business. In the late seventies, I don't think anyone attached any stigma to Arthur's profession. When I found out about it, he became even sexier to me.

Over time, in subtle ways, Oliver's "high art" career relegated Arthur's enterprise to the realm of the sordidly unmentionable, and Arthur himself to the role of Art Wife, helpmate of the Genius. Oliver had never been an especially sexual being. He'd gone flabby and fat with no regrets. He developed a "spiritual" hatred of sex and any discussion of it—despite his habit of finishing most evenings, without Arthur, getting loaded in a Christopher Street leather bar.

Arthur had grown a belly, but dressed to dissemble it. He exuded nervous energy. He functioned in perpetual crisis mode, and so had a stubborn will to sort things out, make things work. Arthur was one of the four or five people I did not consider stupid about how reality is organized. This did not, of course, exempt him from the pain of living in a stupid reality.

He could never sit still. Arthur glided across rooms, restlessly dodging and ducking and spinning on his heels. He hovered and flew up from tables to scurry, emptying ashtrays, refilling glasses, clearing plates. This restive choreography, ingrained from years of whipping up meals for Oliver and their art-world friends, obsessively tended to small details. Arthur's meals involved many stages of vigilant production. When everything landed on the table, continual, intrusively long phone calls followed, which Arthur grabbed in whatever private space he could improvise.

In the distant era when they entertained often, Arthur was a spectral presence, or a spectral absence. This evaporative quality endured, even tête-à-tête. But on this occasion, Arthur let the answering machine pick up his calls. When he finished fussing, he actually sat at the table and said what he had to say in one go.

Intense light flooded the studio from the peaked skylight. Oliver's paintings glowed in the skylight. They were pretty. And somewhat vacant. Vibrant circles, triangles, amorphous shapes in pulsing colors. A piquant flow of urination, on a monitor Arthur duped tapes from, issued from two undernourished, naked Puerto Rican males in some grotty Queens basement. They pissed on a person described in the video's expository dialogue as their "construction boss."

Arthur's abbreviated season on the island had caused him enough perplexity and humiliation that he couldn't quite let it pass, nor could he quite make sense of it.

"We had the whole summer ahead," he began. "And already the usual intrigues were happening. Valerie was working Sylvia White into a corner. She started accusing her of having designs on Henry, to make her feel unwelcome. She'd gotten Henry to show Sylvia that 'polite' cold shoulder of his. But then Valerie made up with her. Very unusual. Invited her to dinner for intense heart-to-heart.

"It was roughly then," Arthur continued, "that Freddy Waste showed up."

Freddy Waste—that really was his name—had pestered the fringes of the Manhattan art world since time immemorial. He was all his name implied, i.e., nothing much. He was the most emotionally obtuse, implacable pest ever to wash up on the island. Disdained by all, Freddy spent years crashing parties, even intimate dinner parties, where he was openly reviled and insulted and usually asked to leave. Freddy never left. He quietly defied people to physically eject him, which of course they wouldn't. He'd become a Manhattan fact, like herpes.

Years passed; Freddy's oblivious insistence on being where he wasn't welcome finally wore people down. They found it embarrassing to loathe an individual so insignificant and boorish. "What a *waste,*" Baudelaire Junior screamed whenever Freddy entered a room. Like water dripping on stone, Freddy slowly bored a hole in the social wall thrown up against him.

This walking personality disorder resembled an inflatable bowling-pin-shaped clown with sand at the base which, no matter how many times or how hard one punches it, instantly bounces upright, wearing the same shit-eating grin. Since he would clearly never go away, people began finding uses for him.

Freddy had toyed with various "jobs" that amounted to running errands for the rich: art bidder at auctions, antique shopper, that kind of thing. A walker, more or less. Lately, he had set himself up as a decorator. It was a period when having no taste was no impediment to success in that arena. Everything Freddy decorated had something indefinably horrible about it. He loved doing bathrooms in deep fecal maroons flecked with gold splatters, dining rooms in scumbled mints and Pepto-Bismol pinks that resembled dried vomit.

Freddy arrived one creepy afternoon, stepping out of the hydrofoil's foul air with Dickie Piedmont. Dickie Piedmont had also been an art-world fixture for decades; unlike Freddy, Dickie was welcome everywhere, prized for his zany humor, his whispery falsetto, his general clownishness. An insatiable alcoholic in the era of Jesse's party snapshots, Dickie was a professional photographer who'd scraped by for years in demeaning restaurant jobs. Several events, some fortuitous, some disastrous, had slightly lowered the volume on Dickie's personality, made him more or less rich, and leached a degree of giddiness out of him, though he remained a basically silly individual. Silly enough to travel in Freddy Waste's unthinkable company.

The first event was a blood test revealing Dickie's HIV-positive status. The second was conversion to total sobriety, in the AA program. During his dryout, Dickie aligned himself professionally with Chrissie Blodgett. Since they both came from Albany, canny art dealers confected a mythical "Albany School," throwing in two other artists Dickie and Chrissie had distantly known in Albany.

In the myth, these four had shared years of impoverished support and related stylistic development. After this marketing scam kicked into motion, enhanced by the early death of one of the four Albanians, as people were wont to call them, the remaining three became famous, to varying degrees. They now hated one another's guts, for one trivial reason or another.

Arthur sensed trouble as soon as the new arrivals checked into a waterfront hotel and trekked up the steep, narrow-stepped hillside where Henry and Valerie Willey maintained their many-splendored, multibuilding compound. Arthur recalled the sinister arrival of Mr. Jones and his apelike servant on another island, in Joseph Conrad's *Victory*.

"I couldn't shake the impression that they'd been *summoned*," Arthur told me, lighting his seventh cigarette in twenty minutes, as the naked Puerto Ricans on-screen used their employer's mouth as a urinal. "Invited. Even though Freddy Waste has never ever been invited anywhere."

Arthur's casting methods, consistent with a certain trailer-park mise-en-scène, created long existential lapses in the action when, for example, models hired for active penetration failed to achieve erections. On the monitor behind Arthur's head, the "fat pig bottom" fellated his two golden-showering partners in tedious rotation. One fleetingly stiffened. He positioned himself at the pig's buxom rear end. He abruptly deflated, ineptly simulating penetration. The camera swiftly panned to the ongoing blowjob at the pig bottom's front end.

"Most people who buy this stuff aren't into penetration anyway," Arthur assured me when I pointed this out. "They mainly want to see piss humiliation."

Insidiously, said Arthur, over a week Sylvia regained her status as court favorite, "the summer friend" who very well might be invited back next year. The Willeys ruled the island socially, unless you escaped and made other friends, in which case the Willeys dropped you. Each year, the imperious couple lured to the island several compatriots, some single, some coupled. The fortunate ones got to witness, rather than undergo, the psychological destruction of the year's chosen victim. Meanwhile, Freddy and Dickie joined the ritual breakfast routine at the More Hot, followed by a cliffside lunch at the island's smaller village (one walked to it, or took a water taxi, according to Valerie's whim) at whichever taverna endured Valerie's patronage that year.

There were two tavernas in the village. Every summer, Valerie initiated a feud with one or the other, and patronized the supposedly rival establishment all summer. Valerie had no interest in the little local people, Arthur said, or she would've figured out by this time that both tavernas were owned by the same family.

Dinner was usually eaten at a restaurant at the bottom of a

dark plummeting valley—southeast or southwest, Arthur never could get it straight, of the hillside enclave where their houses stood above the port. If you missed your footing on the cement walkway, you tumbled through brambles and tall weeds and other stinging, scratching flora. At the very bottom, like the Phantom of the Opera's dining room, sat a flagstone oasis of quiet: a peaceful, well-stocked bar inside, tables outside, a kitchen offering halfway edible paella, tapas, and so forth.

Dickie and Freddy irritated Arthur, without becoming completely odious. "That was the bitch of it." He laughed. "They brought just enough of what you didn't want that you had to take it in stride, like a good Christian, when what would have come in handy," he said, quoting a surrealist poet, "was an eraser to wipe out human filth."

At meals, Freddy flaunted a tiresome gift for describing works of art, churches, and other landmarks he'd recently viewed crossing Europe, peppering conversation with invasive, stupid questions, idiotic jokes that scraped everybody's nerves. He dressed in splashy Bermuda shorts and Sea Island shirts and flip-flops that dangled from his stubby, ugly feet.

Dickie had a compulsion to deflect serious talk into streams of Dadaesque absurdity, funny but meaningless, as if anything involving two consecutive thoughts that weren't the buildup and punch line of a joke offended his idea of a good time. Dickie's presence wearied Arthur. Not because Arthur wanted to talk about big metaphysical questions, but because he resented having to laugh his head off at dinner, when he already had to make an effort not to radiate misery in every direction. Dickie insisted on turning any meal into a hen fest of dueling witticisms.

All the more surprising, then, that one night at the Willey compound, a night when Arthur had to take the hydrofoil to

Gibraltar to deal with some family crisis by telex and local attorney, this same manic Dickie Piedmont, ridiculous Freddy Waste, and far-from-teetotaling Sylvia White *took part in an intervention,* orchestrated by Henry and Valerie, aimed at stripping Oliver of every defense, confronting him with the drunken outrages he'd committed in the past, the decline in his productivity, and his increasingly withdrawn personality, and offering—no, *demanding* that he accept their munificent offer—to pay for a month's rehab at Hazelden.

"All behind my back," Arthur said. A raspy congestion betrayed a nibbling doubt that he fully deserved his indignation. This was the part of Arthur that had been trained for years, by people like the Willeys, to think of himself as nothing. "Because no matter how fucked up my relationship with Oliver is, if I'd been there I would've defended him, I would've insisted we leave and never speak to these bastards again."

Oliver described the evening in gruesome detail.

"First Valerie served her famous Mediterranean clay pot chicken. With the olives and capers and lemons all over it. You know what a whiz Valerie is with chicken—well, I guess you don't." It was true. I avoided people like the Willeys, who collected friends and discarded them like kids trading baseball cards. "Rice pilaf, endive salad. The girls"—the two Willey brats—"went off to the disco, and everybody else gravitated into this salon they have, with a huge marble floor and fat lounging pillows.

"Valerie wore her painting slacks and a sweatshirt and had her hair tied back in the pigtails she started wearing when she became a *painter,* as if she were about to attack a canvas. Everyone else had casual linen, whatever they normally wore to dinner.

"Valerie carried in a fruit bowl and some bottles of sparkling water and set them down on this knee-high glass coffee table.

203

She squatted on her heels facing Oliver and said, 'Oliver, Henry and I are very concerned about you, we've asked everybody here to help you see why, and persuade you to do something about it. Which Henry and I are willing to help you with, financially, morally, and spiritually.' "

According to Oliver, Henry then nodded gravely. Even spiritually and morally. For some reason, Oliver told Arthur, I thought somehow they knew I had cancer and I didn't.

Sylvia White had seemed least at home in this situation, squirming through many of the ugly details Henry and Valerie spun out, at times giving them a comic twist that somewhat belied their spiritual and moral gravity.

"It's the drinking, Oliver," Valerie told him in a harsh voice. "As I'm sure we don't have to tell you. It's reached the point where people can't stand being around you. And Arthur *enables* you. He doesn't go over the edge like a maniac the way you do, but he *allows it to happen*."

"That night you passed out with your face in the salad bowl," Henry put in quietly.

"I've seen you some nights in New York," Freddy Waste jumped in, gleefully, "when you didn't know where you were, you were so drunk people had to bring you home in a cab to make sure you recognized your own door."

"You don't even remember the time you fell," said Valerie. "Right out there on the steps." She started to giggle, but forced her face back into a stern mask of matronly exasperation. "You got a lump the size of a doorknob on your forehead, scrapes and bruises all over."

"That night you called the Australian in the More Hot a pig's asshole and threw a table at him."

"Remember the boat picnic when you puked into Dorothea's penne?"

Oliver told Arthur he'd stared at the Bokhara carpet covering the marble floor and tried to think of some rejoinder. Shame reddened the lardless areas of his face.

"I've been there," crooned Dickie Piedmont's reedy, cotton-soft hissings after an otiose silence. "I really fought getting help. For a long time. And my life kept sliding downhill. My boyfriend was no help, because as long as I was a drunk he could twist that to manipulate me. I'd go out to clubs, stagger home with strangers, have sex without protection. Finally, bingo, HIV."

"I do *not* have HIV," Oliver shrieked, finally bristling, though he felt he had something worse, like the Ebola virus. "Arthur and I don't even have sex."

"Lucky you, from what I hear," Freddy maliciously brayed, incapable of controlling himself. Oliver winced.

"Let's not stray from the point," said Valerie, more softly than was her custom, though her voice still grated as if some zircons she'd swallowed had scraped her vocal cords. "Your alcohol problem is wrecking your life. You're destroying your liver and your kidneys, and driving away all your friends. *I* drink," Valerie acknowledged, "*Henry* drinks, but not to get drunk, we don't knock back one after another until our brains are scrambled. The bottom line is, at the end of the month, *we can pay off our credit cards.*"

She stopped for a commanding breath. Sylvia White's color had been draining steadily since the onset of this gang bang, as she recognized herself in everything Oliver was being accused of.

"You have to understand," said Valerie, "we *love* you. Everyone in this room loves you, Oliver. If we didn't love you, if we didn't care what happened to you, we wouldn't bother doing this." Valerie went blank for a moment. "We'd drop you," she added thoughtfully.

"I love you, too, man," said Freddy Waste, suiting action to word, by his lights, by slapping Oliver heartily on the back.

"I love you, too," Sylvia White ventured nervously. "And I don't even know you."

Valerie began pacing the room, like a solo performer on a Shakespeare stage.

"You are loved, and you are valued," she chanted in oracular fashion. Her voice was least abrasive when spouting clichés.

"But you have to learn to love and value *yourself*," Dickie Piedmont declared with the pat wisdom of the recently dried. "And you can't do that when you're guzzling a quart of gin every day."

"Oliver doesn't drink gin," snapped Valerie pedantically, somewhat rupturing the atmosphere of uplift. "But Dickie's basically right. Until you learn to love yourself, you can't really love anybody else."

By this time tears were streaming down Oliver's bloated face. He felt like an elephant being poked with metal spears by sadistic zookeepers. But they weren't through with him.

"You can't put yourself back together by yourself," Valerie declared, stabbing the air in Oliver's direction with a little finger. With the other hand she plucked a greengage plum from the fruit bowl and took a hearty bite.

"Realistically," said Henry, emerging swamilike from a long, detached-looking silence, "you need to go somewhere professional for a time." Henry helped himself to a plum, as if the ingestion of plums marked the conclusion of the entire matter. "Away from the temptations and stresses that set you off."

They had, it turned out, already done some research and knew how the program worked at Hazelden. It later emerged that Betty Ford cost more than they were willing to ante up.

"When you have Arthur *enabling* you," concluded Dickie Piedmont, with stress on his currently favorite word, "and having a cocktail whenever he wants one—which is his perfect right, this isn't about him, it's about you—you'll never break this addiction by yourself."

"So," Arthur told me, "this plan hatched itself without a word of consultation between me and Henry and Valerie, but Oliver and I discussed it for days. He was terrified of detox. Oliver's terrified of travel as far as that goes. He gets so hysterical on an airplane he practically bolts for the door before they finish boarding." As a superior mind, Arthur said, which Oliver certainly was, he was filled with horror imagining the quotidian touchy-feely regimen at such programs.

Oliver defiantly hit the vodka, lounging on their terrace, for three consecutive days and nights, eating nothing, resigned one minute, defiant the next, and unusually sentimental, clinging to Arthur, declaring Arthur the only person he had ever loved and trusted. Arthur saw desperation seeping out of him like pus from a cyst. Despite his contempt for Henry and Valerie, he had to conclude they were probably right. Oliver woke one decisive morning in a bed full of vomit covering Arthur as well as himself. It wasn't a first, but they both recognized it had to be a last. Matters could only get worse. The truth was, Arthur said, that Oliver had disgusted himself for several years, more than anybody at the "intervention" would ever have guessed.

Within a few more days the Willeys had packed Oliver onto a flight to Minneapolis. Nothing remained for Arthur to do except come back to New York, *voilà*.

"I certainly wasn't hanging around there for the rest of the summer," he said. His departure cleared the way for the Willeys to quickly purchase the house he and Oliver had rented before

Sandy McKenna, who owned it, died of cancer, and her daughter Sophie could inherit it. Valerie had already promised Sandy that she would take Sophie into the Willey family when Sandy passed on. So instead of inheriting a valuable piece of real estate, Sophie inherited the Willeys, who turned her into a Cinderella figure, pre–glass slipper, for her new, younger stepsisters. But that's a story for another time.

"What do you think Oliver will be like," I asked, "when he's clean and sober?"

Arthur's face did not light up with joy. He looked more depressed, if anything.

"The same," he said through his cigarette smoke. "Withdrawn, sullen, selfish, uncommunicative, hostile. Monstrously inconsiderate, self-absorbed, infantile. Shall I go on?"

"You don't think when the booze is out of his system—?"

"The alcohol has nothing to do with it," Arthur said. "Everybody thinks it does, but it doesn't. I love him. I don't imagine I'll ever not love him. But he's got the same shitty personality now when he's sober, I've seen it. By the way, I got some odd letters from Jesse. I'll let you read them."

"What happens with you and Oliver when he gets back?"

Arthur covered his forehead with his cigarette hand. He ran his fingers down his face.

"I can't take too much more," he said. "I'll be the one who disintegrates. But do you know what it's like trying to end something that's been your whole life for twenty-five years? At our age? The idea of being alone is absolutely terrifying."

I nodded.

"I expect I'll end up alone," I said. "I think you get used to it. Some parts of it you even get to like. It's depressing to have to take care of everything in life by yourself, but you also have your freedom. I've watched you become unhappier and unhappier, it breaks my heart—"

"And right now," Arthur said self-disgustedly, "I cling to a fantasy that Oliver comes out of rehab with fabulous qualities he's never possessed in his life."

I could never summon the right words, the right help. I could never save anybody.

"I know anything I say won't make any difference," I said, "but I have to say it anyway. I don't give a shit about Oliver. He's always been nice to me, I've always liked him. I used to even enjoy talking to him when he still talked to people, but that's a long time ago. But I do care about you. You're fifty-four years old, Arthur. This is the only life we have, and it's short. Very short."

Arthur knew that, too.

65

Jesse saw people going away and people coming back. The road to the cottage ran past the bay on one side and the isthmus on the other, like the highway in Florida when they went to Wakulla Springs. When he dreamed about that time, the road always looked as if it would dip down where the two bodies of water met, at a point beyond the horizon. People in the street were running. The pavement stretched up the hill to the cathedral, flanked by low-rise offices and grimy restaurant windows, turning hazy with smoke. Dozens of students were running, clapping sweater necks and handkerchiefs to their mouths and noses. He felt the sting of tear gas, and clawing inside his throat. At the top of the hill, another broad street curved up into the cathedral park. Far away the Virgin of Quito, several thousand tons of dull aluminum, gleamed on a mountaintop. Below where he stood, trim boys in green uniforms paraded on the grounds of the military school. A satellite dish poked from a cluster of stucco rooftops. He stood at the edge of the ocean and heard water running in the bathtub. He read a paragraph of *Journal du voleur*. On the TV, crowds ran under the spermy arcs of water cannons. He stepped into the helicopter beside the river. The bells echoed across the water. They came to a seafood joint with the best broiled mullet on the peninsula, if you scraped off the huge gob of butter in the middle. From far above, the little islands near the airport were ringed with the white spokes of docks and boats. He always wondered about these islands, who lived on them, how you could find them if you rented a car and drove there. What manner of life.

PART
THREE

THE FALLS

66

A final letter from Jesse to Arthur, mailed from Paraguay near the end of his travels, has the first line or two torn away. The upper page has adhered to the fold-over envelope glue; "unless the horse the horse of course is the famous Mr. Ed" are its first legible words. It's a long letter, in impeccably regular script, written on old-fashioned, humidity-crinkled airmail paper.

It mushroomed into an uncontrollable mental chant around the sixth day in the Essaouira apartment, "A horse is a horse of course of course," and I thought, if this is the kind of bubble gum your brain becomes when you luck into your sleaziest image of paradise, there is something dangerous going on. Mohammed and Omar were on their month's vacation—one good thing the French introduced to their colonies, at least, the month off—and they obviously were tickled pink at the thought that they'd struck a gold mine, or at least a purse that would carry them through their holiday in un- believable high style. Brand-new rental car, food and hashish and liquor all paid for, a tight little fanny to fuck day and night be- longing to a relatively unrepulsive foreigner. They were just kids, eighteen and twenty.

They seemed absolutely guileless, and yet my not having a clue about things brought this occasional ripple of apprehension. Unlike any Muslims I'd had sex with—at that point, count- ing Tunis, Alexandria, and Algiers, enough to

populate a small oil-rich emirate—they identified themselves as gay, referred to themselves
as gay men. They somehow kept up, knew how
open people are about this in Europe and America, and had European boyfriends they corre-
sponded with, and I think they both wanted out
of Morocco to a city like Amsterdam or Copen-
hagen. Where they'd be treated as human ref-
use, no doubt, but maybe they would still be
better off than in Essaouira as far as being
openly gay is concerned.

At the same time, when I asked Mohammed if
he was really a Muslim—did he really believe
everything in the Koran, and so forth—he said,
"Of course," very firmly, like, "What else
could I be?" I have only heard that degree of
unquestioning conviction from a *Catholic*, fag
or otherwise, in Goa. I think Goa is the only
place on earth where people take Catholicism
seriously. There are even atheists lurking
around in the Vatican, I'm sure. I'm not saying either of these guys would willingly take
up arms against the infidel or anything, but
you have to wonder. I don't know what that
country would be like these days if you looked
Jewish, and Morocco used to give the Jews
refuge.

Omar's auntie, who'd rented me the apartment, was cheery as Santa Claus about the
whole setup, the nature of which, unless I
missed something very arcane concerning the
laws of hospitality, could not be mistaken for

anything different than what it was. Nothing
overt right in front of her, naturally, but
nothing in the way of pretending they were
showing some dumb tourist the town, either.
Everybody was sweet and funny and high-
spirited and easy. And stoned senseless from
sunup to beddy-bye. Except me. I'd quit smoking cigarettes in Rome. I knew the first toke
of hashish would blow that to hell. I never
liked dope anyway, two puffs put me to sleep.
They, however, were perpetually blasted and
having the time of their lives, amazed by what
they could suddenly get away with, domineering
about where we went and what we ate, but considerate enough, and, to put it delicately,
they couldn't get enough hole, which more than
made up for any little irritations, at least
for a while. When one of them wore out, the
other one appeared like magic in the bedroom
doorway, sporting a foot-long stiffy primed
for a marathon. They weren't terribly bright.
Not stupid exactly, but dim the way potheads
get dim over time, fuzzy, sloppy with food,
and that added to my "objective" certainty
that they were harmless. Things went like the
wettest dream I'd ever had for a little over a
week. Perpetual gratification by my image of
perfection times two.

But as a wise person once told me, if you
suddenly feel paranoid, don't wait around to
find out that it isn't paranoia. Your body
tells you things, your instincts. One day they

left the apartment to buy food. I sat in the parlor, staring at the wall. I realized I hadn't experienced a moment of actual silence since this whole thing started except when they were both asleep. What felt like a minute later, I had driven halfway back to Marrakesh, where after one night in that den of sinister enchantment I hit the road back to Tangiers. I left a stupid note, in mangled French, I was thinking in English and forgot certain words. Thinking as I wrote it: Get the fuck out of here now, or you'll never be seen alive again. It's possible they'll be puzzling over that note for the rest of their vacation. Or maybe they just blew a spliff and forgot I ever existed.

One of the more ridiculous things—but how do you measure ridiculousness in such a situation?—was the purse. It was a green nylon zipper bag, exactly the wrong shape and size such bags always prove to be, no matter how much thought you put into it beforehand, somewhere between a handbag and a very small piece of luggage, kind of like a video camera case, containing the traveler's checks, passport, air ticket, and whatever else valuable I had. There was absolutely no way to conceal it, or keep it out of view, and trying to put it anywhere that looked like a hiding place would've become an obvious statement of suspicion. That stupid little bag became charged with such negativity that I sometimes thought the bag

was living this experience, and I was a lump
of human exigua the bag had to drag along with
it. Bringing the bag anywhere instead of leaving it in the apartment also became a statement. It might mean, say, that I believed
Auntie would loot it and blame it on thieves.
Try going to the beach with such a bag, or
locking it in the trunk of a new car any wise-
ass would love to hot-wire and take for a joy-
ride. And it made me crazy when I tried
separating certain contents of the bag from
the bag itself, passport here, air ticket
there, traveler's checks somewhere else, playing this mental game about which of these
things did I need most, what layers of compli-
cation would ensue if I lost the passport but
still had the checks, or lost the checks but
still had the air ticket, or had the air
ticket but no passport, or the checks and the
passport but no air ticket. And quite often
the boys switched from French to Arabic, it's
what they normally speak to each other. This
had been a major horror of the desert, with
everybody yabbering in Berber, which I guess
is some kind of Arabic too, not knowing if I
was invited somewhere as an honored guest or
being guided to the nearest ravine to get my
head sliced off, and, given the kind of person
I am, whatever kind that is, I have to admit
this was also one of the desert's seductive
charms. The willful daily act of pushing forward into fear territory because the beauty

and silence of the landscape make life or death somehow arbitrary. The spell of the place is that strong.

But in Essaouira—even though it wouldn't have led anywhere anyway, I know this is one of those episodes I'll wonder about for the rest of my life. How would it have been if I'd stayed.

And then you ask yourself. Am I tough or fragile? A coward and an idiot, or a person with good instincts who saw something bad coming from a long way off? Tangiers was more squalid and awful and finished than it was ten years ago, and it was awful then. I checked into the Minzah. Then a screwup happened with the plane reservation. I wasn't listed on the flight. The travel agency in the Village had mucked up the return coupon. Then, one night at the Minzah, I ran into this couple who said they'd met me a few months earlier in New York.

Very young, him maybe twenty, her a couple years older. For a few days I fell into the routine of drinking cocktails with them late in the evening. That's when I started smoking again. A whole summer of holding out without much misery. But they looked so glamorous puffing away at their Gitanes that I just had to. I had no memory of this couple. I definitely had met them at a party, because I remembered the party. They were planning to take the car ferry to Algeciras, then drive to Seville and certain little mountain villages, and go to La Mancha or wherever Cervantes had his theater, taking their time for two weeks getting to Madrid. Did I want to come along?

I could have bought another ticket for New York. Instead I gave in to that strangely lazy craving to find out where something unanticipated will lead. I say strangely, because it should take more energy to improvise your next move than to do what you've already planned, yet sometimes it doesn't. So I just went with them. Seville, Toledo, the whole trip. They were deeply into fucking each other all the time. Love often craves an audience.

No doubt it was the height of imprudence to leave Madrid and go to Buenos Aires instead of coming home. Certainly it was the height of insanity to end up coming here. But I realized after these months of brainless pointless sex that I was looking for something else all along. Something to fill the God-shaped hole, if that doesn't sound too crazy.

I've got to leave soon and put something in my stomach. Asuncion is a really difficult city to find decent food and not a place you want to wander around in after dark. The park I see from my hotel window has about a dozen bookshops set up in huge white tents, and some grossly unsanitary sandwich stands, that disappear at night. Everything's rolled up or shuttered down and carted off and the park turns into Homicideville. There's another park

a bit beyond that one where couples sit at
night, just below the plaza of a luxury hotel.
It's a calming place to sit watching enormous
bats flying around people at eye level like
tame birds. But if I go to that park, I have
to take a taxi home to avoid the other park,
and taxis are scarce at night as there's a
huge amount of carjacking. Whores all over the
place. The scariest whores I've seen anywhere.
Somebody gets killed in the park under my window every night. Almost always a stabbing
death. Most men over twenty-five here look like
killers. The ones under twenty-five look like
killers in training. They all cultivate this
slick, gangstery look and attitude. The women
over sixteen are all fat and bored. Queers are
obvious, isolated, scared shitless in the
streets. They mince uncontrollably like
they're stuck in the 1950s, followed wherever
they go by waves of verbal ridicule from shop-
keepers and construction workers. Fortunately
I can "pass." I don't carry my body that way,
and I'm foreign.

All the affluent streets off from the city
center have gold plaques on the walls that run
in front of the houses. Virtually every last
name is German. I've seen blue-eyed Guarani
Indians walking around. There's a kind of se-
crecy here that's creepier than Romania during
the Cold War. I always thought I'd go anywhere, but I'm not even tempted to visit the
countryside. Every day I walk to the river,

then up into the shopping district, and poke around in the outdoor markets, by day it's almost a normal place, there's one park where old men play chess with wooden timers and they sell these beautiful hammocks and things. But the light is too bright. Somehow the streets are laid out like a sinister stage set and unpleasantly metallic enough that you have to wear dark glasses. There's too many bogus-looking electronics stores and places selling fake designer clothes, and you feel shadowy things gathering energy for sundown everywhere people are congregated. I suppose I'm beginning to sound like Bram Stoker, but this fucking place is evil. When I left Madrid, I thought I'd go to Buenos Aires, and then La Paz, and then maybe fly home. But in La Paz or Sucre or somewhere I suddenly thought, "Nobody I know has ever gone to Paraguay." Well, now I know why.

Tomorrow or the day after I will take a bus to Iguazú to see the Falls. It's pointless coming this far and not going to the Falls. You have to cross the whole country, but I think that only takes about five hours. The buses all over South America show horrible movies on overhead televisions, films you know were made in America but strictly for Third World consumption. Spy thrillers and action movies featuring actors you've never seen, all shot with incredible ineptitude but somehow a lot of money went into making them. I've seen

these movies in North Africa and India and
Chile and everywhere, they're all shot in Los
Angeles and everyone in them looks like a
waiter or a bunny from the Playboy mansion.

This will probably reach you two years after
I put it in the mail. I'm sure you're still
away, but it would be foolish to send you a
letter from here to the island. Miss you oo-
dles, Arthur. I didn't find God down here either. Just the usual God-shaped hole.

Given that Arthur had left the island far ahead of his plans,
there was nothing surprising in the fact that this reached him
when he was already back in Manhattan. There was, unrelated
to the vagaries of international mail delivery, a small frisson
attaching to the fact that he received it a few days after Jesse
himself returned to New York and got attacked. I am getting
ahead of myself. Occupational hazard.

67

At nine on a morning rife with promise of a clean, clear day, the sky over New York turned cheese green, like a gangrenous limb, and a sodden wind sheared through the city, dying minutes later into peppery drizzle, followed by blue sky, fast clouds scudding out over the Atlantic. Insulting sunshine followed.

"That green," people told each other all morning. "That green looked like the end of the world."

"Did you see the green?" Edith Eddy breathlessly asked me on the telephone, ever keen on occult manifestations. Of the many summer exiles who showed up in New York in advance of the fall "season" that year, Edith was the unlikeliest. Some messy situation had run awry, no doubt, but Edith had never before abandoned the Cape before October. "I thought, okay, I expected the apocalypse anyway, but does it have to turn out to be *green*?"

"What the fuck was that green all about?" Anna quizzed Malcolm as they left the Cedar Street apartment to begin their day. "And the wind threw the curtains up to the ceiling."

Miles had an early appointment chez Seagrave. In the coffee shop opposite the Turtle Bay building, customers analyzed the green sky with nervous levity, referring to extraterrestrial invasion, distant chemical plant explosions, overturned railroad cars stuffed with atomic waste, global warming, a freaky collision of weather fronts.

"We're probably getting our own aurora borealis, now those ice caps are melting," the waitress said in a bored voice as she handed Miles his takeout cup. "They say the ice shelf that broke off the other day was the size of New Zealand."

Seagrave had been showering and dressing in his quarters beside the office, and missed the green moment.

"It's just weather," he told Miles. He retracted the vertical blinds of the wide office window. He waved at the choppy river below the giant Pepsi-Cola sign on a bottling plant on the opposite shore. "The sky turns a little green a lot of times before it rains."

"I'm putting the house in Rhinebeck on the market," Miles declared. "I need to move back to the real world."

"Good," said Seagrave firmly.

"I mean I needed that isolation for a while. I don't regret the time I spent there. But I don't even like to go up there anymore."

"Sell it," Seagrave urged, as he had many times. "It's been bothering you forever."

"It's so desolate. I feel like John Gielgud in *Providence*, crawling through endless rooms in my bathrobe and clinging to a vodka bottle."

"You're preaching to the choir," Seagrave said. "It's a healthy move."

"I thought I'd always like it, but . . ."

"Sell," Seagrave repeated, laughing. "Sell sell sell."

"I mean, I have the place here, after all."

"I think we've covered this subject," said Seagrave. "So, what will you do now?"

"I can't even imagine."

"I take it you're not keen on that play anymore."

"No, it's a dead end. I suppose I could write something. Maybe a novel."

"There's an idea."

"I could, oh, go back to the country, shut myself up with the spirits of the dead, something like that—"

"One minute ago you were selling the house," Seagrave said. "For months you've been telling me how much you hate the place and need to get away from it."

"Well," said Miles squirmingly, "maybe not just yet."

"Do what you will, but you won't get anywhere if you make decisions and keep going back on them," Seagrave said. "The question is, what do you actually want to do?"

Miles scratched his chin.

"Maybe that's the problem," he said. "Maybe I don't need to do anything. Maybe I just think I do."

"Everyone needs to do something," Seagrave said with mounting impatience. "Some meaningful activity seems to stop most people from sliding into depression."

"It never seems to stop me," Miles said.

Seagrave had to laugh. Miles was the latest of several patients to exhibit, recently, dramatically, a circular rut in his mental process. Seagrave watched their thoughts swallow their own tails as if seeing all his careful work unravel under some collective, unseen pressure. He felt clinically at sea.

"The thing is, I don't hear my voices anymore. I used to hear voices, when I wrote. In my head. Now I don't hear them."

"You *don't* hear voices," Seagrave said. "That's what you're telling me is your problem."

"Exactly."

"Well, that I can't help you with."

68

Malcolm. Anna. Malcolm. Anna.

Numbers flutter on the Mondrian-inspired grid of frosted glass in Union Square that covers the upper west quadrant of the Megacomplex where Malcolm works. This decorative row of ascending digits is a chronometer in the most useless sense, translating pure duration into mathematical eternity. Numbers accrue. Figures increase. But the time these numbers occupy bears no relation to the date or hour, to seconds or centuries.

Malcolm, dressed in black cargo pants, sandals, his white-on-black Virgin logo T-shirt, sips a Starbucks latte near the south edge of Union Square Park, reading the paper before work. People climb out of the subway like Neanderthals lumbering from a prehistoric cave to squint at the sunlight. They fan out through a maze of cement barriers surrounding an eternal street repair. The numbers, Malcolm considers, can only suggest infinity, as there's a finite number of panels. So the whole mechanism is circular and pointless.

It is a morning of doggie bag news: shootings with no "ironically" misidentified targets or heart-tugging pathos, unpromising boycotts of genetically modified crops, septic boils of violence bursting in faraway realms of pus disappearing under mounds of wreckage and dust. Wherever people attempt life, debris piles up. The local lake explodes, flash floods send millions scrambling to places they're not wanted, warring tribes hack off each other's limbs with machetes. The disgruntled and hungry decapitate local relief workers, or burn down the only hospital within a hundred miles.

People indistinguishable to any foreigner see glaring, evil differences between one another's facial arrangements, the shapes of their hands or feet. They can never know peace until these devils' villages are strafed with mortar fire, their huts inciner-ated, their women raped, their children starved, wells poisoned, crops destroyed. Whichever tribe controls the radio station on a given week sends its evil twin into suicidal flight for border camps that contain no food, no potable water, no antibiotics, and no defense from the recreational slaughter of their host country's restive teenage military personnel.

In more advanced nation-states, it seems like a good idea among especially holy persons to blow up school buses, fire-bomb mosques and synagogues, fire missiles tipped with de-pleted uranium into large divisions of surrendering enemy soldiers. This is all doggie bag news because yesterday's pile of dead flesh isn't nightmarish enough, the victims weren't Amer-ican (one American corpse equals five million foreign ones), and none of the incidents portends a truly gratifying, numerically genocidal catastrophe. The takeaway is hardly worth the doggie bag.

The center front page photo on such a day always offers whimsical relief from the customary, prize-winning shots of ter-restrial carnage. Today's distraction: color images from the mi-raculous Hubble telescope. The Hubble has captured the Tadpole Galaxy, in shades of purple, like a twirling hubcap of astral gases; the Swan Nebula, a twinkling archipelago of rain-bow speckles strewn across milky streaks of ether; and "collid-ing galaxies called the Mice," which suggest the collision of a Glendale street map with a satellite picture of Pasadena. Space has the gel-filtered gaiety of an Ice Follies extravaganza. Even out there where there is nothing, something's always going on. Maybe, Malcolm thinks, our own life-sustaining orb is one of the colliding Mice, floating so imperceptibly toward impact that in forty million years or twenty minutes, it will be a dead rock smashing into another dead rock.

Malcolm eyes the Megabuilding, the flipping numbers.

A line from a movie he can't quite place pops into Malcolm's mind:

"Who needs all this shit?"

He looks again. Almost certainly the building moved, jumped a little to one side.

Malcolm is "tapering." Letting some of the pointy edges push out of the buffer zone.

The glass grid has a gray metal tint worked into it. Its opacity looks like flat aluminum from a distance of more than a block. This surface has begun visibly to breathe. It's as if a giant bubble presses the building's skin from inside, causing the whole wall to swell outward.

He will not call Nahib on his cell phone to cop enough smack to smooth out the day. This avenue of relief is turning scary. Malcolm vomits much of what he eats lately. He's losing weight. Nahib has always encouraged Malcolm to take a little more. Nahib, he thinks, is losing touch with other people's realities and filling up with desperate little obsessions. Like a bucket catching rainwater. Every time Nahib brings a delivery, he tells them of his religion, the sin he's committing by dealing drugs. Yet he isn't just a dealer, he's a pusher.

Malcolm plans to straighten his keel with positive thinking, vitamins, vegetable juices, even masturbation in a Megastore toilet stall if that will lever his brain from the Zone. He will wear cheerfulness on his complicated face. He will not mistake liquefying material in his rectum for small incipient farts whose release would be harmless. Dope constipates him; going off dope turns his intestines to water.

Malcolm has responsible things on his mind. He's taken a homily from a paperback on gnosticism as his thought for the day: "Every moment in our lives is counted, for each is a door opening onto immortality or the void."

Malcolm bought the book, doubting that he'd read it. He gave it to Anna, who devoured several chapters.

"You realize," she told him, holding her place with a finger as she made a disgusted face at the refrigerator's chaos, "this is all the stuff we've been talking about for, like, a year now."

"Read on." Malcolm sighed, having skimmed several right-hand pages. "They believed Jesus Christ never had a bowel movement. Some of it's right on, some of it's wack."

Anna took a bottle of cranberry juice to the sink and hunted a clean glass.

"Was he too, like, divine, did they think? To crap?"

Malcolm searched under a stack of magazines for a notebook he used for drawing storyboards, found it, tried slipping it out carefully, and sent the hill of periodicals cascading to the floor.

"I fucking *hate* the physical world," he said, with jarring violence, scooping up the spillage. "Why can't we leave our bodies once in a while? All these . . . *things*. Everywhere. All the time."

Anna looked him over appreciatively across the cooking island. Her throat hurt. She coughed as she sipped juice. Lately, the apartment was losing its polished, spare, everything-in-place quality. She tried to isolate the moment when Malcolm began spewing a kind of strangled rage, like the obscenities uttered uncontrollably by a Tourette's victim. Not long ago, she thought, or had it been a long time? An insidious trick of drugtime, this lost certainty of when.

"So did the Virgin Mary ever take a dump, at least?" she asked. If such questions were the heart of gnosticism, she thought, perhaps it wasn't for her.

Malcolm irritably restacked the magazines. *I-D*. *The Face*. *Dazed & Confused*. A host of knockoff publications. "I'm young and sexy and design clothes and furniture you don't need," murmured one. "I'm in a band that sounds like everything you ever heard!" screamed another. "I star in a new movie only imbeciles would pay to see," crooned a third. Malcolm and Anna bought these magazines, cloned in baffling plenitude every month, to get a read on "trends," refinements in advertising methods, stuff they could parody in their videos. That there hadn't been, for months, any of "their" videos, just idle plans that evaporated as they spoke of them, was a fact of which even the sight of the magazines made them sharply conscious.

Instead there had been many tortured midnight whisperings, unresolved, veering steadily south on the compass: *Is this getting us anywhere? Can either of us clean up for more than a week if we stay in this thing? Am I pulling you down? Are we pulling each other down?* Their lines had become interchangeable, the problems unfixable. They could not discuss the hollow atmosphere that had seeped into the apartment, into the time they spent together. They neutralized the growing tension with these light exchanges, pretend playfulness. Or bridged the chasm for an hour or two before sleep with sex, even the bad sex it mostly was now.

Malcolm flopped on the couch with his notebook. Anna looked at his prone body and remembered her desire for it in a distant way.

"The Holy Ghost knocked her up, right? It wasn't the Angel Whatsisname. He was like, the Announcer."

"The Spirit entered her," Malcolm said quietly. "Vaginally, rectally, up the nose, it's a mystery. I think they used to paint it going in her ear like a little hummingbird. All science fiction movies are just riffs on the Virgin Birth."

"How so?" Anna realized that she was bored. Bored with the conversation, bored with Malcolm's prattle, bored with her own responses.

"The 'that's incredible' aspect. Like, we see there can be time travel, but nobody believes it. Aliens can come and destroy our planet, or grow themselves as duplicates of us, but nobody believes it. Haley Joel Osment sees dead people, nobody believes him either. Virgin birth, that's incredible. And Jesus came out the vagina, that must have added a lot of skepticism."

"What if they had nailed him to a privy, instead of a cross? The history of Western art would be completely different."

Malcolm drew some blank panels across a page.

Anna coiled herself into an armchair and drew a vaguely phallic form on a paper bag.

"Maybe he wasn't even crucified," she said. "Maybe he did have bowel movements and died on the toilet."

"Holding a cell phone," Malcolm added. "A lot of people would come back to God if they pictured him, you know, gasping his last words into the phone to his agent. They've nailed him, he's washed up in showbiz, he's taking a final shit. 'Why, Irving, hast thou forsaken me?' "

Malcolm recalls this scene and, without really noticing what he's doing, fishes his phone from a pocket and pushes Nahib's number. Just this once, he thinks, and that's the end of it.

69

Denise's voice was unmistakable. It had all five boroughs and three Catskills resorts in it.

"We came back," she said.

"I'm glad," I said. "I hate to think of people being far away."

"I have to ask you a kind of a delicate question. Maybe not delicate really, more of an annoyance probably, but I'm having trouble coming up with any answers."

"Annoy away," I said.

"About Caroline, actually."

"Oh. What, she—"

"Caroline is having a . . . *rocky* time. Things have not been going well."

"What sort of—"

"Aside from being broke, which is a whole issue in itself, she's on what I would have to call a downward spiral."

I pictured Caroline as an extra-long corkscrew whirling through the air.

"How downward are we talking about?"

Denise cleared her throat. I could hear her lighting a cigarette.

"Well, sad to tell," she said, in an aggrieved way, "all the way down. A hit-the-sidewalk-from-the-eighteenth-floor, Andrea Feldman type of downward spiral."

I thought of Andrea Feldman clutching a rosary and a can of soda as she hit the pavement. Too hideous.

"Denise, she can't be using heroin," I said, thinking that of course she could be. Like most people, I think of heroin as practically satanic, people using it as already dead.

"She did drift into it in New Mexico," she said. "But no, she isn't using now. She can't afford it, anyway. She's not the type to steal for it. Vodka, yes. She thinks if she buys those little miniatures it isn't serious. But she buys thirty at a time. She's very depressed. *I'm* very depressed. The sight of all those little bottles everywhere. There's been more than one I guess arguably psychotic episode."

"Euch, she has to see someone."

"I thought with your crash-and-burn expertise you might have a name or two."

"I used to have a whole Rolodex, but you know, most people died or cleaned up a long time ago. The only shrink I know is Laurence Seagrave."

"Should I know who he is?"

"He's written books. He studied with Lacan. He's helped people I know."

"Have *you* seen him?"

"I saw him last year," I said, "at a bat mitzvah in Hollywood. Professionally, no. I'm related to him, actually. His brother is married to one of my cousins. But I know people who go to him. Miles goes to him."

Denise coughed meaningfully.

"Miles isn't the poster boy for mental health, that I know of," Denise said.

"Miles is nuts," I agreed. "But Miles hasn't killed himself, either, and I've been half-expecting that for a long time. I'm not pushing this guy on you, there may not be anything he can do."

"Can I impose on you to call him for me?"

"I can call, but I'm thinking, if Caroline is really out there, Larry doesn't treat psychotics. No one does. Psychotics you just sort of watch. Like television."

"At least he could watch her for an hour and tell if she's psychotic or not," Denise said.

233

"Anybody can tell that," I said. "Unless they're psychotic themselves. She might be better off on a ward where they can keep an eye on her."

"That's probably true," Denise said. "I just can't tell. There's also the money problem. Some days she seems definitely out there. Then a lot of the time she seems like she's in the here and now."

"I think you should take her to Bellevue," I said. "Before she enters the there-and-then category. I think they *have* to take people, even if it's just a few days."

"She won't go."

"Make her go."

"I can't. She's not a midget, I can't pick her up kicking and screaming and cart her off to a hospital."

"Has she made an actual *attempt*?"

"She tried to electrocute herself in Albuquerque," Denise said. "But I tend to think that was more of the traditional cry for help."

"I don't know, anything that involves electricity seems more of a serious, you know . . ."

"Sure, but maybe not if you know there's no current running. She probably knew that. Unfortunately, I haven't been able to ask her. But okay, as a *prelude* to a psych ward, could you ask Seagrave if he would just evaluate her?" Denise was pleading now. Or coming as near pleading as Denise would. I have noticed that people from show business families consider pleading the lead-in to a comedy routine, and avoid it in real life as much as possible. "At this point I'll try almost anything."

"All right. I'll call and ask, and then if he says yes, you can call or she can call."

"Great. Thanks. Incidentally, I'm sorry I've been out of touch."

"I miss you when I don't hear from you," I said. "But obviously, you've had your hands full."

And when you didn't, I thought, I still didn't hear from you. I wondered again if there was something about me that people chose to avoid, except when they needed help.

70

Another telephone voice: smoky, ravaged-sounding, flecks of grating tinsel in it. Jesse. Will I come to his apartment? Right away? It's "kind of important."

Jesse lives in a U-shaped gothic gingerbread building two blocks from my tenement. Its apartments remind me of the Dakota: not as grandiose, very nearly though, with actual halls, rooms scaled for grown-ups rather than scullery maids.

Dark, despite many windows, Jesse's is full of furniture I associate with heirloom properties in Berlin or Vienna, valuable pieces. Isfahan carpets, art deco standing lamps, chandeliers, framed pictures, and other wall decorations worth a sultan's ransom: Balinese and African masks, small paintings by Soutine, Renoir, and Caillebotte, a Degas pastel, photographs by Nadar, Man Ray, Eggleston, Jesse's portrait by Robert Mapplethorpe, another by Peter Hujar, another by Lynn Davis, a Gerhard Richter painting of a burning candle, a Picasso plate, a Giacometti drawing.

Jesse has taste, and the money to indulge it, though I seem to recall that he stopped buying expensive things several years ago. Jesse has two black eyes, a scary contusion on his forehead, a purple bruise on his jaw. A split lower lip that looks like it's scabbed and broken open several times. He can barely walk. When he opens the door, I stare at him and wonder for an instant if he's been made up to look like this or has actually been beaten to the proverbial pulp.

This is, perhaps, not an ideal place to mention that I don't entirely like Jesse. But it figured in that moment, disturbingly, as a sort of stress mark. When you see someone you have mixed feelings about in real extremity, there is, sometimes, a terrible, inhuman moment that sneaks in ahead of your sympathy. A ripple of cold, totally shitty satisfaction. It passed.

He could not say what had happened. He didn't know, didn't remember. Not when, nor how, nor with whom. In New York, for sure, some days after returning from his travels. I conjectured that he'd picked up a bad piece of meat in a hustler bar, or something of the sort. On the other hand, the unmolested state of the apartment indicated that money had not been the issue. Or else the apartment hadn't been the location. He'd been struck hard enough, or been blackout drunk enough, that he could not bring a single detail of the assault to memory. I could tell, too, that he wasn't dissembling out of embarrassment. Jesse has always been, if anything, tastelessly frank about the minutiae of his own worst behavior. He really just couldn't remember.

I took him to the bathroom and studied his eyes in strong light. Jesse was only about an inch shorter than I am, but I kept thinking, He's so tiny. Painful to think of someone small being hit again and again by someone larger. Yet some of the biggest monsters have been small. Stalin was small. Pol Pot. Movie stars look enormous on-screen, and they're often minuscule. Same with monsters. He had a concussion. Possibly worse. He didn't want to go to Beth Israel. I forced him. You can force people who aren't midgets to go to a hospital, unless you're afraid of them. It isn't pleasant, but you can. Jesse was, on the other hand, smaller than Caroline.

Several grim and miserable hours passed in the ER. There was a gunshot victim (male, Dominican, left leg), and a pregnant woman (fat, Caucasian, blue cornflower sundress) who'd gone through a windshield, bleeding out ahead of us. Less obviously traumatized persons were ranged about the place, by themselves, in clumps, fretting, chewing gum, flipping through torn, much-fingered magazines about celebrities and their romances, their breakups. I wondered for the millionth time why a minimum-wage slave would care if Benjamin Bratt and Julia Roberts were "on the rocks." I mean, I knew why. That's actually what I wondered about.

Eventually a doctor who strongly resembled Adolf Eichmann looked Jesse over as if frisking him for hidden weapons. Since Jesse's insurance was in order, he was admitted for tests, scans, stabilization of vital signs, whatever. He begged me to return in the morning.

"Don't let me die here," he said, with a vexing flourish of melodrama.

"You're certainly not going to die," I said. If it were that easy, we'd all be dead, I thought.

Jesse instantly reeled off the names of several people we'd both known who went into New York City hospitals for nonlife-threatening conditions and never came out again. Well, yes. A rich area of medical mystery and epic litigation. All right. Yes. I promised.

And I did—dutifully, loyally, inconveniently—sit by Jesse's bed for at least two hours every day they kept him (eight in all; Arthur often joined me to relieve the tedium), and took care of him rather longer than necessary after he came out.

I have, I see, come back to the place where I started, though the end is not yet. I suppose I offered to look after him awhile, after they discharged him. I'm sure I did. Offer. Persuade, even. I spent a day in his apartment sorting pictures and papers, though he had no need to bring them here. Since he had some cracked ribs, Arthur and I carried everything he wanted to Eleventh Street.

Yes, this is where we began. Yes. We moved my little writing room into my bedroom, improvised a little alcove boudoir for Jesse. Arthur hung a curtain across it. Most of Jesse's damage would heal. Not all of it was physical, of course.

And it was, you see, a chance for Arthur to escape Oliver. It was, in fact, the only chance. Jesse's apartment miraculously empty, and paid for every month by his trust fund. Jesse did need some looking after, for a while at least; and Arthur needed to make a move, or he really never would. Was there an element of calculation here, an aspect of expedience? To answer that you would need to define what a good person is, and whether purity of heart requires having only one reason for doing anything. What constitutes a good person? Answer that.

71

I've made such promiscuous use of other people's letters and memories that the sequence of that summer's final weeks and days, what happened when, what happened first, has gotten knotted up.

Late August that year would have been unbearable without the air conditioner.

It's all balled up, my mother would say.

I am walking with Anna in the park at Twenty-third Street and Park Avenue. It's the middle of a soggy, sweaty afternoon. We have just disrupted the sleepy desuetude of El Quixote by appearing in the bar at what the staff considers siesta time, even though the place is open. In the bar, Anna downed three margaritas, which tipped me that she isn't using dope. People on dope can't keep alcohol down.

Anna's whitish hair is very short. She's got some kind of clever T-shirt on, sandals, a pair of black clam diggers. She tells me everything's fine. *Tout va bien.* She's had the idea of moving to Los Angeles. Her mind's pretty much made up, she says. Unrelatedly, her mother's getting a divorce, and her brother's buying a house in Ibiza. She says nothing at first about Malcolm. The park benches are full of people drinking coffee, resting behind baby strollers. The air smells of diesel exhaust. Men gathering aluminum cans haul transparent bluish plastic bags on their backs.

Anna wants me to meet her father. He's staying at the Hyatt near Grand Central. Before he leaves, she says, we have to have a dinner. Ginkgo branches overhead throw dappled shadows on the walking paths. I ask how Malcolm feels about Los Angeles. He wants to go, she says. But he's not sure if it's the right time for him. Anna knows it's the right time for her. She needs to get involved in something new.

"Everything here is kind of finished for me," she says. "Maybe Malcolm needs to stay and get himself sorted out. You know, it's possible we've played it all out already. He's trying to kick. It's hard for me to disenable him. I'm always tempted if he does it, and if I do it he automatically does it. If he came to L.A. . . . it's easy to fall into holes in L.A."

A few days earlier, she says, an heiress she knows offered to rent her a floor of a former factory she'd bought to turn into lofts, available as of September first.

"That's what got me thinking seriously about Los Angeles. If I were going to stay here—you'd have to see this place. It's gigantic compared with Cedar Street. I really couldn't turn it down if I were going to stay, because the rent she's asking is nothing. Do I want to commit to staying for another year or two years or whatever, or just go now and get away from everything here, that's the question. I guess I've decided I need to go."

For no sensible reason, Anna's announcement washes over me as another abandonment: another person leaving me. It's crazy. I never even see her. She's always seemed more real on the telephone, calling when I've been somewhere far away, than on the rare occasions in New York when she's been physically present.

I look at her slightly equine face and notice how small her breasts are in her novelty T-shirt. She becomes evanescent, disappearing even while she walks beside me. She's leaving, I think, joining the legions of ghosts that haunt all this city's streets. She's occupied my life as a voice whispering secrets from an invisible world I've only caught a blurry view of at scattered intervals, that I've crowded with imaginary details and dramas that have no actual resemblance to it. Now, just when she's become a little more real to me, she withdraws even further into shadows.

It will be worse from now on: I will have to catch myself in the act of picturing this other person's life the way I've habitually run it like a movie in my head, and remember that even the locations I've set it in no longer apply. We walk out of the park and into the arcade beside the massive insurance building. I see myself dissolving in the heat of the day, becoming a ghost myself, an image on a sidewalk, vanishing like a watery illusion on a desert highway.

72

The apartment's a mess. The density of rude matter reminds me of a stretch limo compacted in a giant crusher. I try to toss my own senseless clutter out, even things I might miss later on. Bales of paper objects which could have tax receipts or something else important jammed in their interstices. I urge myself on, thinking, Imagine that you had a fire; whatever's left is what didn't burn. How else can this place accommodate two? More to the point, how can I reduce the physical residue of my life to near-zero? I may want to get out of here someday.

Nothing lasts forever. Not even rent stabilization.

Jesse's restive. He'd like to go home. As soon as one situation clears, another clouds over. We get on better than I expected, living in close quarters. He's considerate. Funny, too. Sometimes we cook a meal together. It's the doldrums of summer, when the sails drop and you can sometimes have a quiet, simple conversation, and days and nights have a suspended momentum that's a kind of grace. But I sense his impatience, a gratitude anxious to say good-bye. By some miracle, Arthur's found an apartment to rent, in the neighborhood, but he can't move in until September first.

I consider asking Miles if Arthur can stay in his upstate house, so I can get Jesse out of here and solve Arthur's interim housing problem at the same time. Miles sounds horrible on the phone. Like a drunk with DTs. He feels trapped like a rat, he says. He describes dropping down a dark, endless tunnel. I know it's not a moment to ask him to give up his country refuge for a couple of weeks, even though he says he hates the place, never wants to see it again, and tells me only his sessions with Seagrave stop him from "sliding off the edge." I know Miles won't relinquish any options when he's reached this pitch of agitation.

I don't know where Jesse goes when he leaves the house. His bruises have healed. He looks scarecrow thin, but his eyes shine. He moves without visible discomfort. Most mornings he disappears early. I hear him letting himself in at four or five in the afternoon, sometimes later. I wonder, naturally, if he's staying out because he wants to, or thinks he'll get on my nerves. He couldn't be more on my nerves than I am. It's a relief to have someone sleeping nearby. In a way. He could stay in his own place with Arthur, it's bigger than mine, but some undefined mental obstacle blocks that possibility. So we're stuck in this temporary configuration that feels like eternity.

One morning after Jesse goes out, Edith Eddy buzzes from the street door. She's the only person in New York who ever "drops over" without calling first. She has her take-out coffee, her muffin, her look of holding in a Vesuvius of difficulties. Edith's messily permed hair, her imperishable fine features, her actressy manner of gripping her coffee container, all are at war with the inner Edith, who can't find any future, who runs the length and breadth of her maze without discovering the exit.

She alludes to an opaque, operatic sequence of events on Cape Cod that sent her reeling back to her East Village apartment: something with Chrissie, the Empress of Photography, but other complications as well, a love affair that sounds one-sided, dejection . . . the story has a burning pot roast and a station wagon in it, a jealous bisexual husband . . .

Edith leaves large pieces of this dire narrative blank, it's barely a story I can follow, she knows I've heard dozens of similar tales from her, that I'll become impatient if she drags it out.

I know, too, that Edith Eddy is suffering. I have only now

realized how little difference it makes if we engineer our own unhappiness or have it inflicted on us.

She has, she says, seen Denise. This surprises me only because Edith and Denise are friendly atoms that graze each other at long intervals, every two or three years, and surely it was only a year or two ago that they split the rent on a cottage in East Hampton? No, five years ago. Edith knows exactly which year. She can date it because that rental didn't quite work out, and it was the same summer Edith split for Alabama and sang with a famous blues quartet, staying away for nine months. I've lost track of everything. Caroline, she says, is on a ward at Bellevue. Denise has taken the bold step of contacting Caroline's family, moneyed people in Connecticut, distasteful as it must have been. *My* psychiatrist, the way Edith's heard it, helped get Caroline admitted.

Edie won't say she feels betrayed by Miles's fickle cancellation of the play he never started, that he promised her a leading role in, that she thought she'd be coming back for in September. Too embarrassed to admit what slender threads she hangs her hopes on, without making alternative plans. But he *has* betrayed her, I reckon. Miles knows the way she is and filled her with his own fantasies, to make them temporarily more real.

"It's not so much that he's a shit," I tell her. "But you can't take anything Miles tells you seriously. He believes things when he says them, but that burning will he used to have, it wouldn't be enough anymore, even if he still had it."

Edith nods: resigned, depressed beyond measure. She never stops calculating her odds of survival, if she does this, or does that, or takes off for Timbuktu. Then, in a very Edith way, her mood abruptly brightens, as if another, carefree Edith had woken up inside her from a restorative nap.

She's suddenly curious about Jesse and his "mishap." Edith

has seen little of Jesse since their long-ago days in Miles's theater company, except in crowded rooms and distracting situations. She asks how long he's been staying with me, and why he hauled all these boxes here.

"I mean, he lives in a fucking palace," she says, with the touch of bemused envy Edith brings to any mention of the better-off-than-she. "If you put the closets in his place together they'd be bigger than this apartment."

I have given this a bit of thought, but only a bit: various complexities in the current mix put me into a funk if I dwell on them.

"My guess is, he didn't want Arthur fishing through them. I know he's got pictures of Oliver and stuff in there, maybe— well, no, that can't be it. But it's peculiar, Edie, they're such close friends and suddenly Jesse acts like he doesn't trust Arthur. Or, more as if he doesn't feel comfortable around him."

"Arthur isn't even like that," Edith says. "He wouldn't dig through Jesse's shit."

"That's true," I agree. "Arthur isn't really that interested in other people's secrets, certainly not enough that he'd go through their things." We trade a look that confirms our shared weakness of character. "But of course, we would."

We dive for Jesse's boxes, like bratty children ripping open Christmas presents while their parents are still asleep. In regressive complicity, or perhaps a throwback to the demonic abandon of our youth, we messily rummage through his memorabilia, sifting out photographs of ourselves and numerous people we've lived half our lives around, making scathing comments about our friends and enemies, occasionally going numb at the sight of a dead person, or of ourselves when we were young and beautiful. After exhausting our interest in the pic-

246

tures, we discover several palm-size notebooks, miniature ring binders, full of Jesse's precise, Palmer-method handwriting.

Jesse has told me about Iguazú. About the Falls, and his prolonged stay in a restaurant/hotel in an isolated clump of habitation deep in the rain forest. He has described, with uncharacteristic intensity, his nighttime visits with the elderly, fat, Brazilian proprietor of the place, who sat on the veranda day and night, fluttering a palmetto fan in front of his face while sipping rum and Coke. Ceiling fans sliced lazily overhead, as small lizards clung motionless to the walls, gobbling flies with lightning tongues. The old man had been a travel agent in Africa and East Asia for many years, and had returned to Iguazú to run the family business. So perhaps it's not surprising to find, in one of the little notebooks, what appear to be transcripts of the old man's nightly musings, though there's something queer about the way Jesse's written them down, without commentary or description.

> *Tour groups. I do not like the tour groups, my friend, but without them this little establishment would quickly disappear. And the weddings! And, not long ago, a funeral dinner. Not all of these weddings turned out to be happy occasions, either, I assure you.*
>
> *Those are the laughing sisters, señor. Pay those laughing sisters no mind. They have been laughing that way at every possible thing for as many years as I recall, exactly like two hyenas in the Congo, for no reason that anyone has ever discovered.*

Edith and I pass the notebook back and forth, reading the entries aloud.

"That sounds a little fabricated," I note with a certain perplexity. "You think he was trying to write a novel or something?"

"Or just passing the time," says Edith. "I write down weird things that pass through my head. Mainly about people who died, little things I'll suddenly remember about them. It keeps them alive for me a little bit. Of course, when I die they'll be lost anyway. You might get an archive somewhere, but I sure as hell won't."

I think to reassure her that some sort of Edith memorial trove will outlive her, but it does seem rather doubtful, though I'm sure she'll float through many people's memoirs. I wonder if she knows what an indelible impression she's made on the lives she brushes up against between her disappearing acts.

Oh, the backpack tourists, it is often too much. "Is there agua caliente?" *I tell them, "This is Argentina, of course there is* agua caliente, *you are not in Bolivia or Peru, we are not savages here."*

"That sounds real," Edith says. "Tourists bitch about the water everywhere. Even up in Provincetown."

Countess Sacco has lived in Iguazú for many years. I believe she is Canadian by birth, but pretends she was born in Paris. She was married to a count, who died so long ago we have all forgotten the story of his life. An Italian, that much I remember. All Italians are counts and countesses and so forth. I do not know what happened to Countess Sacco in her long life, but she now detests and fears glass of any kind. She lives in a world without glass. In her home there are no glass windows. And no drinking glasses, only goblets of metal. She is a little bit afraid of plastic as well, but not so much. You see the problem. It is impossible for her to travel, as there is glass everywhere in the world. When an interesting person comes to Iguazú, we try to invite him to her home. This is a problem, because interesting people seldom come to Iguazú. Almost never. She is a very

cultured woman, but as you will see, somewhat tiresome in her ec-
centricities. Because it is not just the glass, señor. I think the glass is
the least of her difficulties, although it is obviously an important one.
I would prefer not to say more about it. You will see.

"What on earth," I say for lack of any keener perception.
"But you know something, that's just weird enough to be real."

"Jesse always liked telling stories," Edith says. "I could never
tell which ones were true. In rehearsals years ago, he always
showed up with these bizarre rumors about strange phobias
people had. I mean, this glass thing even sounds vaguely familiar. I remember once he said he'd followed a woman around
in a supermarket for an hour because she had no face. Literally
no face. She'd gotten it burned off or something and she had
no features, just teeny eyes and holes where her nose and
mouth should have been. You say he got knocked on the head?"

"Yeah, but not down there. But you never know, maybe he
did. And then got knocked on the head again up here. I'll tell
you something, that's my deepest fear. Getting a severe blow to
the head. Losing my brain functions. And I fell twice last month
on those fucking marble stairs out there, smack on the forehead."

You want to know if that is an auténtico *slice of Argentine beef?*
Auténtico? Nothing is auténtico *anymore, my friend, not anywhere*
in the world. Maybe in a few little pockets of unimportant space,
here and there, in Bhutan or Madagascar or what have you, you
may find auténtico. *Auténtico bubonic plague,* auténtico *Ebola vi-*
rus. Perhaps this rooting everywhere for auténtico *is more effort than*
it is worth anymore. But the Falls . . . they make the Falls a kind of
water Disney World, with the families coming here from Chile and
what have you. . . .

This is my old mother coming. She is ninety-six, can you imagine? She will only speak Portuguese, she won't speak to you in English. She will want to come here and sit at that table and sing her old Portuguese songs. She likes to sit on this veranda and drink rum all night, at her age . . . but what difference can it make? My father died fifty years ago. But I remember him very well. My mother has not been entirely alone all those fifty years, you can very well believe me when I tell you.

"Now, that could be real," Edith ponders.
"*Auténtico,*" I correct her.

It is very remarkable, my friend, how the water will carry voices away, as if they were not even there. All day and night, the people come here and chatter like monkeys, in Italian, French, English, Greek, every language you will ever hear. Unfortunately, because I have lived so very long, I understand most of what they are saying. Very stupid things, for the most part. They prefer to hear themselves making idiotic noises to hearing the roar of the Falls. I believe the falling water makes them nervous. It will go on crashing down like that long after they are dead and forgotten about, and they do not like to be reminded about that. Happily for me, my ears quickly attune themselves only to the water. And so all these voices become like the chirping and squalling of little senseless birds that have migrated to Iguazú for some unknown purpose. Of course, here in the hotel it is different. I have to look after my customers and tend to their various needs, it is my business to listen to them.

Permit me to say something, my friend. It is something that you in your wisdom—I do not claim to possess any—have probably considered many times. Water is the basis of life. Some would tell you carbon, but what is carbon in comparison to water? There are chemicals that make us into one form of life or another, but all these

*chemicals find their way into the water. I will tell you, señor, why I
have lived so many years in this ridiculous place, running this ridiculous hotel, with that incessant roaring of the Falls, did I tell you
before? That my father perished on those Falls? Perhaps I mentioned
it when we spoke another day. It is not important. Only a detail.
For him, an important detail. The truth of the business is that if I
do not leave the Falls, it is because I feel the pull of life here more
strongly than anywhere in this world that I know. It is probably not
a coincidence that these same Falls that represent life for me also
represent the death of my father. I am not trying to conceal anything,
and why should I, at my great age? These are not simple things to
explain to anyone who has not lived, as I have, so many years at
the Falls. To hear these incredible torrents of water crashing down,
not for three days, like the tourists, or for one year, but for thirty
years, my dear friend, and my mother over there, singing her sailor
songs, my mother has lived at the Iguazú Falls for sixty years! Ten
with my father, after that another fifty.*

I can easily visualize the old man, dressed in shabby clothes,
fanning himself in the sopping tropic night. But I don't believe
in him. Neither does Edith.

"He made all this up," she concludes.

"It's almost like a veil hiding something else," I say. "Whatever
was really going on down there."

"When we did those plays with Miles," she says. "Oh, I hate
to think how many years ago." If only, I think. If only, Edith,
memory wasn't your image of perfection. "Jesse was the only
one who wasn't in awe of Miles. I always remember that. Miles
was such a tyrant. But Jesse wasn't afraid of him."

What webs we weave, I think.

"There was a reason for that," I tell her. "It was supposed to
be a big secret at the time, but after all these years . . ." And, I

think, after all this endless stringing vulnerable people along, whipping up anticipation, disappointing people, and leaving them high and dry. "Jesse financed all those plays. He put up all the cash for every one of them. He was in love with Miles. Miles used that to get money out of him."

Edith's eyes open wider than I thought they could.

"Was that when you—"

"Were sleeping with Miles?" I know the laugh I eject sounds bitter. "Honey, me and a million others. But no, I came along many years after the crash of the *Hindenburg*. After that comeback play with Paul that turned out to be the swan song. What made Miles really crazy was, after Jesse got fed up and cut the money off, people were lining up to offer Jesse acting jobs. And Miles went absolutely nowhere for ten years."

73

I have heard so many peculiar stories about Anna's dad, his survival of two separate bolts of lightning and the psychic powers they supposedly installed in his mental hard drive, that I half-expect meeting him to be a drag. I dress in jeans, a black T-shirt, and a black Gaultier dinner jacket that's basically transparent. The weather's cooled, but it's still August. Jesse's taken the jitney to East Hampton, to spend the weekend with a friend. I'm getting nowhere with my book. I am starting to worry about cash.

Of course I'm curious to meet the legendary Christophe, but can't shake the fear that, as with so many such contrived meetings, two people who are "bound to like each other" won't. I hope the evening doesn't include any demonstration of Christophe's precognitive talents. I do not wish to know the future. I suspect it will be bad. I am also skeptical about any paranormal or magic gift, the mere mention of which recalls a droll evening I spent drinking with Taylor Mead several years ago.

We were in Marylou's, a joint on Ninth Street that enjoys an undeservedly shady reputation. A familiar figure walked in. The late Bob Williamson was many things to many people. To most of them, he was a world-class bore. Taylor groaned when we saw him moving along the bar toward the dining room, trailed by a comely young Russian. Bob paused at the sight of us, briefly growled and muttered a few yards of his impenetrable, incessant monologue, reminiscent of W. C. Fields, then retired to a table with his young protégé. Some hours later, he brought the Russian over and introduced him as "the next great magician."

I thought of Bob as someone who was forever running a new scam. He had the look of a man who spent too much time at racetracks. The type who appreciates "a fine cigar," as if there were such a thing, and can't really tell a Cohiba from a ten-cent cigarillo. Well, maybe he could. The dead take their secrets with them.

The Russian boy whipped a deck of cards from his jacket and fanned them near Taylor's face.

"Pick a card," said the boy.

"Oh, go to hell," said Taylor, sparing us whatever cheesy marvel would have followed.

At the Odeon, as the world outside turns twilight orange through the blinds, I find, at a round table near the back, sitting between Anna and Malcolm, an attractive, smallish man in an elegantly tailored blue business suit, impeccable pink shirt, Sulka tie, white-haired, tanned, who resembles the actor Terence Stamp in his current later years. He stands up to shake hands, greets me effusively, and says he read one of my books on the plane coming over. I'm instantly inclined to like him.

"I could only find one in Italian," he says apologetically. It was *Rent Boy*. I bite my lip. I realize I'm making the face of a "naughty boy" embarrassed by the exposure of a childish prank.

"I would have given you a different one," I tell him. "To start with, anyway."

I assume a book that would have shocked my parents would shock Anna's father. Forgetting, of course, that we are nearly the same age. But no: Christophe found the book very funny, very acute about "the nastier side of capitalism." There's a hint buried in this remark that Christophe considers his own activities part of the comical side of capitalism.

No, there's nothing alarming or tiresome about Anna's father. No mention of his near-death experience. No occult inventory of my desktop. Christophe has a confident air, not exactly imperious, but firmly convinced of his own reality. He looks like somebody who has never had to search far for a woman, or for people who craved his company. He's charming, affable, enjoying New York as only someone who doesn't live here can: seen some Broadway shows, traipsed around museums, even taken the Circle Line tour. I like the Circle Line tour myself, though I have only taken it once. The rest of tourist New York is like eating blowfish, as far as I'm concerned: a little taste, prepared in a certain way, makes your lips tingle. If you eat the whole thing, you drop dead.

Anna radiates an ebullience that could be real. She's made an effort to get her hair a nonchemical color, and wears the Little Black Dress very young women slide on to look worldly beyond their years, and unavailable. She's on her second glass of chablis. Malcolm's extremely quiet, subdued, self-effacing, uncomfortable. In his usual sandals, ripped and patched jeans, and a strangely disconcerting green crepe woman's blouse.

Christophe and I talk in a comfortable way about Daniel Schmid, whose family owns hotels in Switzerland: Christophe knows Daniel, has seen his movies. He has, in fact, met my friend Ingrid Caven, who starred in many of those films, and knows the writer Jean-Jacques Schuhl, who lives with Ingrid in Paris.

It appears we have many friends in common: before long, I feel like a grown-up, with Anna and Malcolm reduced to silent children, though Anna puts in a bright question now and then.

"I really admire Jean-Jacques's *restraint,*" I tell Christophe, "in not publishing anything for twenty-five years."

More chitchat about long-forgotten films.

Malcolm would normally grow animated at any talk touching on movies. The fact that he doesn't is a bad sign. He listlessly picks at a watercress salad and drinks only ice water. Christophe tactfully includes Malcolm in the rambling conversation, but these efforts don't elicit much beyond a kind of affirmative grunting. Malcolm looks as if the Odeon's gleaming wood and delicate low lighting, its faint resemblance to a luxury liner salon, is somehow drowning him, as if our voices are pushing his face underwater. Soon after the entrees arrive, Malcolm turns as green as a black person can.

Anna notices first. She asks if he's all right. She asks in a voice only people who sleep together use: as if they shared the same body.

"I think Malcolm needs to—" I make as graceful a gesture of vomiting as I can manage.

"I'll go with you to the loo," I tell him. The word "loo" comes out because of Christophe, I suppose, though plain "toilet" would be better. Malcolm nods his stubbled chin urgently, covers his mouth with an overstarched napkin, and scrapes back his chair.

"He just had an attack of food poisoning a few days ago," I hear Anna telling her father, who strikes me as the kind of guy who knows exactly what the problem is, without needing the gift of second sight.

We make it downstairs to the men's room and Malcolm heaves his salad into a toilet bowl. I hold the middle of his back, quite uselessly, until whatever he's put in his stomach all day comes up.

Sweat pours off his face. He is so impossibly beautiful that watching him vomit has a sick sort of allure.

He sits bent over on the toilet seat. I find myself kneeling on the black and white octagonal tiles at his feet, my hands on his thighs. I wipe his face with toilet paper. I caress his hair, his arms. There's nothing sexual in any of this. I almost wish there were. I think of all the opportunities I've had to make love with this man. There was once a time when I would have taken on a relationship with such a person, at exactly this point in his disintegration. I have not vanquished all my demons, but I have expunged the attractions of the damned and beautiful: too much suffering, too much desire, zero gratification.

"What the fuck am I going to do." Malcolm's choking voice depresses me beyond words. He breaks into sobs. He's crying. He's sweating and crying at the same time.

"Hon, you need to get help," I tell him. "There's every way in the world to get help for this."

There isn't, there are waiting lists miles long, and every sort of shitty obstacle, but this is what I have to say, or else I will have this blubbering, inconsolable, horribly dear lost soul on my hands, and no hope of getting him back upstairs.

"She's leaving me," he cries, "and I'm going to have to face everything alone."

I never have the right words. I never can save anybody.

"Anna loves you," I tell him. Anna loves Anna, I think. "She's afraid you'll both become addicts."

"I *am* a fucking addict," Malcolm wails. It's the first time I've ever heard an addict admit it, except at an NA meeting. "I thought we were chipping, you know? Just chipping. Then she stopped, and I went right on doing it. Nahib always said you had to do at least ten fucking envelopes a day to get addicted."

"A drug dealer is the worst source for that kind of information, Malcolm, his job is to keep you paying him. Okay. You're addicted. So you kick. You do the detox, and you quit. You're very strong," I tell him, thinking it's a lie. Everything I'm saying is a lie. My nose should be longer than Malcolm's penis by now. "You're young and talented, and I know it's a cliché, but you have your whole life ahead of you."

He's not very strong, my poor, lovely thing. And, sad to tell, he isn't very talented, either. Worse still, I think he knows that. He doesn't have the drive to get where he wants to go without talent. It would not surprise me if the life ahead of him involves selling his body again, a life that brings a lot of fast and easy money that evaporates as soon as it comes.

"I feel dead," he whispers. "I feel like I'm already dead."

Well, I think, we're all dead already, in a lot of ways, but best not to mention it.

We stay in the toilet for a long time. I'm worried Christophe will pop in if we remain another minute. Malcolm assembles himself as well as he can, splashes cold water on his face, makes himself presentable in the mirror. He wraps me in a hug. He tells me I'm the best friend he ever had. I hope this isn't true, but I'm afraid it is.

The rest of dinner goes past in an embarrassed, let's-cut-our-losses-here sort of blur, we're rushing to get through it now, talking in a farewell style as if we're already out on the street hailing cabs.

I shake hands with Christophe on the sidewalk.

"It's been very pleasant meeting you," he says with a smile. "I meant to say before, I'm sorry for your loss."

I'm speechless, for once in my life. I run scrambled versions of my last conversations with Anna through my brain, try to remember anyone I knew who died in the past six months, anyone close enough to matter: the trouble with death is, there's so much of it all the time that unless a particular extinction cuts very deep it turns numb inside you and disappears.

"I don't know what Anna told you—" I begin to say, completely puzzled, but Anna's holding open a taxi door for him, and Christophe slips into the cab with a wave.

I stop at The Bar on Second Avenue, desperate for a drink.

I find friends there. I drink way too much. Fortunately my friends leave, and no one familiar replaces them. I manage to crawl home by one in the morning.

My calico, Lily, is curled on a pillow, and I want my bed, and to ignore the flashing light on the answering machine. I push the play button anyway.

"Gary, Edie, call me when you get this, I'll be home all night."

"It's Edie. Listen, it's important, call me whenever you get in. Even if it's late."

"Gary, it's a little after midnight, I'm going to be up for a while but call me whenever you get this, if you wake me up it doesn't matter, it's really really important."

She's heard a good joke, I think, or she's leaving for Montana and wants to say good-bye for a change. But I know Edith cherishes her hours of unconsciousness, so probably it is important. It takes a while to find my address book, and even longer to decide if I'll make the call. She picks up on the first ring.

"Edie, hi, I wouldn't call this late but your message said—"

"No, I'm awake, are you alone?"

"Yeah, alone and plastered as shit. Jesse went away for the weekend."

"Listen, I have some really bad news. If you want me to come over there, I'll be there in ten minutes."

Everything sinks inside me. Something's happened to Arthur, I think. Someone's been in a plane crash. I have time to consider the bad news may be Edith's own bad news: ovarian cancer, whatever.

"Tell me," I say.

"This is so awful. I'm so sorry I'm the one to tell you this. Miles is dead."

"Miles is *what*?"

"He died. I'm so sorry to tell you this. Especially when you're drunk. You'll remember tomorrow, won't you?"

I was drunk. I'm not anymore, suddenly.

Miles cannot be dead. It just isn't a possible thing. I was so fucking mean the last time I talked to him. Miles is part of me. Miles loved me once. I love him. Still. Despite everything. He made it so impossible these last years to be kind. I still should have tried. He's dead.

"Oh God, Edie, how did he do it? I don't even want to know really, but I have to."

He practically said he had nothing left to live for. How would he do it? Pills? A gun? I know he wouldn't jump out a window, he has an awful fear of heights. But then people often do it using the one thing they're afraid of. Somehow this question of method seems even more urgent than the fact that he's dead.

"He didn't do it. He had a heart attack on a crosstown bus. He made it to the ER at St. Vincent's, but it was too late. He died five minutes after he got there."

74

Friends and Colleagues of Miles Sutherland
invite you to a memorial celebration
of his life
at St. Mark's Church
on
Saturday, September 8, 2001
3:00 P.M.

The date strikes a few people as unseasonably early, but conflicts in everybody's schedules, the confusion of planning an event that involves Edith, Denise, Jesse, and, to a lesser extent, Arthur, all lobbing stray ideas into the hopper, along with suggestions from Miles's other, far-flung associates regarding "what he would have wanted," and the possibility that his send-off might otherwise have to wait on some favorable blank space in the oncoming fall calendar—all these elements move the thing forward in a scramble.

Burning questions include: full bar, or only beer and wine? Chips and dip, or a full buffet? Should the actual church interior, the main auditorium, be reserved for the afternoon, or is the smaller room, often used for poetry readings, off the side entrance, more serviceable?

This last question, it is queasily acknowledged, darkly echoes the one that haunted Miles in his later days: could he ever fill a big room to capacity again? Or should he, in death, be spared the potential embarrassment of a skimpy turnout? The smaller room can, in a pinch, more easily be made to *look* full.

The heat, the wearying effort involved in drawing *tout* Manhattan in from the Hamptons to fill the whole church, the expense: everything argues in favor of the back room, with its draped Regency fireplace, its huge round ceramic relief of the Annunciation, and its resemblance, in most other respects, to the plain white cube of a smallish art gallery.

I recuse myself from most of this planning, and also decline to speak at the event. I do not wish to play the widow, a part hundreds of others could claim with as much justification. And all the summer's internecine dramas, despite my role in most of them as passive sounding board, have exhausted me in a way that I can't recuperate with vitamins and epic bouts of sleep.

My reticence in this matter is probably one reason why, on the list of five speakers, Tova Finkelstein manages to become the star eulogist. Denise, who coordinates most of this organizational mess with obdurate efficiency (we've both buried plenty of friends, planned their memorials, made certain our dead got some kind of dignified farewell), contacts Tova in Bari, Italy, where the Conscience of America is directing a Pirandello play, simply to break the news. Tova snaps that of course she's already heard about Miles's demise, and demands to know what plans are afoot to memorialize him.

"Well," Denise tells her, making it sound as microscopic as possible, "we're putting a little thing together next week. But I'm sure there'll be a bigger memorial later in the year that you'll be able to get to."

Tova takes imperial umbrage at the suggestion that she cannot, on a moment's notice, and with barely a blip in her jet-setting schedule, board any plane to any destination in the universe, and insists on flying in for September 8. She indicates, in no uncertain terms, her availability as a speaker. Well, who will tell her no? In the fallow aftermath of Labor Day, one major brand name on the menu will, no doubt, help swell attendance. Tova is, Denise reports, histrionically upset and grief-stricken. And a total bitch at the same time.

"After all," Tova grandly proclaims, "I *was* his mentor." She adds that she's "angry" at Miles for not taking better care of himself. This from a woman who, Miles once told me, never had anything more in her fridge than a bulb of fennel, and chained Marlboros after her own double bypass.

By this time Jesse has reclaimed his apartment. He has not, however, removed his boxes of pictures and notebooks, which become yet another vaguely funereal clump of inconvenient junk in my apartment. Arthur has shifted to his new place on Seventh Street. He's borrowed two thousand dollars from me, for the deposit and other expenses. As so often happens when you lend money to a friend, Arthur immediately made himself less available. He resents my largesse and thinks I grudge him the loan. I know how his mind works. So I am now alone with my cat, memories of Miles, and a half-written novel that seems utterly beside the point.

The "memorial committee" calls daily, many times, separately and in groups. Should there be bowls of nuts? Pumpkin seeds? Fruit baskets? How many kinds of cheese? French bread or crackers, or both? Should the reception afterward run two hours, or three? Should we scatter Miles's ashes at dusk, which still falls a little late in the evening, or proceed directly from the reception to the scattering place? And which river should receive Miles's dust, East or Hudson?

On this point I am adamant.

"The East River. Miles wasn't wild about the lordly Hudson."

The unavoidable morning of the day arrives on battered wings of a murderous hangover. Denise asks me to go with her to the women's psych ward at Bellevue. Caroline's being released into Denise's care for the day, so she can give a eulogy.

I meet Denise at First Avenue and Tenth. We cab to the brimstone megalopolis at Twenty-seventh, its own Forbidden

City of death and madness. Bellevue, to my mind, is the vertiginous, eternally twilit Edinburgh of de Quincy's opium nightmares, the lair of Stevenson's Body Snatchers, and Frankenstein's laboratory all rolled into one big factory of horror. I never pass Bellevue without imagining that if I ever walk into it, even venture into the foyer, sumo wrestlers in hospital whites will grab me and lock me up for eternity behind its shit-brown walls.

Caroline, however, is nowhere within that ancient stone maze. She's on the seventeenth floor of a twenty-five-story building called the New Bellevue, a regular Lefrak City of health care that's been erected, apparently, by modernist elves, behind our backs, so to speak. The Bedlamite open wards are a thing of the past, like Olivia de Havilland in *The Snake Pit*. The Lysol-cheery rooms of this new Morbidity Lite, 4,400 in all, never contain more than four patients each, sometimes only one or two.

I expect the first Mrs. Rochester, zombified beside a flickering candle in a brass holder. I anticipate a degree of friction between Caroline and Denise. After all, Denise made the call to Connecticut, involved the people who wrecked Caroline's mental health in the first place, the people whose money is keeping her here, and for which there will eventually come a large emotional price tag: some increment of undeserved forgiveness, nauseating gratitude, maybe even an apology for telling the whole world all the nasty things that happened in the house in Fairfield.

Nothing goes as I imagine. Nothing ever does. The now-ex-girlfriends embrace and kiss with a kind of sexual hunger that seems completely out of whack with the occasion. After this carnal tussle subsides, I give Caroline a peck on the cheek. I feel full of emotion yet completely cold and removed. I can't feel her skin. It's a movie. Life has reached the condition it's been pushing toward all our lives. It's nothing but a movie.

Caroline. Such a good person. Saddled with such an ill-favored life. She doesn't look especially crazed, just sad. There are no bars on the windows. The room's flooded with light. But I know that window glass, plastic, whatever it's made of, would bounce a person twenty times her weight back onto the carpet instead of shattering.

Her face beams genuine pleasure when Denise produces, from the box she's brought, the dress she picked from Caroline's wardrobe for the afternoon. A size-eight, sleeveless black silk sheath, with a straight skirt, kick pleat on the side, scooped neckline. A pair of black pumps come out, and, from Denise's handbag, a string of seed pearls in a cotton-lined box.

"It's really the only thing to wear to a memorial," Denise says, though she herself has opted for casual drab, maybe to make Caroline look more resplendent.

I wear my gray Armani suit, the only real suit I own. I bought it in Macy's in San Francisco fifteen years ago. It still looks fine. I don't, but I don't care. The suit's enough.

St. Mark's. I've been in this room so many times that all its details have dropped from memory. The arched windows gazing into the rear garden. The big circular fans, blowing.

I have dreamed of you so much—I can't keep the Robert Desnos line from enunciating itself in my head—*that you have lost your reality.*

Whether he loved me or not doesn't matter anymore, does it?

Am I afraid of his death? We only came here to die, after all.

No, I'm not afraid. Today I'm not afraid. I don't think I will be afraid again. The worst has happened, even if ugly surprises await.

The organizers have opted for fruit. Nuts. Varicolored vegetable paté, nonpotato chips in bright chemical colors. Enough food for ten times the number of people rambling in, around thirty by my count.

Caroline holds my hand. Her palm's sweating. Denise squeezes my arm. I know most of these people. So many of them that I can't focus anything. Anna's here somewhere. Her worldly goods are boxed up on Cedar Street awaiting UPS. And Malcolm's here, in a spiffy suit. He isn't going to California. He kisses me on both cheeks. With death you get both.

Yes. I know most of them. Each with his or her own idea of Miles. I feel I know most of these gray folding chairs, as far as that goes.

Mouths smile: life goes on, I guess they're saying. Hands wave strangely in my direction. People I dimly recognize shoot consoling expressions that stop short of lugubrious. There's a familiarly awkward milling around, awkward chitchat, the personalities reserved for the one serious thing life has to offer, and the volume of it, the disconnected words spitting through the air, make me want to collapse. I'm too tired to be here. I feel . . . nothing and everything. They feel the same way. Malcolm's at my back. He presses fingers along my spine.

This is grief. A little spinal massage and a garbage scow of abandoned sentiments. I know what I'm supposed to display, the expressions people expect on my face. But I can't have my emotions on cue. What I really feel is immense impatience for this all to become a gray memory instead of something happening right now.

They've made a kind of leaflet, a foldout on cheap paper

Miles would've hated, with a fairly recent photograph of Miles on the cover. A Timothy Greenfield-Sanders photo, very elegant and natty in the original print. Miles never took a bad picture, but the reproduction is too grainy, almost a smudge. Inside, a statement written by an anonymous friend. By a committee, actually. The statement inside's a little off the mark, somehow. Not dishonest but perhaps disingenuous. Scattered all over the back page are quotes from Miles's published works. Witticisms from his plays. Some famous things famous people said about him once upon a time.

I must keep this immobile stoic look on my face just a few hours longer. I can't cry, so I must appear too stricken even for tears. If I manage this, I can meet my own death in the street with a big, welcoming, shit-eating grin.

Commotion surges behind me. Whispers susurrate through the seated audience and standees. That quickening excitement, like the lights going down before an opera. I know that Tova Finkelstein has made her entrance.

This milling and yabbering takes far too long. . . . Large, manly Tova traps me in a bear hug. I have not seen Tova Finkelstein in years, except in magazine photographs, and the years have not been grossly unkind to her visage, despite ill-health and a late-blooming predilection for using a candy pink lipstick shade that doesn't suit her olive skin at all, but rather floats on it like a torn Post-it note stuck to her mouth. Tova never used makeup in her life. I'm not sure why she's taken to it in her seventies. It doesn't soften her manliness on television, or in life. Dressed, as always, in black slacks, a black turtleneck, her signature Vietcong outfit that would make any other human sweat in this weather. I notice a tall, freckled, Southern-looking young man with corn-colored hair and an expression of vigilant obsequiousness, hovering at Tova's elbow: her latest walker, no doubt, whom she half-turns to with, it seems, a halfhearted inclination to introduce him. She changes her mind. He makes a weak smile that seems an apology for his presence, if not his existence. He becomes the vapor of a claque.

At last the volume drops. The industrial fans that serve for air-conditioning whoosh above the dying din.

"We're here today"—Denise's amplified voice from the plain wooden podium sends everyone standing scrambling for seats— "to remember a complex, brilliantly gifted, troubled, difficult, generous, and beautiful man, Miles Sutherland."

I've taken a chair at the end of a row near the back, beside Caroline. Her hand in mine is trembling and wet.

The speakers know their order of appearance. This eliminates the typical "emcee" verbiage between eulogies. Jesse first: he's had a facial, and spent a thousand dollars at Commes des Garçons for the occasion, had his hair whipped into a leopard-spotted caprice of black and white. He looks like a million dollars, as the saying goes. He has a million dollars, so I guess he should.

"Bette Davis once said when someone asked her why she smoked," Jesse begins, " 'Darling, if I didn't smoke I wouldn't have had a career.' I could say Miles Sutherland was my Bette Davis cigarette, because if he hadn't given me my first acting job, I probably wouldn't have had a career. I certainly wouldn't have had as interesting a personal life as I had for many years if Miles hadn't consistently rebuffed my sexual advances."

A wave of strangely prim amusement rises in spots through the audience. I'm sure it's news to most people that Jesse believes he has a career and bewildering that he thinks they'd believe Miles rebuffed Jesse's sexual advances.

"Miles could be a royal pain in the ass," Jesse goes on. "But the operant word would be *royal*. He was a member of the aristocracy of literature."

Well, it's nice to think so, anyway. Jesse expatiates in this vein for about ten minutes, poised, funny, somber and shaken by turns, plucking the right cliché from the air when he can't think of anything more original to say, and he refuses to cry, he chokes up for a moment and stops dead until he gets his voice under control: a pro. Most of what he says is true, most of what isn't true he doesn't say.

Oh Caroline don't please don't please fall apart. She lets go of my hand and moves for the podium a bit uncertainly, as if she's forgotten where she is, and her long glossy hair, her freckles, her loping walk, for some reason it's Caroline I'm thinking about, Caroline, alive, whom I'm actually mourning instead of Miles, and as she positions herself at the microphone, raising it to suit her height; I'm afraid she's just going to shatter like a mirror into thousands of unreadable reflections. But no.

"I didn't see much of Miles in the last few years," Caroline begins, in a hoarse voice that eventually shakes out its rasping frog. "But he was very much with me in my thoughts, and his support for my work was important at a time when I thought everything I wrote was worthless. A lot of people felt that Miles wrote himself out, but the truth is that the confusions of this world . . ." She falters. ". . . became very hard . . . very hard for him to sort his way through. He was looking for a way to continue, and I think, had he lived, he would finally have found it. . . ."

Outside, wind shirrs vegetation in the church garden. The hint of a cool breeze washes in through the arched open door. Arthur, several rows forward, looks back at me with a furrowed face. What's that face, I wonder: does he really imagine I could speak here, today, now, that I could possibly say anything without breaking down?

A magazine editor Miles once worked for has, for no reason

I can think of, been asked to add her two cents to this mercifully limited array of recollections: she's short and fat and ugly, the kind of Old School dyke who keeps every one of her previous girlfriends somehow glued into her life drama. Everything she says about Miles could be said about almost any corpse, but I suppose she's the perfect mediocre foil for the next act.

Tova springs to the podium with that air of aplomb and confidence, competence and take-no-prisoners intellectual regency that—along with an extreme sexual beauty that still has its remnants engraved in her face—has made her an international icon.

Caroline switches seats with Denise. Now Denise clutches my hand. She knows this is the hardest moment of the day. The hardest one to take, I mean.

"I have to say," Tova announces, clear and brittle, as only Tova can be, "having listened to the other speakers today, moving as some of what's been said has been, that something I hoped would be expressed here hasn't been, so I seem sort of designated to say it."

Oh fuck you, whatever it is, I think. I'm positive Denise is thinking the same thing.

"Miles's early career encompassed poetry and prose essays of great promise. His plays, though they bore the heavy influence of the Theater of the Absurd, also had a unique quality of wordplay and a prehensile use of language that one could compare without hyperbole to some of Gertrude Stein's operas and plays.

"He was a physically beautiful man, and in his case I don't think this helped his productivity. I think his forays into film acting and screenwriting were mostly unhelpful to him as a writer. He spent a lot of himself on the hunt for gratification and the admiration of people who didn't really matter, and his disappointments in that area of his life weakened his confidence in his work. Still, he conquered a tortured, ten-year spell of writer's block to write the almost sublime play *An Evening with Jorgen Delmos*—a play I had an indirect association with, as I planned to direct the great actor Paul Sanders in a subsequent one-man performance. Paul's death unfortunately intervened. In a sense, our project would have been a continuation of what Paul had begun to attempt with the piece Miles wrote for him."

"Could she be a little less humble?" Denise hisses in my ear.

Tova is hardly finished with Miles. For this world's Tova Finkelsteins, no revenge can ever be complete, no forgiveness ever possible. She explains her own reachy thoughts at epic length, as is often her wont, secure in her charisma, her aura of celebrity. She could recite the phone book and cast the same spell, something like the fascination of a freeway pileup. The longer she speaks of Miles, the note of not very subtle put-down becomes ever more audible.

Tova's Miles was, in effect, someone who "could have had a real career," had he been as relentless, as disciplined, as smart as Tova herself. She manages to suggest, in an ingeniously understated way that is nevertheless so outrageous only Tova could perpetrate it with utter indifference to the pain it causes, that a fatal heart attack was probably the best thing that could've happened to him.

And on and on and on. Everything Miles ever said about this woman is true, I realize. I had never quite believed him. She's insufferable. The world is about her, Miles is about her, the day and the night and the sun and the moon are all about her and nothing but her. After the eon of the void, Tova concludes her oration, her Balanchine prance on Miles's grave, with the face Maria Malibran must have worn after a supreme operatic triumph. I think she actually expects the room to explode with applause. Thankfully, it doesn't.

271

And then she leaves. Leaves the podium and heads for the rear, nodding sagely, even smiling a sad smile broad enough to show her bad teeth to a few literati scattered through the audience. Will she stay for the conclusion? Perhaps even sip a club soda and mingle at the reception? Certainly not. Not for Tova to mix with "the little people" munching pumpkin seeds and discussing their microscopic lives.

She sweeps out of the place with an air of having performed yet another thankless, incalculably huge, exhaustingly generous favor to humanity, her eyes expertly hooded to project humility on this mortal occasion—a paradoxical humility, considering her cosmic importance—her long, tall, spectral walker (in line with many others for a huge career shove, whatever it is he does) proceeding a few steps behind Tova's rather large ass, until he scurries ahead to thrust open the exit door for her.

It's left to Edith Eddy to close the show. Somewhere in the middle past, it became the thing to wind up funerals with Edith Eddy singing her heart out. It's something she does well.

Edith has made no concession to fashion. She has a black eye, for some reason. She's wearing a man's suit too short at the sleeves and trouser cuffs, white socks and men's shoes that are probably a size too large. And she's carrying the urn—an ugly pewter urn—containing Miles's ashes with her. She plants it in full view of the assembled bereaved, on the edge of the podium, with a firmness that screams anger.

She grabs the microphone out of its holder. She paces in front of the podium, staring at the floor. She gathers breath. Fumbles around for her opening note. Bursts out a cappella. She doesn't need an orchestra, or even a banjo. Her voice blasts everyone out of low-burning melancholia. It has everything of torment and loss and exaltation in it, and a strange softness that conjures the slow decomposition of dead flesh.

everything must change
nothing remains the same
everyone must change
no one and nothing remains the same

Edith doesn't get far into it before everyone sitting in my row starts drooling tears. I suppose I'm crying. I feel wet. I climb out of my chair and move directly to the buffet, and as quietly as possible pour myself a stiff one.

nothing no one remains unchanged

I lose it. Yes. I can see the sumo wrestlers in hospital whites, moving swiftly to drape me in a straitjacket.

so few things you can be sure of
except the rain comes from the clouds
sunlight from the sky
hummingbirds do fly

When Edith reaches the finale—quite a difficult crescendo to carry off without instruments—a patch of dead silence follows. Broken, I'm afraid, by the sound of my own maniacal laughter, which I cannot stop or even restrain by gulping an entire paper tumbler of Stoli. Caroline weeps. I think she's weeping for me. Denise palms damp from her eyes.

It's some kind of memorial. Part mud bath, part masochism, part farrago of feelings. Of all kinds.

There's Miles in his urn. In plain sight, dead. Or at least, the thing they've put what they call the cremains in. The audience rises. Half bolt for the exit, the other half for the buffet.

I eat some grapes. I see people watch me eating grapes. I

start eating them with a great show of appetite. Hey, they're all digging into the grub. We came here to mourn, not to starve.

One final thing to do, and this threatens to dissolve in confusion as people decide who will share a taxi with whom, and the odd procession that forms at Twenty-third Street and FDR Drive has shrunk to five: me, Denise, Caroline, Edie, and Jesse. Everyone else has either cabbed to the wrong location, or decided to skip this piece of the ritual. I'm sure we said Twenty-third and the river. Come to think of it, though, Twenty-third runs to both rivers.

We walk past the gas station, the big white boats, under the pylons of the drive, down along the flagstone esplanade, where the path's lined with reeds and evergreen plants and eventually a stone jetty protrudes into the water, and there's a pebbled strand where a bit of tide sloshes back and forth. A forlorn street lamp. Some metal benches, empty. A jogger wearing a Nike headband. Of course we can't get down to the water, can't climb over the railing and jump down. There was a time when we would have, but this isn't that time. That time was a long time ago. A rotted log directly below rests on a bed of moss.

"I thought there'd be more," Denise says. I don't know if she means mourners or ashes, as Edie has lifted the cover of the urn and we can all see in the twilight the gray chunky powder that was Miles.

The water. The pebbles. The darkness falling quickly now.

Night falls ink blue by the time a strong enough wind blows up along the river, though the white rocks below glow strangely on their bed of sand.

And finally the wind takes him.

In a world that *really* has been turned on its head, truth is a moment of falsehood.

—Guy Debord, *The Society of the Spectacle*